Miss Farrow's Feathers

Susan Gee Heino

Laughingstock Publishing

Cover design by Lewellen Designs

Excerpt from *Miss Wheaton's Whiskers* by Susan Gee Heino

ISBN: 978-0-9886175-4-4

Dedication

To Chirp.
You fell into our lives just when we needed you most
and you fluttered your way into our hearts..

Other Regency Romance
by Susan Gee Heino

Yuletide Lies

Miss Wheaton's Whiskers

Passion and Pretense

Temptress in Training

Damsel in Disguise

Mistress by Mistake

Chapter 1

Hampshire, England, 1818

Meg Farrow choked on a feather. Handy, since she needed one just now. She'd heard that passing a feather through flame provided just the right odor to rouse an insensible swooner. Poor insensible Mrs. Sedley-Stone certainly did need rousing just now. She'd swooned—but good—and the smelling salts hadn't worked.

It was just as well, though, considering that the very uproar that had sent the woman into hysterics was still roaring along. Or *soaring*, rather. Papa lunged about the drawing room waving a net while the large, yellow-headed parrot squawked loudly from atop the window cornice where it had come to rest. Their usually unflappable housekeeper screeched from the far corner, flapping her arms twice as much as the bird.

Meg's head was beginning to throb. Two weeks of this had been more than any of them could take.

"Bartholomew! Come down here right now," Papa ordered, shaking his fist—his fist!—at the bright-eyed parrot.

The bird cocked his head, ruffled his feathers, then let Papa know exactly what he thought of that idea. Heavens, but this creature knew words Meg had never even heard before—and she spoke three languages. On the settee, Mrs. Sedley-Stone had just begun to stir. Apparently she *did* know some of these words, because they made her swoon all over again.

"Watch your ruddy language, you bone-headed devil," Papa shouted at the bird.

"Papa, for heaven's sake," Meg chided.

Gracious, now even Papa had been corrupted by the parrot's influence. What were they to do? The whole village was talking about it. Innocent passers-by could not come within a hundred yards of their house but they were accosted by the most egregious verbiage, uttered loud and clear in a high-pitched raspy voice. It filtered through the doors, through the windows, out into the street. Anyone who didn't know better would think this was not the parsonage, but a common wharf-side alehouse.

Those who did know better would likely not have bothered coming so near to begin with. Sadly, Bartholomew's saucy tongue was well known in the community. Even sadder, it used to be contained to Glenwick Downs, a good two miles out of town. Now that their dear old friend, the Earl of Glenwick, had passed from this life and gone to his reward, Bartholomew had passed into the Farrow's possession and into the confines of the parsonage.

With him came the language. And the squawking. And the random feathers strewn all about the house. And other miscellaneous unfortunate things, the least of which was the swooning Mrs. Sedley-Stone. Meg was doing what she could to remedy all of these.

The insistent pounding at their front door did not help matters. When it was clear their housekeeper was far too preoccupied with being terrified of the parrot to tend to the arduous task of answering the door, Meg took a deep breath and abandoned Mrs. Sedley-Stone. It wasn't as if she would notice, after all, considering she was unconscious again.

Meg left the small drawing room and the chaos it contained. Of course the sound of Papa's bellowing and the bird's corresponding profanity were little diminished by the distance between her and the entry way. It would take far more than fifteen feet and one simple wall to stifle all that.

Most likely this was the very reason for all the pounding. She expected to find the local magistrate at their door, here to fine them for causing such a disturbance. Or perhaps word of their new house guest's unchristian-like behaviors had reached a higher authority and this pounding was to bring word from the Archbishop, threats against Papa if he didn't reform the dreadful bird right away. Most likely, though, it was one of their long-suffering neighbors with a hatchet and a sudden craving for exotic poultry. At this point, she would half welcome that.

In any case, it would be of little benefit to keep the insistent pounder waiting on the other side of that door. She patted her hair back into place, took a deep breath to calm her frayed nerves, then opened the door. Wisely, she took care to step back just in case there truly should be a hatchet involved.

There was not.

Nor was there a magistrate, Archbishop, or any close neighbor. There was, in fact, no person she'd ever seen before. The gentleman she found at her door was quite clearly a stranger.

Not that he looked strange; quite the opposite, in fact. This particular gentleman looked perfectly ordinary. He had all the requisite features, arranged in what most would consider a pleasing manner, and he wore very adequate clothing. They suited his elegant form quite well, as a matter of fact. His hat perched just right atop his head, which Meg couldn't help but notice was a good six feet off the ground, and his eyes were very much an agreeable shade of blue. Indeed, nothing at all strange about this man.

What was strange, however, was that he stood at her door appearing completely unruffled by all the ruckus in the background—as well as by her unseemly staring. In fact, while the housekeeper screeched and Papa sermonized behind her, this gentleman gave her a smile. Then he surprised her by speaking her name.

"Miss Farrow, I presume?"

Maxwell Shirley knew from the young lady's eyes—rather fetching brown eyes, as a matter of fact—that he'd guessed correctly. Miss Farrow, indeed. Then again, it was hardly a guess. He'd been told the Reverend Mr. Farrow lived at this home with a small staff and an adult daughter. And the parrot, of course.

Since the fresh-faced, demure young woman who answered the door could hardly be the staff—or the parrot—he felt it safe to presume she was Miss Farrow. She was just as he'd been told; well-dressed, lovely, and perfectly proper from top to bottom. Or so she would seem.

Max gave her a warm smile that had served him well with proper-seeming young ladies before. She responded by blinking those wide nut-brown eyes at him. Excellent. Perhaps this part of his journey would prove every bit as productive as he hoped. He was about to launch into the carefully benign greeting he had prepared.

His speech, however, was interrupted. A most distracting uproar came from the rooms behind her. Except for the slightest twitch in her left eye, she did a remarkable job of ignoring it, though.

"Er, yes. I am Miss Farrow," she answered him sweetly. "May I help you, sir?"

He cleared his throat, ready to get on with what might prove to be an uncomfortable interaction.

"Yes, I hope so, miss. I'm here to see..." he glanced at the paper in his hand and tried to appear charmingly awkward. "Mr. Farrow, I believe."

A crash sounded from somewhere inside. This time Miss Farrow appeared concerned and glanced over her shoulder. "I'm afraid he's—"

But a man's voice called from behind her. "I'm right here. Is there someone at the door?"

"Yes, Papa," she said, turning and pulling the door open wider as she did so.

Max could now see the parts of Miss Farrow's delightful form that had been hidden by the door. Delightful, indeed. He could also see the modest but carefully polished woodwork of an average-sized entrance way, along with a rather stiff, red-faced gentleman who, for some reason, was clutching a net. The unnatural shrieks and squawking from the interior of the house continued, though with slightly less fervor than at first.

"May I help you, sir?" Mr. Farrow said, puffing his way through the house to stand beside his daughter.

Max decided he'd do well to forget—at least for now, anyway—the young lady's delightfulness. It was time to be merely charming and eloquent. Perhaps he might find opportunity for delightfulness later on.

"I hope you may help me," he said to the man. "I am here to speak with you on a most important matter."

It was likely a waste of breath. Mr. Farrow wrinkled his brow in confusion. The man clearly had not heard a word Max had said, thanks to the uproarious squawking that echoed throughout the interior of the house. A stream of impressive profanity accompanied the squawking. Max's ears perked to the chaotic din and it might just be about time to ask after it—as any normal person probably would—when a middle-aged woman in an apron came running out of a doorway and into the entrance hall, hands flailing over her head in a most Methodist manner. Quite unconventional, to say the least.

Indeed, though, it was quite welcome. All of this further convinced Max he'd come to the right place today. Miss Farrow clearly possessed the attributes to do what he suspected she'd done, while the good Reverend Farrow was obviously in possession of what Max had been seeking. Now Max was going to find out just what else these questionable clerics possessed… or how honestly they'd come by it.

"I have some questions for you," Max continued loudly, once the profanity had waned and the moaning Methodist had disappeared into the rear of the house.

"Questions about what?" the gentleman asked, leaning in toward Max in an effort to hear him clearly.

"I was told you were the person I needed to speak with about—" Max began to explain, but had to stop.

A large green and yellow bird suddenly sailed through the doorway that had just produced the flailing woman. It landed gracefully on the older man's shoulder and cocked his head, gazing with round, red eyes at Max. A parrot. By God, it was *the* parrot. Max smiled.

"Er, was that your parrot making all the fuss, sir?"

Miss Farrow blushed. Mr. Farrow cleared his throat.

"What? Oh, er, well... yes, and I apologize if—"

The bird slapped him in the face with his wing as he leaped off the reverend's shoulder. It was too sudden for Max to do anything but stand stock still as the bird aimed straight for him and settled itself onto his shoulder, digging in his claws and brushing up against Max's hat. It slid downward over his eyes.

Max reached for the bird, pushing him aside just enough to right his hat, The bird uttered a moderately tame curse. Max tried to hide his pleasure. So the old bird remembered him, did he? Good for him. Now if Max could but trust that his only nice coat would not suffer some unlaunderable defacement.

As it turned out, however, his ear was the item in most immediate danger. The bird nibbled it and Max swore involuntarily. Damn. Not the best way to ingratiate himself into the good minister's favor. It did, however, seem to garner some sympathy from Miss Farrow. She waved her hand at the bird, trying to distract him from his very intent ear nibbling.

"I'm so sorry, sir," she said. "He has a preoccupation with ears, I'm afraid."

"I assure you," Max said, gently swiping at the bird. "I'm not opposed to a little ear nibble every now and again."

But he had little time to consider how Miss Farrow might take his admission. Instead of his swipes succeeding in removing the bird, they merely served to gain its attention. Max was rewarded by a two toed grip around his finger. The bird stepped up onto his hand and allowed Max to bring him round to eye level.

Miss Farrow gasped. Mr. Farrow cleared his throat again. The bird cocked his head in the opposite direction and stared into Max's eyes.

Good old Bartholomew. How long had it been? A dozen years at least. And clearly the bird's vocabulary hadn't improved one bit.

"Good gracious," Mr. Farrow exclaimed. "You've

tamed him!"

"Er, he's not actually a bad creature," Max said, then wondered if it was wise to give so much away already. "At least, so he would seem."

"You know parrots?" Mr. Farrow questioned.

In truth, Max knew nothing of parrots in general. He did, however know *this* one. Hell, he'd learned much from old Bartholomew in his younger days. After a bad night at the gaming table or a disappointing day at the races, he was rather thankful for the colorful descriptors he'd gained from conversing with the creature in his youth. Just now, however, he opted for a more vague answer.

"I know a bit of them, sir."

His words seemed to have a profound effect on Mr. Farrow. The reverend grasped Max by the free hand and pulled him into the house. The sudden movement upset Bartholomew, sending him into screeching and flapping and the repetitive recitation of two damnable lines of what Max knew to be the mildest part of an even more damnable rhyme.

Miss Farrow blushed again. How interesting. Max would not have guessed her to be the type to own familiarity with the rhyme in question.

His curiosity about Miss Farrow's various knowledge, however, was quickly diverted by Mr. Farrow's barrage of questions.

"Can you help us, sir? Have you experience with this sort of thing? How long do you expect it to take?"

Perhaps if Max had been able to make heads or tails of the man's rambling he could have answered intelligibly. As he could not, and as he had found Miss Farrow's warm brown eyes with their mixture of innocence and admiration to be somewhat of a distraction, Max rather babbled his response.

"I... er, that is..."

Thankfully Bartholomew disrupted things by leaping off his hand and flying up onto the nearby stair rail. He joyfully bobbed his yellow head up and down while he completed the rhyme. Miss Farrow blushed again.

"You can help us, can't you?" Mr. Farrow repeated. "You did come about the advertisement?"

Advertisement? Good gracious, were these people trying to sell the bird? Indeed, Max was glad to have arrived when he did. What a disaster it would be if Bartholomew ended up sold off to some stranger. He only hoped he had enough ready blunt to cover the sale. He was hoping not to have need for contacting his solicitor until he had a better idea of the situation here. He needed to know who could be trusted, and who could not.

"Er, yes. Yes I did come about the advertisement," he replied. "What terms are you suggesting, sir?"

Mr. Farrow beamed and shook his hand excitedly. "Excellent! Thank heavens, sir. Come in, come in. We can make whatever arrangements you see fit, considering the urgent nature of things. Meg, go see if Mrs. Cooper has calmed herself enough to get us some tea. She can bring it to the drawing room."

Mr. Farrow began leading Max toward the doorway where all the hysteria had played out so recently. Max politely removed his hat and followed, giving Miss Farrow a bow and feeling somewhat disappointed to be losing her company already. She, however, appeared in no great hurry to rush off at her father's bidding.

"But Papa—" she began.

Her father shushed her. "Go along, pet. I'm sure Mrs. Cooper is fine. You know she's a durable woman."

"Yes, Papa, but—"

"And perhaps some cakes, if she wouldn't mind. It's a

bit early, I know, but tell her some cakes for our guest might be just the thing."

"Of course, Papa, but—"

Mr. Farrow led Max into the drawing room. Miss Farrow followed but Max had the distinct impression she would rather not have. He soon understood why. There, sprawled gracelessly half on and half off the settee was a large woman in bold, matronly garb. It appeared she had at one point been entirely on the settee, but had slid off. Her garb, however, had not. The thick fabric of her gown had remained affixed to the silk of the settee and was now wrapped unceremoniously about her thighs. The effect was not nearly as enticing as a purely verbal description might lead one to think.

Fortunately, the woman appeared to be sleeping and unaware of her dishabille. Unfortunately, the sound of their voices woke her. Her eyes popped open as they entered the room and it was clear she was at first confused by her surroundings. Slowly she took stock of things. She blinked at them and gradually her puffy, blotched face was overcome by an expression of mortification, evidenced by more blotches.

"Good gracious," the surprised reverend said, clearly as mortified to find the woman this way as she was to find herself. "Mrs. Sedley-Stone!"

"Yes, Papa, that's what I meant to remind you," Miss Farrow said, rushing past them to go to the aid of the woman.

Max wasn't at all certain what his response to this vision should be. He knew it would be most improper to stare at the woman whose legs were all but exposed before them, so he looked away. But to look away with so much vigor and enthusiasm might be equally rude. So, rather than turning dramatically around and gouging out his eyes to wipe the image from them, he could only quietly avert his glance in the most gracious, polite fashion possible.

That put his gaze squarely on Miss Farrow's previously noted form. This time it was the backside of her form, to be precise, as she bent in all innocence and Christian charity to help right the older woman's clothes and return her to a more appropriate, seated position. Whether or not it was rude to stare at this Max really did not care. His eyes were not about to re-avert at this point.

"Forgive us, Mrs. Sedley-Stone," the good reverend said in most formal tones. "I cannot express how sorry I am for any discomfort you may have—"

His beautiful apology was interrupted. Bartholomew swooped back into the room and landed directly atop Max's now hatless head. He cringed at the feel of the bird's claws digging into his scalp, while his eyes stung from his hair being brushed down into them. The bird squawked loudly, then most eloquently recited a stanza—in perfect pentameter—declaring what should be done when a woman of dubious morals is found with her skirts up about her this way. It did not involve innocence or Christian charity. Nor did it involve improving the woman's morals. It was, in fact, a line from a song best sung in the company of good friends, aberrant amounts of alcohol, and absolutely no ladies.

None of these conditions were applicable at this time. Both ladies were frozen in stunned disgust. Mrs. Sedley-Stone fell back onto the settee, fainted away. Her turban rolled off onto the floor, but this time her gown stayed where it should be. Miss Farrow sighed, then turned helpless to shrug at Max.

"This happens a lot, I'm afraid," she said.

Mr. Farrow slapped Max on the back. Bartholomew's claws dug in deeper.

"But we have hope now," the older man said brightly. "The Almighty has been gracious, and we have seen our salvation."

Max couldn't quite tell for certain, given that his hair was still down in his eyes and the bird was now turning circles on him which added green and red tail feathers to his visual obstruction, but he got the idea Miss Farrow's expression was not nearly so hopeful as her father's.

"I knew if I advertised, things would work out," the reverend went on. "We needed a parrot trainer, and now here he is. Come, young man. I'll show you up to your room while my daughter handles things down here. You may bring the bird, if you like."

It did not appear as if Max had any choice. Bartholomew was stuck fast to his head and Max could not see to do anything but follow where his new host would lead. So Mr. Farrow needed a parrot trainer, did he? Apparently they were not selling Bartholomew, after all.

Well, this was an interesting turn. Perhaps the old man did have some idea what he was about, after all. No wonder they had put up with the bird's unseemly habits despite the obvious hardship they caused.

Mr. Farrow must know—or at least he must suspect—the same thing that Max did: Bartholomew was the key to a treasure. A treasure, no less, that someone had already killed for. With luck, Max would get the bird to reveal what he knew about both treasure and murder.

Hopefully it would be before the murderer killed again.

Chapter 2

So this so-called parrot trainer was to live here, in their home, was he? Meg wasn't certain she liked that idea. Oh, she supposed she *liked* the idea, but that was entirely the point. She *did* like the idea; whether she ought to or not.

The young gentleman was here to train Bartholomew, for heaven's sake. A parrot trainer. Honestly. What sort of respectable gentleman made his way in life as a parrot trainer? She'd have to keep a close eye on him. And *not* because her eye found his broad shoulders so very easy to keep on.

What did it matter to her that his shoulders were broad and his eyes as blue as a warm August sky? What business was it of hers to even notice such things? She was all of five and twenty, after all, not some young miss to giggle and blush for any stranger to come cross her path. Never mind that she'd been dangerously close to doing both the whole time she'd been in his presence.

Why on earth should she have such a reaction to this stranger, this... this parrot trainer?

And now he was to be living in their home! Gracious, but she'd best get her lingering eyes under control. She was a sensible adult, after all. Her life was devoted to Papa and to looking after the people in their village. She was not about to have her head turned by some stranger who would be here only a short time, just long enough to purge the unpleasantness from poor old Bartholomew. If he could, indeed, do such a thing.

Could he? Was he truly a parrot trainer, or just someone looking to take advantage of Papa's hospitality? She'd best make sure Papa had asked for some references. Blue eyes or not, the man was a stranger and Papa was far too generous for his own good.

But Bartholomew had acted quite docile around the new gentleman. Perhaps this stranger could actually do what he said. How wonderful that would be! Of course, even if the man were the greatest expert in his field, she hardly imagined the task could be accomplished over night. Bartholomew was a difficult case. The gentleman would likely be staying a while.

How did she feel about that? Her life had no room for broad-shouldered gentlemen who made her weak in the knees, or sent prickles up her spine simply by giving a smile. She'd nearly been ruined by such things once; she was not about to let that happen again.

If Papa said this man was to stay here and train the parrot, so be it. The task was quite needed. She'd simply have to keep her distance and see that his work was uninterrupted. Such instant reaction as she'd had to this man convinced her of one thing for certain: the sooner he accomplished his task and went on his way, the better. She'd make sure nothing came in the way of letting that happen.

Unfortunately, Bartholomew had other ideas. Meg had barely gotten Mrs. Sedley-Stone coherent enough to huff herself out to her carriage and head off to her home than the bird came sailing back into the drawing room. She grabbed up a fan from the table and tried to shoo him out of the room, to no avail. He perched atop the mantle and demanded Meg fetch him some rot-gut and a nipper of jack. He addressed her as "wench," which had become his particular name for her.

She glared into his beady, red eyes and was addressing him as a totty-headed cockerel when their gentleman guest came into the room. Meg felt immediately guilty for berating the gentleman's student, but the man seemed to quite understand. He smiled at her and she felt the annoying flash of weakness grab hold of her knees. Drat, but this was going to be much harder than expected.

"Forgive me, Miss Farrow," he said. "I seem to have lost my new charge."

"Yes, I see that," she said briskly. "Perhaps we should lock him up in your room."

And you with him.

"I'm afraid training is not quite that simple," the man replied. "Especially since this is your bird."

"He isn't my bird, sir. Didn't my father explain? We've only recently inherited him."

"Indeed, yes. Your father told me. My condolences on the loss of your neighbor, by the way."

"Thank you. He was a good friend to us."

“Was he?” the man asked. “I was rather under the impression the old man kept to himself and had few friends.”

“He was somewhat elderly and did not go out of his house often, but Papa and I visited frequently. He was always quite gracious.”

“So your father has been vicar here for some time?”

“Just over ten years, sir. Does that have any bearing on your ability to train our parrot?”

“It might. It helps to know how comfortable he is with you, how long he has known you and how well.”

"I see," she said, trying so hard to be casual that she

dropped her fan.

Quickly she stooped to pick it up. Bartholomew burst into another horrible line from another horrible song.

"*Thank God for the view from behind!*"

Oh, that dreadful bird! Her face burned and she wanted to crawl away and hide. She could not, of course, so she tried her best to act as if she had no idea what the bird meant. Obviously she failed miserably. The gentleman knew all too well that she understood.

“I can see why you are so eager to retrain him.”

“It’s been awful, sir," she was forced to admit. "People come visit and they have to endure this… and worse. It’s indecent! We're at our wit's end. You do think there is hope, don’t you, Mr… er, Mr…”

“Mr. Shirley. Maxwell Shirley. And yes, I do think there is hope.”

He moved one step closer to her. She took a step back. Oh, but those eyes! He could likely charm vipers with them. As she had not seen many vipers here lately, she’d best take care that he did not use his talents on her.

“I am quite glad to hear it, Mr. Shirley. Indeed, how lucky we are that you happened to see Papa’s advertisement.”

“Yes, isn’t it.”

“Quite. Now, if you’ll excuse me, I’ll leave you to your work.”

Thank heavens. She could excuse herself before the man had any clear notion of how he affected her. The last thing she wanted was for him to gain any clue of that. A man with brilliant blue eyes was dangerous enough, but for him to realize his own power… well, that would be regrettable.

Max was most careful to hide a smug smile. Miss Farrow liked him; he could tell. This was quite a good thing. He could get her to trust him, to share certain things. His first priority was information, of course, but he'd happily take anything else she might end up wishing to share. He was quite keen for that, actually. For now, though, he'd best tread lightly.

"Er, one question, Miss Farrow," he called after her as she tried to scurry from the room, abandoning him with the blasted parrot.

"Yes, sir?"

"I… that is, as I'll be staying here, it appears, would you tell me when dinner is?"

"What?"

"Unless I am to eat in my room, if you prefer."

"Er, no, of course not, Mr. Shirley. We dine at six, and you are certainly welcome at our table. Papa would have it no other way."

"Thank you, Miss Farrow. No wonder my… er, the parrot's former owner was such a good friend. You are kindness embodied."

"We are Christian people, sir, and you are our guest. Surely that is not so rare."

He gave her his warmest smile. "You are quite rare, Miss Farrow, in every good way."

She blushed again. How charming. Well then, he would lay it on thicker.

"I suppose this must be why your neighbor chose to entrust you with his parrot."

Now to ascertain, did she know how valuable the bird might turn out to be?

Apparently not. She gave a distinctly unladylike snort. "If the man had truly been our friend, he'd have left the parrot to an enemy. Thank you for such flattery, Mr.

Shirley, but I have no need for it. I am happy you are here for the bird's sake, and I would hate to delay you from tending to your task."

Damn. He'd painted it a bit too much. Clearly she had beauty as well as proper gray matter. He'd best take care to remember that for the future.

"I appreciate that, Miss Farrow. You must be eager to see improvement."

"You have no idea, sir."

He tried not to smile. Indeed, he believed he did have an idea how dreadful it had been cohabitating with Bartholomew. He remembered his youthful visits to the earl's home. All the more reason, though, for him to question their motive for keeping the animal now.

"Obviously this is why your father advertised for a trainer."

"I told him to advertise for a *buyer*," she said. "But he would have none of it. So, here you are, sir, and we are thankful for it."

She was inching toward the door even as she spoke. So she was impatient to be rid of the bird as well as him, was she? Well, he would not make it easy for her. She might not know the bird's true value, but her words made him suspect her father just might. He would be wise to question her just a bit more. Besides, he was rather enjoying the game.

"I hope I am up to the task, Miss Farrow. You must realize a case as difficult as this will not be an easy matter."

"I have no doubt of it, sir. But just how long do you estimate you might need in order to reform our degenerate bird?"

"What sort of time frame do you expect?"

"The sooner the better, Mr. Shirley."

"Unfortunately, I can't begin to estimate just yet."

"Hmm. I rather expected as much."

"Are you in any great hurry, Miss Farrow? I mean other than the annoyance of the bird's, er, dysfunction, are there any pressing matters I ought to be aware of?"

"Whatever do you mean?"

"I mean, why are you in such a hurry to convert him, Miss Farrow?"

"Why? Because our house has become a laughingstock. His language is vile, his demeanor is surly, and you saw Mrs. Sedley-Stone. We will never live it down. Of course I'm impatient, Mr. Shirley. Whatever other reason could I possibly need?"

"So you have no incentive of a... financial nature?"

"Oh. I see what you get at. We are not wealthy, sir, but never fear that my father will pay you for your service to us here."

“But of course I didn't mean that... after all, he is a man of the cloth. I trust him implicitly.”

"Do you now? And I suppose you expect us to feel likewise. Well, let me just add that my father will pay for your service as long as you actually provide it. We'll need to see proof that you are indeed making good headway. Soon."

"Certainly, Miss Farrow. I assure you, I'm quite good at what I do."

He paused just a moment to let her think what she would at his words, then held up his hand to invite Bartholomew to fly to him. The bird did, and then proudly—and loudly—announced himself a right pretty bastard.

Miss Farrow rolled her brown eyes. "Oh, yes. I can see you've had quite the improving effect on him already."

“As I said, it will take time, Miss Farrow. I have my work cut out for me.”

“Indeed you do, I’m afraid.”

"But I am quite capable. You'll see."

Yes, indeed, she would see. Max had done a good many things in his life. *Fail* was not one of them. Especially not when a lovely brown-eyed miss was involved.

Chapter 3

"I think Mr. Shirley will work out quite well for us," Papa said when he wandered into the drawing room to interrupt Meg from the letter she was writing.

Oddly enough, she'd just written that very phrase to her sister in Kent. Except for one thing: Meg's phrase included the word *not*. She did *not* think Mr. Shirley would work out quite well for them.

From what she had been able to determine of Mr. Shirley's character over the past three days since his arrival, was that the man was a sort she knew only too well. He was well-spoken, enchantingly turned out, and completely amused with himself. The only person his sort tended to work out quite well for was, well, himself. She'd had a gullet full of this sort of gentleman.

Still, he did have a way with Bartholomew. The bird seemed quite comfortable with him, and vice versa. Not that the man's influence had done anything to curb the bird's language or his annoying tendency to sneak up behind Meg and then bark like a dog, or comment on the view. It was more than annoying, actually. Just yesterday she'd poured tea down her front when Bartholomew did that during a visit with the very elderly Mr. and Mrs. Melling, and already this morning her hairbrush had gone flying. The bothersome bird had managed to get into her room while she was dressing! She refused to even contemplate how that had been managed.

Something would have to be done.

"I'm pleased that you like him, Papa," she said carefully. "But doesn't it bother you that the man would arrive here for a position in our home and not bring any references?"

"He explained that, my dear. The parcel containing his references was lost on his journey. He's contacted his previous employer to forward another. It should just be a matter of a few days more. You'll see, pet. All will be in order."

"I hope so, but—"

"You worry too much. Anyone can see that Bartholomew is quite taken with him. And frankly, so am I. In fact, I wonder why you seem to be so very cool toward him."

"He is a strange man in our home, Papa. I should expect you might be glad to see me so very cool toward him."

"He is a fine young man, by all appearances. I should think you'd appreciate that."

"I prefer to appreciate people on something more than mere appearance, Papa. And his appearance is..."

"It's very fine, isn't it? Yes, I thought you might notice."

"Honestly, Papa! I was not about to say that. Heavens. I was going to say his appearance is rather... convenient."

"Indeed it is. Miraculous, I might even say."

"And I say it is suspicious. Doesn't it strike you as odd that you barely had that advertisement placed and he should appear at our door?"

"But that's what advertisements are for, dearest. I should think you'd be pleased that the Almighty saw fit to answer our need so quickly. And with someone so charming and attractive."

"Who still has done nothing to disrupt the atrocities coming from Bartholomew's mouth... or other parts. Really, Papa, I hope you insisted those references come quickly."

"The English post does the best that it can. Be patient. I think we are well on the road to success with our feathered friend."

At that point, Bartholomew came flapping into the room. It was almost to be expected, really. She'd gone for nearly an hour without suffering any indignities from him. This bird would be the death of them all.

And as for Mr. Shirley... well, she could only wonder what sort of destruction he might bring. The man rushed into the room after the bird and came to a jolting halt when he noticed them there. She refused to acknowledge how his dark, glossy hair fell over his brow, tempting her to right it, or how the room brightened from the hint of the smile at his lip when his eyes happened upon her. Despite three days working with the unteachable parrot, the man's coat was still impeccably pressed and his neck cloth elegantly tied.

Papa's description of the man's appearance as "fine" was quite modest, indeed. But no. Meg would not let herself judge the man on his appearance, no matter how fine it was. Papa might call him miraculous, but she would use other words. Dangerous was certainly among them.

Bartholomew seemed to have no such concerns about the man, though. He ignored him quite easily, swooping up to his perch on the cornice and squawking away as if a formidable, broad-shouldered gentleman was not bearing down on him. Meg was glad said gentleman had turned his attention from her and back onto the bird.

"I'm so sorry," Mr. Shirley said, obviously attempting to explain how—once again—he'd lost track of his pupil. "I was reading from the Scripture in hopes Bartholomew might mimic me, but I'm afraid he took umbrage at the story of the Hebrew children devouring quail in the wilderness."

"Perfectly understandable," Papa said, nodding as if he often experienced the same thing while addressing his own faithful flock. "The unenlightened often times kick against the pricks."

"Er, what?" Mr. Shirley asked, obviously not much of a Bible scholar.

"A prick was used to goad oxen," Meg informed him. "A stubborn ox would kick against it."

"I see. In that case, yes, you are correct. Bartholomew is certainly kicking the prick."

She bit her cheek and forced herself not to comment.

Papa, however, did not appear to see anything comment-worthy about the situation. He simply shook his head and gave a sad smile.

"I'm sure your influence is having some positive effect on him, Mr. Shirley. We must all remain patient."

Mr. Shirley—of course—agreed. "Indeed, sir. Bartholomew's patterns did not develop overnight. He was attended by sailors for many years, and I daresay the old earl did very little to curb the bird's ramblings."

Obviously Papa had been thorough in explaining to Mr. Shirley many details from Bartholomew's history. Yes, the bird had been carried all over the world on a ship full of merchant sailors. It was there he had learned his abhorrent vocabulary, and when he'd passed into Lord Glenwick's possession, the earl had thought the bird horribly amusing. He'd encouraged the outbursts and the endless recitation of one bawdy ballad after another. It was no wonder retraining was proving so difficult.

Not that she was defending Mr. Shirley. She still had

her suspicions about his abilities, as well as his non-existent references. There was no question, however, about his familiarity with the profane. Bartholomew spouted off a surprisingly tame verse and Mr. Shirley chuckled under his breath. Apparently he knew the rest of the rhyme which, sadly, was not nearly so tame.

"When you smile at him that way," she warned the gentleman. "It only serves to encourage him."

"What he said was not so very bad."

"Perhaps not, but the words that come after it are."

"Ah, so you are familiar with that particular stanza?"

"Not by choice, I assure you. Bartholomew has several favorites that we've been repeatedly subjected to."

To prove the point, the bird recited one of these—a thankfully mild phrase Meg had heard far too often. She sighed and waited for the bird to finish, but Mr. Shirley seemed not to mind. He seemed, in fact, to be interested in the mindless chatter.

"I heard him say that yesterday, the same phrase," he noted. "*Dot marks the spot.* Does he repeat this very often?"

"Too often. And several others that are equally nonsensical. Plus, of course, the various bouts of profanity."

"As I've noticed. However," Mr. Shirley said and was clearly quite engrossed by the subject matter. "He does seem to favor certain phrases from rhymes, but not the entire rhyme. I wonder why that is?”

"He's a parrot, sir. I hardly think he can be credited for having deep reasoning behind his words."

As a self-professed parrot trainer, she wondered that Mr. Shirley did not already know this. She'd make certain to point it out for Papa later on. More and more she was convinced Mr. Shirley was not at all what he alleged.

But he gave no indication of being put off by her suspicion. "Of course Bartholomew does not understand the words he speaks, but he certainly understands our reaction to them. He knows what gets him attention and what does not."

"Obviously he cares very little what sort of attention he gets from us," she noted. "Quite often he gets something thrown at his head."

Mr. Shirley tsked at her but she felt no guilt whatsoever. Anyone would be held blameless for such action after weeks of living with the bird. Especially since they never actually hit the bird with their projectiles. So far.

"I've not seen any violence from you, Miss Farrow," the would-be trainer pointed out. "But I have seen you deliver him biscuits to buy a moment of solitude. Oh yes, I've seen you do it. Don't tell me that does not encourage the bird to misbehave."

Papa nodded somberly. "Indeed, you are right, Mr. Shirley. I'm afraid we've been unwittingly rewarding his reprehensible behavior. Meg, have you considered this? No, I daresay neither of us have. We've been so desperate for anything that might buy us a moment's peace we haven't stopped to think what we might be actually teaching him."

"I'll not take any credit for the little monster," Meg declared. "He was corrupted long before he got here."

"The earl certainly did get a chuckle from some of the bird's more colorful sayings," Mr. Shirley said, then quickly amended his words. "At least, I can imagine that was the way of it. Likely it is the explanation for why the bird still persists even after years away from the sailors who initially trained him."

"Your instincts are correct," Papa said with an approving nod. "That was indeed the case. Lord Glenwick did enjoy a bawdy lyric."

"But we do not," Meg was quick to add. "So if there is something we ought to be doing to help curb Bartholomew's enthusiasm for the improper, please instruct us."

Mr. Shirley cocked his head as he seemed to consider this. Bartholomew did the same from his perch above them. Meg wondered who, in fact, truly was the teacher there. Mr. Shirley's words did little to resolve her confusion.

"Perhaps the bird's persistence in repeating these phrases that he clearly no longer hears on a daily basis are a result of his feelings of insecurity."

"His *what*?"

"Insecurity. He's lost a beloved caregiver, the home he knew for many years… it stands to reason the poor creature feels insecure."

Papa nodded knowingly. Apparently he thought Mr. Shirley's drivel was perfectly reasonable. Exactly when he had become an expert on the sensitivities of parrots she really had no idea.

"The poor thing," Papa said with an empathetic sigh. "He has suffered great loss, indeed. What can we do to comfort him?"

Now Mr. Shirley did something Bartholomew could not. He smiled. It was a distinctly roguish smile, too. Meg wondered that Papa did not scold the man for giving her such a look.

"You should sing to him, Miss Farrow."

"*Sing* to him? *I?* What, lullabies and nursery rhymes?"

"Most certainly not. Those things would be meaningless to him. No, I should think the only hope of comforting dear Bartholomew is to give him the things he is comfortable with. Sea shanties and ale songs."

She could scarcely believe her ears. Was the man

demented? He couldn't be serious.

"Sea shanties and ale songs?"

"But of course."

Papa was actually rubbing his chin in pensive agreement. "It would stand to reason that might be seen as comforting for the poor animal..."

"Honestly, Papa! You cannot encourage such things!"

"Mr. Shirley does have a point, my dear," Papa said, to her amazement. "And you do have such a sweet, soothing voice."

"Not when singing sea shanties and ale songs, I don't," Meg grumbled.

How could Papa possibly be in favor of such a thing? He seemed even more smitten with Mr. Shirley than she was. Not that she was smitten. Certainly not.

"Perhaps I should clarify: you must only select the songs and verses that are not particularly, er, offensive, Miss Farrow."

As if she would do anything other than that! Honestly, the nerve of this man.

"And which lines would those be, sir? You've heard for yourself the sorts of things that bird articulates."

He nodded. "Indeed. But surely not every line familiar to Bartholomew is offensive."

Meg snorted. She hoped Mr. Shirley might mistake it for a ladylike sneeze, but of course it was likely he did not. What could he expect? These were not nursery rhymes spewing from Bartholomew all day long.

"It is true," Papa said, judiciously ignoring her snort. "That there are occasionally phrases that do not seem to be a part of some coarse verse."

"Good! Excellent. Then those are the words Miss Farrow should use for comforting him."

She held back the snort this time. "Well, don't expect

that to take very long. I'm afraid I will run out of comfort in a matter of minutes."

"But surely not everything the bird utters includes vile reference," Mr. Shirley persisted. "Although, perhaps you know more about these things than I do."

"I most certainly do not! I simply know that certain seemingly inauspicious phrases he employs fit with the particular rhyme scheme of some others that are a bit more... indelicate."

"Yet not everything can be connected to a greater whole?"

"Oh, who knows?" she snapped. "He is always natting on about something and, quite frankly, I try not to hear it."

"Well, I think we could all help the bird if we do hear it," Mr. Shirley said. "The more we can understand about his habits, the more we can hope to break him of them."

Meg frowned. She wasn't at all certain she liked this line of reasoning. Papa, however, seemed to find it encouraging.

"I say, Shirley, you do know your business. The apostles spoke in other tongues to be understood by the alien, so clearly we must do the same. Yes, we will do all that we can to learn the bird's tongue, as it were, so we can then expect to begin teaching him ours."

"Quite so, sir," Mr. Shirley said, beaming. "You understand my method completely. Now, Miss Farrow, if you'd be so kind as to take out a clean paper. I'd like to create a list of some acceptable, unconnected phrases Bartholomew says."

"Excellent," Papa said. "Your method seems productive indeed."

Meg pushed her letter aside. Apparently her afternoon would be spent not in gentle correspondence with her sister, but in recording the litany of Bartholomew's odious banter. Perhaps Papa might approve, but she did not. Mr. Shirley's so-called "method" was all too clear to her.

The man's intent was to charm Papa and make them do all his work for him. No doubt when Bartholomew remained corrupt, Mr. Shirley would still pocket his fee and claim they were the reason for his failure. He would be gone and no worse for the wear. They, however, would be left a few shillings lighter and still stuck with a foul-mouthed bird.

She was just about to announce they'd not fall prey to his foolishness when Mrs. Cooper interrupted. The housekeeper cleared her throat and came into the room, delivering a newly arrived letter into Meg's hand. Meg recognized the bold, masculine handwriting immediately.

Ah, but this was a welcome interruption indeed.

Max watched her blush. What an interesting turn of events. Who might be sending letters to Miss Farrow that would put such an enchanting glow into her fair cheeks? From where he stood he could not see the writing on the letter so he had no hope of determining the author's full identity. There was little doubt, however, as to the person's gender.

So Miss Farrow had an admirer, did she? And if the tell-tale patches of rose in her cheeks were any sign, she returned the sentiment. The fact that she tried so hard to keep from displaying her reaction—as well as the subtle way she tucked the letter into the drawer of her little writing desk—seemed to indicate that her sentiments were not widely known in the household. At least, not especially known to her father.

Hmm. Perhaps Max could find some way to make use of this knowledge. If Miss Farrow had secrets, surely she'd be eager to keep them. Whatever he might do to push her toward focusing on that rather than on his non-existent references she was so ruddy interested in would surely work in his favor.

The stars seemed in his favor as Mr. Farrow gave his unwitting assistance.

"Come, Meg, Mr. Shirley asked you to help him compile a list," the man said.

She startled, so lost in thought it appeared she had momentarily forgotten them.

"Oh... yes, Papa, but I..."

"Miss Farrow has just received a letter," Max said. "Perhaps she ought to take a moment to read it before we continue."

Now she blushed deeper. "No! That is, no need to take time away from our business just now. I can get to that later."

"Are you certain it is not a pressing matter?" Max asked with the sweetest of tones. "I would not like for you to miss out on something important."

"Is it important?" Mr. Farrow questioned. "Is it from Mary? Are the children well?"

"They are fine, Papa. I received a letter from her just yesterday and everyone is quite well. No, this is nothing. Indeed, let us focus on aiding Bartholomew. Tell me, Mr. Shirley, just what sort of list had you in mind? I'm happy to act as secretary for us. Perhaps you had a lyric in mind that you think we should examine?"

Perfect. Miss Farrow seemed ready to do anything to take their attention off of her letter. He could certainly work with that. In fact, he'd be more than happy to help her.

Do *anything.*

Chapter 4

He'd watched her all evening, but Miss Farrow hadn't gone after that letter. She seemed perfectly content not to know its contents. Max, on the other hand, was getting quite impatient about it.

Why was the girl not more persistent in finding a moment out of company to go back to that desk and retrieve the letter? Did she not worry it might be found there? Or had he guessed wrong and the contents did not contain something incriminating?

He hated to think the later. For one, it fit nicely with his suspicions if indeed Miss Farrow was receiving secret letters from some mysterious quarter. For another, his rational mind simply could not fathom that a young, attractive woman might not have an admirer or two tucked away somewhere. That she was not married and instead lived alone with her father just made him wonder all the more at her reasons.

If she had admirers, why had she not married any one of them? And why would this particular secret admirer need to remain a secret? The obvious answer was because he was in some way inappropriate for her. If Miss Farrow was up to anything inappropriate, Max most definitely wanted to be in on it.

But why had she gone all afternoon and most of the

evening without fretting over that letter? It seemed unnatural. A lady with secrets to hide should, as a matter of course, be more eager to tend to them. By the time dinner was finished and Mr. Farrow excused himself to his study, Max was finding himself quite agitated.

"I must meet with Mrs. Cooper to plan the meals for tomorrow," Miss Farrow said, excusing herself and indicating it was high time Max went back upstairs to be tormented by Bartholomew.

"Thank you for a very lovely dinner," he said before she could exit the room.

"You are welcome," she said, and that was all.

There was nothing he could do but politely rise and wait as his hostess took herself off to the kitchen. What an infuriating woman! Did her blushes this afternoon mean nothing? Was that letter so unimportant to her that she would leave it unattended for days and days while he drove himself mad over it? No, surely he could not have misread her so dramatically.

She must simply be proficient at hiding her desires. With that assumption, he left the dining room and started up the staircase. At the landing, however, he paused. Did he hear footsteps? Yes, he believed he did. Perhaps Miss Farrow did not remain in the kitchen with the housekeeper after all.

He pressed himself against the wall and waited. In moments he was rewarded. Miss Farrow did, indeed, emerge from the dining room and crossed the entry hall below him. She did not glance his direction but silently let herself into the drawing room. Ah, but he'd clearly been right all along.

Now the question remained, was she so eager to see the letter's contents that she would read it there, or would she take it up to the privacy and leisure of her own room? He strained to listen. Returning footsteps or rustling paper?

Paper. Good. So she had not been as indifferent to this letter as he'd begun to fear. She was reading it straight away, the very moment she thought she was alone. Most excellent.

He went back down the steps, moving quietly to avoid detection. She would be irked when he interrupted her, of course, but he could see no way around it. The only way to find out just how he could make best use of her spurious actions—and the guilty conscience that no doubt went along with them—was to find out more about that letter. And it's author.

She was at her desk, letter in hand. He could just make out the curve of her lip; a secret smile for her admirer, he supposed. He disliked the man already. Surely anyone who was not suitable for public acknowledgement did not deserve such a sweet smile from a good woman. He did not feel one pang of guilt for interrupting her.

"Finally reading your letter, I see," he said, stepping into the room.

She started. "Er, yes... I had nearly forgotten it."

Ah, so she was a liar and a secret keeper. He could work with that.

"I suppose we kept you too busy to get to it," he said. "I hope it has not turned out to be any matter of great urgency."

"No, it is just a note from a friend. Nothing urgent."

"That is good to hear. The way you were pouring over it when I came into the room made me worry it might be of great import."

"My friends are of great import to me, sir. Now, is there something I can do for you, or would you mind if I excused myself to my room?"

"The list," he said quickly, before she could make an

escape. "I came back to get the list we made earlier."

"Of course. I have it right here."

She pulled up a sheet from the desk. The three of them—four, counting Bartholomew—spent a good hour making a very exhaustive list of phrases spoken by the bird and determining which were fairly innocent and which were, well, not. The first part of the list focused on the most common phrases and Miss Farrow had become quite the expert at blushing as they went through that. Max and Mr. Shirley had been as tactful as possible, of course, but there was no hiding the fact that Bartholomew was a heathen.

The second part of their list was of more interest to Max. This focused more on the phrases that seemed not to be part of any known rhyme or song lyric. These phrases were enigma—no one knew what they meant or where they came from. Max couldn't recall hearing them before, not from school friends, drinking lads, or any of his father's merchant sailors. And more importantly, not from Bartholomew, not in the years gone by when he'd spent happy visits at Glenwick Mannor.

So where had the bird learned these cryptic phrases in recent times while Max had been gone? And who had been teaching him? And just what part did all of it play into the old earl's untimely death?

"I'm sorry you had to spend so much time on such an unpleasant task," Max said, accepting the page she offered. "Especially when you had this much more pleasant letter waiting to be read. Your friend is well, I hope."

"Yes, thank you."

He'd stepped close to retrieve his list and she'd shifted the letter so he might not see it. The minx.

"Is she a friend from the village, or perhaps an old school chum?"

"It's... yes, someone who once lived in the area."

"Ah, the absent friend. It's good you can keep up correspondence. Have you and she been friends long?"

He enjoyed watching her discomfort as she struggled not to correct his supposed misunderstanding that her friend was a female.

"Er, well... we became acquainted shortly after Papa and I came to live here."

"When you were a mere girl. But she lives elsewhere now. Recently?"

"Not very. Several years now."

"Ah. Once out of the schoolroom. Your friend left to get married, I suppose."

Oh, but she didn't much care for that statement, he could tell. He was more intrigued than ever about Miss Farrow's deep, dark secrets. To be corresponding with a married man! But this was even better than he had hoped.

"Yes," she replied hesitantly. "But sadly, my friend suffered some recent losses and is in mourning now."

"Losses? How tragic. No wonder you are so eager to read her words and respond. I'm sure your kind affections will help soothe her, Miss Farrow."

She blushed again and held the letter closer to her, just in case he might peer over and notice the writing. He had, of course, and his first impression was solidly confirmed. Masculine script, and quite a lot of it, from what he could see. Whoever this grieving, distant friend was, he had much to say to Miss Farrow.

"Thank you, Mr. Shirley. But if you wish to work on your list now, perhaps I should retire to my room. I wouldn't want to disrupt your efforts."

"No need, Miss Farrow. Bartholomew is upstairs and I should return to him. I will study the list there and you may reply to your dear friend in private."

She seemed most relieved at the thought of his departure. Of course he'd much rather stay and continue his questions, but clearly she was on edge regarding her secret letter writer. He'd do well to let the matter drop for now, leaving her to think she'd protected her secret. Perhaps she might even think him a friend, responding, as he had tried to appear to, with interest and compassion.

Indeed, it seemed Miss Farrow was a good woman to be friends with.

"Thank you, Mr. Shirley," she said.

He gave a polite bow then simply moved toward the doorway. She called him just before he was gone.

"And thank you for your work with Bartholomew. I am hopeful we will all be rewarded by your efforts."

So she hoped for reward, did she? It was hard to know just how much he should read into those words. He decided it might be best to let them be for now. It might not be prudent to let his imagination get carried away—at least not until he had more definite proof of his suspicions. What this moment called for now was nothing more than a warm, brotherly smile.

That is what he gave her.

"Thank you, Miss Farrow. Your kind assistance makes my task that much easier. And infinitely more enjoyable."

She blushed again. Ah, but she was fetching with that pink in her cheeks. He was more than pleased to have been the one who inspired it this time.

Finally he was gone. She breathed a sigh of relief. Good heavens, he'd asked so many questions! It had been all she could do to guard her tongue and keep from revealing things she had no wish to reveal. Why had he been so inquisitive?

At first she thought perhaps he suspected. But of course that was ridiculous. How could he? *Why* would he? The man was simply being sociable. Was she so very anxious about things that she could not even recognize friendly conversation? Yes, perhaps she was, and she refused to contemplate what that might imply.

Nigel Webberly was coming back to Richington. Of course she should be feeling some anxiety. Perfectly natural. After all, she hadn't seen the man for seven years—not since he broke her heart and went off to marry that heiress.

Not that she had any reason to blame him, of course. She was barely out of the schoolroom—just a starry-eyed girl and he'd never promised her anything. It had always been expected he'd marry well. He was the grandson of Lord Glenwick, after all. Of course she should never have fancied herself suitable for him, never have felt betrayed when he took her off alone and, instead of a proposal, she was given a good-bye.

It had been all Meg could do not to let her father see how devastated she'd been. How awful it would be even now if he came to suspect how she had felt for the man, what she had assumed he'd intended, how she'd regretted the kisses she'd let him steal! Indeed, Papa must be kept in the dark at all costs.

But years had passed and slowly she'd begun to think herself healed from her heartbreak. She'd seen him for what he was; a man who had wealth, position, and more than enough charm to get nearly anything he wanted from anyone he chose to get it. In the end, he simply chose not to get it from her. She'd vowed to never again be swayed by any other smooth-talking, fine-featured gentleman.

Then how on earth had she allowed Mr. Shirely to end up as their houseguest? And she'd been actually civil toward him just now. This was certainly not a good sign of her recovery. The last thing she wanted—the last thing she would allow—was to be on friendly terms with another charming, good looking man with nothing on his mind but taking his ease and then taking his leave. Everything about Mr. Shirley said he fit that description most perfectly.

Yet he had been applying himself to the cause of bettering Bartholomew, hadn't he? She did not believe it at first, but the gentle way he handled the bird and the insight he seemed to have... he did seem to truly care for the creature. Apparently her time spent discussing the situation with the man as they compiled their list this afternoon had altered her impression of him.

She was still not ready to give up on her quest to see his formal references, though, but it was harder and harder for her to completely dislike him. And she had to admit, it might not be a bad idea for Nigel to see her in company with Mr. Shirley when he returned to Richington. Purely for her own vanity's sake.

Not that Nigel was likely to notice. He was indeed deep into mourning. His grandfather, the earl, had died one month ago, and just four months before that he'd lost his young wife. Papa had insisted they send him plentiful words of comfort and condolence, and to Meg's surprise, Nigel had replied with warm appreciation. He continued the correspondence beyond that and over the past weeks he'd been especially friendly. Not that he gave any hint of rekindling the sort of relationship she'd once thought they'd had. That was entirely in the past.

At least, she thought that it was. But on reading this letter from Nigel today, she must admit to some little doubts. Why had her heart sped up a beat when she read that he'd be returning? Why had his tone seemed so much more intimate in this letter than in his letter last week, or the week before that? And what was this nagging flutter that had settled into her belly? It vexed and perplexed her.

Well, she had three days to purge it—three days before Nigel Webberly returned to Richington to claim his title and ownership of Glenwick Downs. How could she pass the time without seeming a nervous wreck? How could she make certain he would not turn up to find her as wide-eyed and love-struck as before?

She could devote herself to assisting Mr. Shirley, to rehabilitating Bartholomew as much as possible. Indeed, that would certainly keep her mind far, far from matters of love and tender emotion. She'd likely be ready to throttle the first man to turn his eyes upon her after surrounding herself with Bartholomew's filth and Mr. Shirley's conceit and false charm.

If the man's charm were indeed false. It had not seemed uningenuous when he found her here a few moments ago... the way he spoke with such interest and earnest concern about her friend—whom he gratefully assumed was a female—it was more than expected from him. Almost endearing, in fact. And that smile he'd given as he left her alone...

Gracious, but was she actually entertaining such thoughts? Clearly not in her right mind. Nigel's imminent return must have her quite rattled. Indeed, that must be it. Even after all this time, Nigel Webberly could still addle her brain. She'd even begun to consider making friends with Papa's reference-less parrot trainer.

Oh, she was addled indeed and had very little notion what she could do about it.

Chapter 5

"Give your old pole a twist, lad," the blighted bird chattered.

Max did what he could to shush him. Damn the feathered rascal! If some progressed wasn't achieved soon, even the ever optimistic Reverend would start to question Max's ability. Not that he actually had any, of course. Over the past days it had become clearer by the minute he was out of his depth when it came to retraining an obstinate parrot. Bartholomew's language seemed to be getting worse rather than better.

"There once was a sailor named Tuck..."

"Not that one again, please."

"...who asked a young wench for a—"

"Cease, for God's sake!"

He grabbed for the parrot, determined to hold its beak shut, if that's what it would take to stop the flood of vulgarities. Bartholomew was too quick. He leapt off the huge, rag covered tree-trunk someone had brought indoors for use as a perch and sailed around the bedroom, flapping and squawking loudly. By God, if the fluent profanity didn't alert the Farrows to Max's failing, this sort of racket surely would.

He gave up, letting the bird settle atop the dressing table mirror and smugly rearrange his feathers. That's how the creature seemed to feel about everything Max did; smug. It was as if Bartholomew truly did know something Max didn't and was perfectly happy to keep it that way.

But just what did the blasted bird know? In nearly a week of Max's efforts to make sense of Bartholomew's random ranting, he was no closer to having an answer to that question than when he'd first arrived at the Farrow's front door. Had the old earl's death truly been the natural consequence of a long, peaceful life, or were Max's suspicions correct? Had Bartholomew been witness to something devious, or was he just an idiot bird who'd spent too much time in low company? The old earl's final correspondence had seemed to indicate the later. He worried something sinister was afoot, and he directed Max to the bird.

Bartholomew knows. He'll tell you what to do.

Indeed, that's what the letter said, along with a few other things that still didn't make a lot of sense. But so far, Glenwick had been wrong. Bartholomew might, indeed, know something, but he sure as hell wasn't telling any of it to Max.

"Come, bird," Max said, drawing a deep breath and maintaining a herculean grasp on his temper. "Tell me where it is. Where's the old man's treasure?"

Bartholomew cocked his head. Was he contemplating Max's words? Had something Max said sparked recognition within the bird's miniscule brain?

"Treasure? Is that familiar to you, bird?"

He could have sworn the bird nodded. Max was almost ready to cheer when the creature spoke.

"Old man's chest. Old man's chest."

By God, perhaps he'd hit on it at last! For one heart-stopping moment Max dared to hope. Perhaps he'd gotten through, at long last.

"Yes, yes! The treasure chest. Where is it?"

"Forever alone on his island fair West."

West. An island! By Jove, finally the bird was making some sense. Max tried not to let his excitement show. It would not do to get the bird all worked up again, would it?

"An island in the West? Is that where the treasure is?"

"I never will go, to stay is the best."

Oh, hell. Now he recognized these words. Bartholomew wasn't giving him some secret directions for finding the fabled Glenwick treasure, he was reciting another bloody sea shanty.

"I'll guard with my life the old man's chest," Max finished, chorusing along with the bird.

Damnation. What sort of fool was he, thinking to carry on meaningful conversation with a blasted bird? Of course Bartholomew couldn't answer his questions. He was a parrot, for God's sake. All he could do was blithely repeat lines he'd heard over and over aboard the merchant ship where he'd lived for a good 20 years. When Max mentioned "treasure", all that did was bring to mind the words of a song—a fairly bawdy one, at that—about a sailor who let a busty female seduce him into losing his treasure.

“Wretched creature,” Max grumbled.

He kicked the heavy perch. It wobbled only slightly on its substantial base.. The bird squawked as if in real terror for his life and flapped around the room again, leaving a well-aimed deposit on Max’s shoulder. Max swore.

All this was just in time for Mr. Farrow to appear in the doorway.

“Everything well in here?” he asked, though clearly he must have seen for himself the answer to that question.

“Well indeed, my good vicar,” Max replied cheerfully, as if he were particularly fond of bird droppings on his coat.

"A vicar and lass fell down into a hole—" Bartholomew began.

Damn it all, not that one! Max stepped in front of the bird and raised his voice, hopefully enough to drown him out. He smiled at the vicar and opted for mindless—but loud—conversation.

"So, it must be getting on toward supper, I should think. Must say, I'm getting rather famished. Are you? Oh, but is it late? I hope I've not kept you all waiting. Whatever is the time, anyway?"

He ran out of inane things to babble about and was, sadly, silent when Bartholomew delivered his last line of the rhyme.

"Perhaps you should climb on my pole?"

The Reverend cleared his throat. Max loosened his cravat. Bartholomew repeated the last line, for good measure.

"He certainly has a vast repertoire," Mr. Farrow said.

"Indeed he does. I'm working to replace the most, er, colorful phrases with things a bit more universally acceptable."

"Yes, as you've had my daughter singing and chanting to the bird at odd hours during the day."

Yes, he had, hadn't he? And she'd hated it; likely hated him for it. Clearly nothing useful had come of it, but Max had no intentions of allowing her to stop. It was the best amusement he'd had for quite a long time, actually.

"If he hears things that are familiar to him—things that we have deemed unoffensive—my hope is that those are the phrases he'll make free use of."

"Make free with whatever she's got, lads."

Oh, good grief. Would the bird never stop?

"He seems to use that phrase quite often," Mr. Farrow

noted. “Surely it isn’t one you’ve been reciting of late.”

“No, definitely not. It seems there are several phrases he employs more frequently than others. I’m not certain what to make of them.”

“Well, old Glenwick had his own way of things. He never minded the bird’s vulgarities, I’m afraid.”

"No, he was more likely to encourage— er, that is, it would appear the bird was encouraged to be as inappropriate as possible."

Mr. Farrow nodded. "I fear that is the case and there is no hope for poor Bartholomew."

Well, that didn't sound good. Was the vicar already decided to let Max go? What would become of the bird? Blast it all, but somehow he would have to convince the Farrows progress was being made.

"You mustn't lose hope, sir. Remember, it took years for Bartholomew to develop these patterns. Clearly he is not going to replace them in a single day."

"Or five," the vicar pointed out.

"Yes, it does seem things are slow going, I'll admit to that."

"Yet you truly believe there's hope for him yet?"

"I do, yes. Most assuredly."

"Well, he does seem to enjoy your company..."

Max tucked his bandaged hand behind his back. No sense alerting the good reverend to the fact that Bartholomew had tried to enjoy Max's index finger this morning.

"I suppose it would not be charitable if we were to abandon the bird after such a short time," Mr. Farrow said after a decisive pause. "Indeed, if you are convinced he is worth the effort, Mr. Shirley, then I will bow to your greater wisdom and experience in the matter."

Max tugged at his sleeve to make certain it covered the

marks on his arm where Bartholomew had tried to "enjoy" that, too.

"Thank you, sir. I am convinced you will not regret your trust in me."

"I'm pleased to hear such confidence. As it turns out, we will rely on you heavily over the next days. It will be most imperative that Bartholomew keeps a steady tongue... or beak, or whatever he has there."

"Oh? Why is that?"

"A guest, Mr. Shirley. My daughter informs me we are expecting a rather important guest. He should be arriving tomorrow."

"How pleasant for you."

"Indeed, it will be. We've not seen him for years, although he was once very dear to us."

"An old relative, perhaps?"

"He was formerly a resident of our village."

Ah, so this was a part of the reason for Miss Farrow's blushes over her mysterious letter. Her gentleman friend—after his recent losses—was now coming back to her. How very interesting. Max was careful to keep the full measure of his curiosity out of his voice.

"How nice for you to meet with an old friend again. Does he still have family in the village?" he asked.

"No, I'm afraid not. When his grandfather passed away last month, that was the last of his nearby relations."

"Last month?"

"Yes. His grandfather, in fact, was Bartholomew's previous owner. The Earl of Glenwick."

"Glenwick was his grandfather?"

By God, he'd not expected that. Miss Farrow's secret beau was none other than Nigel Webberly! Damn. This was going to be sticky. Max had not intended to encounter the man so soon after his arrival in town.

He should have expected him to turn up right away to claim his inheritance, though. After all, that's what one did when one's grandfather died. No one knew that better than Max.

Lord Glenwick was *his* grandfather, as well.

Everything in the house was just as it should be—or at least as close to that as it could be—so Meg forced herself to take a deep breath, pick up a book, and retire to a comfortable chair in the quiet of her own room. Nigel Webberly would be here tomorrow. He'd be back at his grandfather's estate, back in their village, and he'd be coming here to her home.

To see *her*.

Her heart twisted in her chest at the thought of it. How would it feel to see him again? Had he changed in these past years? Would he think she had changed very much? She'd been a fresh little miss when last he'd seen her. She was hardly so fresh now; would he notice? Would she care if he did?

She wasn't in love with him. That infatuation faded after he left, after he misled her then broke her silly, girlish heart to go marry another. It had been ages, in fact, since he'd even crossed her mind. She had no reason to fear their reunion would be anything but pleasant and friendly. At least, she hoped that it would be.

For Nigel, it would more likely be bittersweet, putting him in mind of a happier time. Since his last visit to Glenwick Downs, much had changed in his life. He'd lost his wife and his grandfather was gone. Perhaps being back here would prove difficult for him.

Indeed, she could imagine it would. Along with memories of happier times, his return would surely remind him of an unhappy time, too. His leaving had been sudden and his grandfather had not been very pleased with him over it. That was why he'd never been back in the seven years since. It was so sad. The old man had died never really reconciling with Nigel.

She would simply have to do her best to see that his return was as peaceful and amicable as possible. Not something that would be easy given Bartholomew's behavior. What would Nigel think when he saw the bird again? As she recalled, he'd not been particularly enamored of him in the past. No doubt time had not made his heart grow fonder.

At least he'd be relieved to find they'd taken that burden on for him and he was not stuck with the creature. He'd probably applaud their efforts at reforming him, even if it did mean they'd brought an unreferenced stranger into their home. She hoped he'd applaud them, at any rate, rather than wonder at Mr. Shirley's presence, especially since no improvement would be detected in Bartholomew and since Nigel—more than anyone else—knew all about Meg's weakness for smooth-talking gentlemen.

But she had no weakness for Mr. Shirley. Indeed, she was very proud of herself for the cool manner she'd maintained toward him, even after five days of facing his smiles and suffering his friendly conversation and unruffled demeanor. And the man's appearance... well, surely she should be highly commended for sustaining indifference when up against *that*. On his best day, even Nigel Webberly had never presented so well.

So deep in thought on the subject matter was she that the housekeeper had to knock at her door three times before she was aware the woman was trying to summon her.

"Excuse me, miss, but you've got a visitor to see you."

Good heavens, could Nigel have arrived a full day

early?

"It's Mr. Perkins, miss."

Meg was suddenly unable to comprehend the simple words.

"I'm sorry, Mrs. Cooper. Did you say Mr. Perkins?"

"Yes, from Glenwick Downs, of course."

Ah, *that* Mr. Perkins. Of course Meg knew him. He was the steward for the earl, he attended Papa's church regularly. Whatever could Mr. Perkins want, coming here unannounced? Gracious, could something have happened to Nigel as he was traveling?

She tidied herself and let Mrs. Cooper lead her down to the drawing room where Mr. Perkins had been deposited. He gave a friendly smile when she entered the room. Certainly he did not look like a man delivering dire news. She hoped his looks were not deceiving.

"Good afternoon, Mr. Perkins. How pleasant to see you. I'm sorry, but I'm not quite sure where my father is right now if you were hoping to see him."

"No, Miss Farrow, I actually came to see you."

"Me? Well, I'm happy to help you in any way I can. What is it you need?"

Mr. Perkins cleared his throat and glanced toward Mrs. Cooper who stood silently in the doorway. It was obvious he hesitated to state his business in her presence, although what on earth he could be so concerned about, she could only guess. Still, if he had business that was best discussed in private, Meg knew there was likely good reason.

"Thank you, Mrs. Cooper. If my father turns up to ask for me, you may tell him I am here. I'll call for you if there is anything we need."

The housekeeper nodded and pulled the door shut behind her as she left them. Meg turned back to her guest.

"Now, whatever has brought you here, Mr. Perkins?

Not any bad news, I hope."

"No, Miss Farrow. No bad news that I am aware of, but..."

"But what, Mr. Perkins?"

He seemed uncomfortable, as if he really did not wish to continue. She bit her lip and wasn't certain that she wanted him to. Whatever could he be about? If it wasn't bad news regarding Nigel's expected arrival, then what?

"I'm afraid you are unaware that the earl confided in me regarding... certain matters," he began.

"Certain matters?"

"Regarding Nigel Webberly. That is, I should say, the new Earl of Glenwick."

"And what did he tell you regarding him?"

Mr. Perkins hesitated, then continued.

"You know the old earl loved Mr. Webberly best of his grandsons."

No, she hadn't known this at all. "I only ever heard him speak very highly of both of them. He was devastated, of course, when the older one died in that accident aboard ship some years ago."

"Yes. The elder Mr. Webberly's loss was tragic, but the earl was secretly happy to know that Nigel would be left as his heir."

"I'm sure the earl was happy to have anyone left as his heir," she couldn't help but note. "First he lost his elder son, then Nigel's father, and then the elder of the grandsons perished. It's no wonder the poor old earl became such a recluse."

"His lordship had more than his share of sadness in life, yes. But of course he was never pleased with the elder grandson, going off to live in America when his mother remarried the way she did."

"Yes. I never got to meet that Webberly, he was out of

the country by the time Papa and I came to Richington."

"Well, his choice to leave England was a great disappointment to his grandfather. Perhaps that was why they old earl had such especially high expectations for Mr. Nigel Webberly."

"I'm sure that he did."

"So you can understand how devastated he was when Nigel engaged in... well, when you and he..."

"When he and I *what*, Mr. Perkins?"

"The earl was aware Nigel may have given you reason to have certain expectations. I don't know if you're aware, but this caused a rift in their relationship."

"Yes, I must admit I had suspicions of that."

"So you informed the old earl what transpired between you and his grandson?"

"He was a dear friend. Nigel left us all so very suddenly, you must understand. I was confused so I went to the earl. He informed me of Nigel's engagement and, I admit, my astonishment at the time was probably evident."

"So this brings us to the matter I have come to see you regarding today."

"It does?"

"Yes. You must be aware of the rather, er, sensitive documents the earl had drawn up at that time."

"No, I can't say that I am."

"Well, the fact of it is, Miss Farrow, that he did. And now I regret to inform you, they have gone missing."

"But what does this have to do with me?"

"They pertain entirely to you, of course."

"Me? What sort of documents are they?"

He nervously cleared his throat. "They are documents of a legal nature."

"Legal documents?"

"You are completely unaware of this?"

"Completely, sir. I cannot possibly see what legal documents his lordship could have had that might in any way concern me."

"He did not forward copies on to you? To your father perhaps?"

She was amazed at the very notion of such a thing. What could Mr. Perkins be talking about? She and Papa had been friends with the earl, but certainly there had never been anything of any legal nature between them.

"No, of course not. My father and I were never involved in any of his lordships legal affairs."

"Then he did not tell you of any certain hiding place he may have designated for such things?"

"No. What things? I'm very confused by this, Mr. Perkins."

"So... you are unaware of the arrangements he made?"

"Arrangements? If you are referring to Bartholomew, he merely asked us to look after the bird for him. There were no legal documents made for this, as far as I know."

"No, Miss Farrow. I'm afraid it is another, far more personal matter I refer to."

"What, then? I honestly cannot guess what you might mean, Mr. Perkins."

He was clearing his throat again, tugging at his neck cloth. It was all very confusing. She ran through any memory she might have of documents ever coming from Glenwick, or anything Papa had mentioned regarding such a thing. Nothing came to mind.

"The old earl," Mr. Perkins finally continued. "Made specific arrangement for funding to be set aside in the event of..."

"Yes?"

"In the event that..."

"Yes?"

"In the event that a child should be the result of your, er, acquaintance with his grandson."

Her mouth dropped open. A *child*? So, dear old Glenwick thought that she and Nigel... oh my! But she'd never given him any reason to suspect that. Good lord. He'd gone and put his suspicions in writing? Gracious, now that document was missing and was likely to turn up anywhere. After all, the old earl was dead and his steward, his solicitors, everyone was busily putting his house and his documents in order. Nigel would be here to take over and... oh, gracious. Whatever would Nigel think if he were to find those documents?

Oh, but he'd think she'd spoken all manner of ill things about him to his grandfather! He might think she'd gone straight to Glenwick, carrying horrible tales and accusations, perhaps even in an effort to extort from the man. He would blame her for the rift that ensued between them. Indeed, this was a disaster! Whatever could the old earl have been thinking?

"Oh, heavens, Mr. Perkins."

"Indeed. As you can see, I felt it imperative that I make you aware of this development."

"Yes, thank you, Mr. Perkins. But I must assure you that—"

"No need, Miss Farrow. It is obvious Glenwick's fears were unfounded and I assure you I will be the very picture of discretion."

"Thank you, Mr. Perkins. I... I simply do not even know what to say."

"Say nothing, Miss Farrow. This is a delicate matter, of course, and the less that is said by either of us, the better."

"But what will we do? You understand I cannot have such a thing bandied about."

"No, which is entirely why I came to you. As you

surely have no expectation where the new earl is concerned, then you will undoubtedly want these documents located and disposed of as quietly as possible."

"Yes, certainly. But you said they are missing."

"Perhaps disposed of already by the previous earl; I don't know. I merely thought that perhaps you had some idea of them."

"No, none, sir. Lord Glenwick never once mentioned that he had done such a thing."

Mr. Perkins shrugged, but clearly was very relieved. "Well, then perhaps we are fretting for no good reason. Clearly old Glenwick was under some misapprehension regarding your relationship with his grandson, and clearly nothing further needs to be done with any legal matters he may have drawn up at the time."

"Other than we cannot have people hearing about this! Dear heavens, what will they think?"

"Indeed, I can well understand your concerns. Perhaps... perhaps you might like to take a look at the old earl's papers? You might notice some reference that I have overlooked. I'm sure you would wish to be certain all is contained."

Lord, but if old Glenwick had suspected such things of her, there was no telling what he might have mentioned in correspondence to family or friends. Mr. Perkins was a kind man to be concerned for her, of course, but it did stand to reason he might have overlooked something amongst the earl's papers. It was not his name that would be ruined, after all.

And Nigel—the new Earl of Glenwick—would be here tomorrow! It stood to reason the first thing he might do was go through his grandfather's papers. If anything existed there that might shine a dim light on her, she could never face him again. And Papa... oh heavens, what this scandal would do to him.

Papa's living depended on keeping favor with the earl. She couldn't stand it if her one youthful folly were to bring shame on her father after all this time. Yes, perhaps Mr. Perkins was right. Perhaps she might like to take a look at the old man's papers... before anyone else did.

"Yes, Mr. Perkins. I do wish it, beyond all."

Chapter 6

Max left Bartholomew to chew on his own digits for a while so that Max could steal down to the pantry in search of something—anything—that might distract the bird long enough to hear himself think. He crept down the stairs and his ears immediately perked at the sound of Miss Farrow's delightful voice from the drawing room. She'd avoided him for hours and he'd resented it. Who was she with now? It would be wrong to eavesdrop, of course, but no one could fault him for walking slowly as he passed the door, only slightly ajar.

When he detected a male voice from inside, his slow steps faltered. Miss Farrow was alone with a man! Indeed, how could he not pause with interest?

"Yes, Mr. Perkins. I do wish it, beyond all," he could hear her say.

Indeed, the breathless tone in her voice indicated that whatever it was that this Mr. Perkins had offered, her agreement was heartfelt. Max was enthralled.

"I knew you would welcome my visit," the male voice replied smugly. "I knew I would not regret if I dared to come speak to you on this."

"I'm so glad that you did! But please, Papa cannot know of it."

"Of course. We shall certainly continue to keep the

matter quiet."

"I… that is, I'm afraid I feel quite urgent about this. Do you think we might find time to get deeper into the matter yet today?"

"I should certainly think so."

Max had to clamp his jaw shut to keep it from gaping open. Was he hearing what it seemed he was hearing? His blood pounded as Miss Farrow continued.

"We cannot proceed here, though. You understand, but Papa…"

"Of course. At the manor, then," her gentleman replied quickly. "Will you meet me at the manor?"

"Yes, I can do that. This evening."

"Can you get away?"

"I will tell my father I am visiting Miss Bent. She's been ill, so he will think nothing of it."

Damn, but even Max was impressed at how easily the chit planned her lies. Well, well, well… he knew Miss Farrow was a still water running deep, but he had no idea just how deep she was! And how deep she was in it, apparently.

Just who was this most fortunate gentleman? Max didn't recognize the voice, but that was hardly a surprise. He'd met precious few people since coming to Richington on this visit, and he could hardly be expected to recall acquaintances' voices from all those years past when he spent summers here. It only seemed likely, though, that the manor to which the gentleman referred was the only manor home in the area Max was aware of: Glenwick Downs.

But this wasn't Nigel—even after these years, wouldn't Max know his voice? Besides, Mr. Farrow said they weren't expecting Nigel until tomorrow. No. It couldn't be him. This Mr. Perkins must be yet another man of the lady's very close acquaintance. Just how many men did this modest little spinster have?

And would she like another?

"Thank you, Miss Farrow. I will do my best to see that our, er, meeting this evening goes well," the man said earnestly.

"I appreciate that, Mr. Parker. A satisfactory conclusion to this will surely be a benefit to both of us."

Max firmly bit his cheek to keep from laughing aloud. Or snorting. My, but the chit was cool about her illicit assignations! Obviously she didn't yet know the man who could kindle a blaze beneath her frigid demeanor. At least, she didn't yet know him in the Biblical sense. Not that Max was one to boast, but he had no doubt he could teach the chilly miss a thing or two.

But who was this Perkins and what on earth could he mean to Miss Farrow? There was nothing in her tone that indicated he meant anything to her at all. So why was she planning to engage in scandalous activities if there was no real passion to drive her? Curiosity was driving Max to reckless abandon as he pressed his ear against the door.

"Indeed," the gentleman said. "With luck, the new earl will know nothing of it when he arrives tomorrow."

"That is certainly my hope. I do wish to continue on friendly terms with him."

"I can understand. You would naturally wish that."

Max had to wonder what sort of simpering lout this Perkins fellow was. How could he sound so calm and unaffected? Even a fool could see the young lady was just dangling him along. Was this fool so very desperate he would arrange a secret tryst with her all the while knowing she cared more for another?

Then again, Richington was a small village. Choice material like Miss Farrow was not to be found around every corner. Apparently this Perkins was clever enough to realize that jealousy or posturing on his part would get him nowhere. He'd have to make himself content with what he could get. Still, Max could not reconcile any of this in his mind. What on earth was the woman up to?

"Very well," Mr. Perkins continued with unmanly calm. "I shall take my leave, waiting with impatience until you can meet me this evening."

"I'll be as prompt as I can," the young lady said.

Prompt? Who spoke of promptness when planning matters of passion? By God, the woman was an iceberg. She showed as much zeal as if she were scheduling a visit to the fish market. Max shook his head. What sort of tryst was this, these two unbesotted lovers so casual and indifferent? Why should they even bother to put themselves out for it? He could surely understand Miss Farrow's lack of interest, but how was the Perkins fellow so even and cool? It was unnatural.

Max was contemplating what Perkins must have done or said to tempt her in the first place when he suddenly realized footsteps from inside the room were coming toward him. Damnation! He gathered his wits just in time to jump away, back toward the stairs, and pretended to have just entered the area as the door to the drawing room opened.

A well-dressed—but very middle-aged—gentleman appeared in the doorway. Behind him, Max could see that Miss Farrow was surprised to find someone so nearby. He smiled casually as if he knew nothing and nodded toward the gentleman.

"I beg your pardon, I had no idea there were guests."

With a courteous bow he stepped backward, up onto the bottom step to allow ample room for Miss Farrow and her gentleman to proceed past him toward the front door. They did not. Mr. Perkins understandably narrowed his eye and studied Max. No doubt he had good reason to wonder what Miss Farrow was doing with yet another gentleman in her personal orbit.

She detected the quandary and cleared her throat. "Mr. Perkins, this is Mr. Shirley. He is here assisting my father with, er, a project."

Max bowed once again. “I am the parrot expert, sir. I am assisting with the parrot.”

Mr. Perkin’s brows went upward. “Assisting with the parrot? I was unaware there was anything wrong with the bird.”

“Bartholomew’s fine,” Miss Farrow informed. “But it’s his language, of course. Papa decided we needed to bring in a trainer to reform him.”

Mr. Perkins actually seemed interested. “I see. And have you had much success, Mr. Shirley?”

“Some,” Max relplied.

“Very little,” Miss Farrow chimed over top of his reply. “Bartholomew spouts his rubbish all hours of the day and we are yet to make heads or tails of any of it.”

“But we are trying,” Max finished, determined not to let her malign his competence, despite the fact he admittedly had none—in the area of parrot training, at least. “These things take time.”

“Well, I’m sure that his lordship appreciates all your effort,” Mr. Perkins said. “He will undoubtedly be happy to reunite with the bird once he’s arrived back at the manor.”

Even Miss Farrow seemed surprised to hear this. “Reunite at the manor? Do you suppose Ni—the new earl will wish to keep his grandfather’s parrot for himself?”

Mr. Perkins shrugged. “It would stand to reason he might. The bird was very dear to his grandfather, after all. True, his language is abhorrent, but for sentiment’s sake, I would imagine the new earl will want the bird back.”

Miss Farrow chewed her lip. “Right away, do you suppose?”

"I don't see why not, especially if Mr. Shirley has not been achieving success with his training."

"But I have," Max argued, pointlessly. "Some."

"Then his lordship will undoubtedly thank you," Mr. Perkins said cheerfully then headed for the door. "I will inform my employer of these new developments."

His employer? Ah, so Mr. Perkins worked for cousin Nigel. Max wondered what Nigel would do if he knew just how closely his associate was attending his duties.

"I'm sure we will be happy to see the new earl reunited with Bartholomew," Miss Farrow said, following her guest to the door. "And thank you so much for your visit today, Mr. Perkins."

"Indeed it was my pleasure," the man said, turning to face her and give Max a dismissive nod. "And a pleasure to meet you, Mr. Shirley. I must be about my business now, but I look forward to seeing you again, Miss Farrow."

She gave no hint of looking forward to the same as she returned his nod. "Yes, thank you, Mr. Perkins."

Once again Max was impressed by her coolness. She actually showed more emotion at the mention of the offensive parrot being dislodged from her home than she had at the veiled reference to her scheduled liaison with the bland Mr. Perkins. Who was the fellow that he should presume to know what Nigel would or would not wish to do with their grandfather's prized parrot? Especially if it the good reverend had been specifically entrusted with the bird by the old man himself?

It was all very odd. Max would most definitely be interested in learning more about Mr. Perkins and this entire situation.

"Mr. Perkins is steward at Lord Glenwick's estate,"

Miss Farrow kindly informed Max once the door was shut behind the man and they were alone.

Ah, that explained things. Somewhat. But whatever happened to Mr. Hastey, the steward Max remembered from his own days at Glenwick? He very nearly asked, but of course that would have enlightened Miss Farrow that he had some connection to the place and he most certainly was not ready for that. Not now, when he was only just getting some solid evidence to prove his suspicions.

"Ah, I see," Max said, although of course he truly didn't.

Miss Farrow didn't seem to care one way or another, though. "If you'll excuse me, Mr. Shirley, I have, er, things to tend."

He bowed politely and stepped aside to allow her access to the stairway. "Yes, I'm sure that you do, Miss Farrow."

She frowned at him, then shrugged and scurried past, trotting upstairs to tend whatever it was she needed to tend in preparation for her evening's plans. He almost felt sorry for her, knowing things were not very likely to go as expected. After all, he intended to interrupt them.

Meg absently tapped the table and glanced—for the hundredth time—at the clock. Was it her imagination, or was dinner taking interminably long tonight? And could Papa possibly chew any slower? Heavens, but she was becoming more and more agitated every minute. Surely Mr. Perkins was going to give up on her, to think she was not coming.

And of course she really shouldn't go. Indeed, anything that required her to lie to Papa could surely not be a proper thing to do. Then again, it would certainly not be proper if these papers Mr. Perkins mentioned were to turn up in the wrong hands, their horrible accusations and assumptions coming into public knowledge! No indeed, that would not be proper at all, either.

She had no choice but to slink over there and help Mr. Perkins look for them. She simply had to find them, or at least be convinced they'd been destroyed years ago. It was wrong to lie and to go sneaking around, of course, but she comforted herself with the knowledge it was for a worthy cause. It would protect Papa, of course.

"You've hardly eaten, my dear," he said from his place at the head of the table.

She started. "What? Oh, but I find I'm not terribly hungry, Papa."

"Perhaps this meal is not to your liking," Mr. Shirley suggested. "Could it be you have an appetite for something else?"

"No, of course not. It's just... I have recalled that I had promised to look in on Miss Bent today. You know Miss Bent, Papa. She's been ill, the poor thing. She's really quite elderly now and her niece has had to go into Town for a time. We know times are tough for them and I do worry so. I feel simply awful that I've not been to see them and after I had promised and all... so perhaps I should go over there now. Yes, I should, don't you think? Of course you do. You always tell me to do what is right, Papa, and I did make a promise..."

Mr. Shirley was watching her intently. What was that look in his eye? *Condemnation.* It was almost as if he could detect that that she lied! Could he? No, surely not. How could he? She was merely imagining things. He wasn't condemning her at all. He was smiling, in fact.

"It's refreshing to hear a young lady so dedicated to good work, Miss Farrow," he said. "Too often young ladies seem to care only for fripple and finery and beaux. How pleasant to see you are nothing at all like those pretty packages with nothing inside them but cotton."

"Thank you, sir," she said, but wasn't quite sure that he merited it. Had that been a compliment? She wasn't at all certain.

"You want to go visiting now?" Papa asked. "But it will be dark in two hours."

Oh, bother. She was going to have to elaborate on her lies to convince Papa. Drat. How she hated that! But what other option did she have?

"Perhaps I could accompany you?" Mr. Shirley offered unexpectedly. He smiled again at her, then turned his attention to Papa. "That is, if you think such a thing might be appropriate, sir. I agree that it is not wise for Miss Farrow to be out on her own as evening wears on, but she did give her word to this Miss Bent, and the poor old woman must need visiting. I could surely see that Miss Farrow is safe on her errand of mercy."

Good heavens, this was the last thing she needed! But surely Papa would never allow it. To send her off alone with Mr. Shirley would be even more inappropriate than allowing her out on her own, of course. No doubt she could trust Papa to be sensible about this, at least.

But Papa's sense of propriety failed her.

"You would do that, Mr. Shirley? How very considerate of you," he gushed.

"It is the least I could do, sir, after you and Miss Farrow have been so gracious toward me."

"But Mr. Shirley," she protested, hoping she didn't sound quite as desperate as she felt. "As Papa noted, it's getting on toward dark, and I'm afraid you don't know it, but Miss Bent lives almost a mile out of town. It's nearly as far as Glenwick Downs. I can't possibly prevail on you to put yourself out for such a distance on my account."

But it seemed her argument had the opposite effect as she'd hoped.

"What, so far out of town?" Mr. Shirley exclaimed. "Then I flatly insist, Miss Farrow. You must let me accompany you."

"Most definitely!" Papa said. "And you should take the carriage. It is worth it in this instance, my dear. "

She franticly searched for a way out. "But Papa... it's such an imposition for Mr. Shirley and... and you know how timid Miss Bent has gotten in her old age. Just think what a fright it might be to have a carriage arrive with a strange gentleman."

Papa countered easily. "But you would be there to reassure her, my dear."

If she had been a child she would have stamped her foot and pouted. As it was, she had to settle for a disappointed frown.

"I don't know, Papa. Perhaps I should not go."

Drat. She could hardly *not* go, so it appeared she truly would have to sneak away. Perhaps she could claim a headache and retire to her room early. Would Papa discover her gone if she then tiptoed away? Would he even believe a headache story after she made such a fuss about leaving? Likely not. She wasn't sure what she could do.

"But you must go," Mr. Shirley said. "I can see your concern for your friend and you are to be commended for it. Surely you will not rest well if you have not looked in on her."

"Yes, but—"

"But you are concerned my presence will upset the frail old dear. Yes, I can very well understand that. I am a stranger here, after all. But she lives out of the village, you say? Is it, perhaps, in the direction of the posting house?"

Meg wasn't sure of his intent, but she nodded in confirmation. "Yes, it is, actually. Just a slight ways beyond."

"Excellent. Then perhaps, if your father agrees, I could ride with you that far and you could drop me off at the posting house. I have some letters I should send and can post them from there. Perhaps the distance from there to Miss Bent's house is not too great and your father will not worry of you traveling alone. When you are done, you can simply retrieve me on your return."

Meg was a bit dubious of this suggestion, but Papa latched right onto it.

"Capital! Indeed, a most excellent solution, Mr. Shirley. You are resourceful, indeed. Don't you agree, Meggie?"

"Indeed, it does seem to suit all our needs..."

"Then it is settled," Papa said. "Thank you, Mr. Shirley. I'll send for the carriage immediately and I suggest you set off right away, the sooner the better, to make use of what daylight there is."

"But you know how Miss Bent likes to talk, Papa," Meg said, giving one last half-hearted effort at dissuading Mr. Shirley. "I could be there quite a while."

"No need to worry on my account," Mr. Shirley said. "I've got a book I can bring. Once my letters are done, if you are not back, I can read. Feel free to take your time. Even if after dark, you'll be quite safe with me, Miss Farrow."

"Wonderful!" Papa exclaimed, giving Meg no opportunity to quarrel.

"Fear not, Miss Farrow," Mr. Shirley said with a dashing grin. "I'm an excellent watch dog, you'll find."

Drat him, but that's what she was afraid of.

Chapter 7

His companion was uneasy. Just as he hoped. She was perched nervously beside him in her father's carriage—which turned out to be nothing more than a very modest gig—and her apprehension was palpable. Max was going to enjoy this little drive.

"You'll tell me the way I should go, won't you?" he asked, although he knew it quite well. "You are much more knowledgeable about it than I am, and I'd hate to proceed in the wrong direction."

"I doubt that will happen. There is but one road leading north out of Richington."

"Yes, but if you're not on alert, I might go too far, Miss Farrow."

He watched her expression, wondering if she noticed he intentionally chose phrasing that could have been interpreted more than one way. Amazingly, she seemed completely innocent—or at least quite oblivious. How could she possibly be on her way to an illicit liaison and not recognize his most eloquent *double entendres*? What was he to make of this chit, anyway?

"I will alert you when we have gone far enough, sir."

Indeed, he had no doubt she would. Miss Farrow might be prepared to go entirely too far with her friend Mr. Perkins, but Max had no reason to expect her attitude toward him to be similarly accommodating. What was it about Perkins that appealed to her?

She gave no indication of passion or honest affection for the man. From all he could see, she was mostly indifferent toward him. So why go to all this trouble to meet him this way? Why risk public scandal and shame? There could really only be one logical answer—her interest must have something to do with the man's position.

Mr. Perkins was steward at Glenwick Downs. He had been managing things for Max's grandfather. Obviously, if anyone would know the old earl's secrets, it would be his steward. And since Mr. Perkins expressed special interest in Bartholomew, there was one conclusion Max could draw.

The steward must know of his grandfather's hidden treasure and Miss Farrow must be in league with him to find it. That had to be why she would put up with the annoying bird in her home when clearly she would rather have not, and that was why she would waste her time with a lowly steward. She wanted that treasure and she needed Mr. Perkins to help her find it.

"So you are certain you do not need me to accompany you to your friend's house?" Max asked her after a few moments of uncomfortable silence.

"No! That is, I would hate to worry her, as I said. If you don't mind waiting at the posting house, that would be best."

"Of course. If you're certain."

"I am."

"And you'll be safe on your own?"

"Of course I will. It isn't as if Richington is overrun with highwaymen and the like. Besides, we still have some hours of daylight. I'll hardly be alone on the road but for a few minutes."

Indeed, she was likely correct about that. If Perkins was any sort of a man, he'd be waiting at the front gate for her and wouldn't waste a minute getting to their business. But this caused Max to wonder. What—other than the obvious—*was* their business tonight? Surely Miss Farrow expected more than a quick tussle. Did they have some promising clue, some evidence gained to lead them on to the treasure?

He himself had been less than successful at gaining that knowledge. His grandfather's last letter had indicated quite plainly how the information was to be got, but so far all Max's efforts had come up empty. It seemed, despite his grandfather's conviction that he had passed his secrets along to his trusted pet, Bartholomew was not inclined to share what he knew of the whereabouts of any treasure. Try as he might, Max had not got him to spout off anything but low-minded drivel.

So what clues did Miss Farrow and her uninspiring lover have? Max could hardly wait to find out. He only hoped his grandfather hadn't done much renovation on the aging manor house in the years since Max had last visited. He was counting on the secret passages he'd played in as a child still being passable and, well, still secret.

Meg glanced over her shoulder, not for the first time. Was someone following her? She saw nothing, just the long, evening shadows on the familiar road. Her horse plodded along peacefully, unaware of any potential danger.

Meg's heart pounded, though. She'd left Mr. Shirley at the posting house not half a mile back. He'd seemed content enough, hauling his leather bag containing the writing supplies he'd need to catch up on correspondence. It actually seemed he was looking forward to a couple quiet hours without Bartholomew. Not that she could blame him for that...

She glanced around again, seeing nothing but trees and farm fields and the occasional sheep in the distance. The hairs pricked at the back of her neck, though. Why should she be so on edge? Indeed, if there was anything to fear here, it was Meg's own conscience, clearly quite unsettled by her lies and deceit. This sort of thing was not at all her usual manner and her stomach churned over and over because of it.

She had lied to Papa, lied to Mr. Shirley, and was now heading off to meet Mr. Perkins to work at concealing yet something else. Heavens, how had she come to this? It was no wonder her nerves were frayed and she felt quite a wreck. It would serve her right to develop digestive spasms after this.

But now the horse's ears did flick. Indeed, Meg had heard a twig crunch in the brush behind them, and the animal heard it, too. She glanced back. Again, there was nothing and no one. It appeared she and her horse were alone on the road.

Well, the little creek bed that had been running along near the road veered off toward the east and with it the undergrowth. For the next mile, Meg would have nothing but open farmland on either side. If anyone was following, she would certainly see them, and hopefully be able to avoid any confrontation. She slapped the horse into a more rapid trot and soon left any tree, creekbed, or possible hiding place far behind her.

Glenwick Downs was just on ahead, over the next roll in landscape. She would be within eyesight of the place soon enough, and Mr. Perkins would see she was safe once she got there. There was nothing to fear, except her own guilty conscience, of course.

Her stomach rumbled and churned again. Oh, but this guilt was tortuous! How was she to manage it? By keeping her time with Mr. Perkins as brief as possible, obviously. If she was quick, she might even have time to stop in at Miss Bent's house on her way home. Yes, that's what she could do.

Miss Bent's home was just along her way. She had passed it not ten minutes after leaving Mr. Shirley behind, in fact. If she stopped there on her return—even just to say a quick hello and then be off—she might feel so much better about this evening. Why, she would only be half of a liar, then.

Her conscience felt lighter at the thought of it and her stomach stopped churning. A bit. Mostly, though, she was just eager to get to the Downs and have this unpleasant task over with.

Just as she came around the bend that led to the grand entrance for the Downs, her eye caught on something off in the distance. A figure, moving in the foliage along the now distant creek bed. No, she was imagining. It was a shadow of something, perhaps, but at this distance it was impossible to say what. A deer, someone's hound, a wandering swine... anything, really. Whatever it was should not concern her, of course. It was too far away and clearly not following her. If there had been anything there, it was moving off into the distance, keeping to the shelter of the creek bed as it wound its way toward the lake behind Glenwick Downs.

She, however, was just passing through the heavy stone gate that would welcome her into Glenwick Downs. She could make out the row of mis-matched chimneys along the grand roof even from here. A long, tree-lined lane would take her over a low crest and there the house would be laid out before her. No matter how many times she and

Papa had been invited to visit, the sight always took her breath away.

And tonight was no different. The imposing stone walls of the manor looked like burnished gold in the evening sunlight. The tiled roofs tilted at a hundred different angles, yet seemed perfectly in harmony with one another as they sheltered the many rooms and alcoves of the great, ancient house. Sunlight glinted off the tiles, making shades and shadows, drawing her to wonder at the countless secrets the place seemed to hold.

The windows—it looked like a hundred of them—sparkled the orange and red sunset in their many panes. The grounds surrounding the house boasted manicured lawns and carefully planted groves. The rose garden could be glimpsed just around the corner and she could smell the scent of early blooms wafting her way. The effect was quite grand and Meg knew she never would get over the thrill of being allowed access to such a beautiful place.

Tonight, however, she couldn't allow herself time for admiring. Mr. Perkins was standing on the front steps, waving toward her. Apparently he was as eager to do this as she was. She hoped that meant they could be done quickly. The sooner the better.

Two grooms dashed out to take her horse's head, as if the poor old creature would put up any fuss. Mr. Perkins helped Meg alight from the gig and led her into the house. She had to practically trot to keep up with him.

"I suppose you'd like to get right to business, then?" he asked.

"Yes," she said, happy he did not expect her to bother with silly pretense, as if this were a social call.

He took her directly to his former master's study. She'd never been in this area of the house and couldn't help but stare at her surroundings as they passed a staircase she knew nothing about and a long corridor hung with rich tapestry and pieces of armor that, presumably, had been worn by previous Glenwicks. It was all very ominous and quite masculine—complete with dead animals mounted on the wall. Clearly this was the master's part of the home.

"This way," Mr. Perkins said, then paused to allow her entrance to the one room at this end of the house that appeared to be well-lit inside.

She stepped in and found that the excellent lighting came from broad windows overlooking the elaborate rear gardens. The sun hovered low over the lake just beyond and reflected brightly, sending glittering beams into the dark-paneled room. A huge desk commanded attention at the head of the room, the chair behind the desk rose like a throne. Shelves were lined with all manner of books, stacks of paper, and various odds and ends that must have held great significance for previous lords.

Oddly, though, it was all in obvious disarray. Apparently while the former earl had been meticulous in the upkeep of the rest of the house, this room was not subject to such care. Perhaps here, in his private domain, he forbade access to servants and cared for all of it on his own. Well, given the clutter and the haphazard placement of, well, everything, Meg had to admit he hadn't done a very good job of it.

Mr. Perkins must have noticed her dismay. "As you can see, the old earl left things rather out of order for us."

"Yes, so I see."

"Which is why I've been at a loss to locate the certain documents we spoke of."

"I can entirely understand that. Well, tell me how we should begin."

Mr. Perkins nodded. "Very well. Here is a stack of letters, correspondence between the earl and his solicitor."

"And these indicate that he suspected that I..."

She couldn't even bring herself to complete the sentence.

"The earl was concerned that when Nigel Webberly left Richington so unexpectedly, that he left you in a delicate condition. These drafts indicate he insisted documents be drawn up that would see to the provision for any child that might result."

She cringed to hear him speak those words aloud. It was too horrible! Yes, the earl had known she'd felt a certain fondness for his grandson, he'd shown obvious displeasure that the young man had run off to marry that heiress, but never had he hinted that he suspected anything truly intimate had transpired between them. The thought that such a thing had been preserved in writing—that he'd had his own solicitor draw up official papers for such a thing—well, her stomach churned anew at the very idea.

"Go ahead, Miss Farrow. Read through the letters. Anything you feel might be perceived as, er, incriminating, I suggest we destroy it entirely."

Incriminating. What a horrible word. Still, she supposed it was exactly accurate, given the situation.

How devious she felt! Lying to her father, misleading Mr. Shirley, sneaking out here to prowl through the old earl's papers and search for something that might paint her with an overly colorful brush. Heavens, but the idea of destroying someone else's things in secret seemed very, very wrong, indeed. Still, she must do it to protect her good name—as if she'd ever done anything to truly besmirch it!

Mr. Perkins offered her a seat at a table and began showing her through the letters, the specific portions he felt might be of most interest to her. Of course the only letters available to them were in draft form. Any actual letters from the earl to his solicitor had been sent.

Still, these drafts hinted clearly. The earl insisted on drawing up papers to provide for the anticipated arrival of an illegitimate child. Fortunately, these drafts were vague and made no clear reference to her in specific, but of course the actual legal documents would have needed to be clearer. Thankfully nothing she saw here would sufficiently implicate her. The final documents certainly would, though.

"And these are the only references you have regarding the documents?" she asked.

"Well, there is this," he said, pushing another paper toward her. "It isn't specific, but I believe it might reference the old earl's intent."

She took up the paper and held it into the light. It appeared to be a letter, written in a hand she did not know and directed simply to "G". She assumed that meant Glenwick and referred to the old earl. The letter felt hasty in tone, as if written in great urgency, but the date at the top was smudged, blotted beyond legibility. She read through it carefully.

Your last correspondence was received and your concerns for N are well noted. I am looking into the matter post haste. In the meantime, take what measures you deem best. Even good men can fall prey to the promise of treasure. I will visit you at the earliest possible moment and look forward to discussing everything. I fear I have some unpleasant evidences to support your suspicions, but of course those are best left out of this letter. Until I am with you,

—X

"Who is this X?" she asked.

"I haven't a clue," Mr. Perkins replied. "Did the old earl ever mention anyone with that name?"

"It's hardly a name, but no, I can think of no one who

went by that. Perhaps it is merely a mark, the sender was illiterate and had someone else write the letter for him?"

"Perhaps," Mr. Perkins shrugged. "But the feel of it is rather intimate, don't you think? I doubt the old earl had many illiterate friends."

"True. And the mention of 'N' would seem to indicate a familiarity with Nigel Webberly."

"Exactly."

"But what is this treasure it mentions?"

"Er... I believe that is a gentleman's way of referencing something sensitive, miss."

Her face burned and she quickly changed the subject. "Oh. I see. But when was it written? The date is smudged out."

"Yes, that is unfortunate. I found it amongst these other papers from that time period, though, which is what first alerted me to it."

"The handwriting is different from the other drafts, though. Very bold, decisive—not tidy and reserved like the others."

"I think it rather a mess, myself.":

"Well, clearly it was not written by a secretary or clerk the way those drafts seem to be. This author wrote hastily and with passion. His concern for the earl seems to be personal rather than merely for business."

"Then who do you think could have written it? A good friend of the earl's from that time?"

"I don't know. Heavens, I certainly hope this doesn't indicate that the earl shared his suspicions with others back then!"

"Obviously he did. Perhaps if this 'X' were a confidant of the earl he might know where the document is."

"But how can we find him? Perhaps the solicitor from that time would have a record of who was given a copy of the documents then."

"The old earl's solicitor at that time has since died from old age, and his office was ruined by fire some years ago. Still, we know the earl would have kept copies here of everything legal."

"Yes, I can see that he certainly kept everything," she replied, glancing around at the mess.

"You see my dilemma, Miss Farrow."

"I do not envy your task, sir, but I am relieved on one point for my own account," she had to admit. "No one has mentioned me by name in any of these drafts."

"No, it appears the old earl was careful."

"But how, then, did you determine he was referring to me?"

Mr. Perkins appeared uncomfortable, his face wrinkling into a worried frown. "Forgive me, Miss Farrow, but it was from all the things the new earl has said about you."

"Nigel... that is, the new earl has spoken of me?"

"Indeed. You have been in correspondence with him these recent months, have you not?"

"My father and I sent word of our condolences when his wife passed away. We have corresponded a bit since."

"Well, your concern has meant much to him, let me assure you. After his grandfather's death I have corresponded with him on matters of business. He was most eager to ask after his friends in the village—you, in particular, Miss Farrow. It was the way he mentioned you and spoke of his great regard for you that made me begin to think perhaps you were the woman referenced in these letters. When I spoke to him about it—":

"Good heavens! You spoke to him about it?"

"I was discreet, of course. I merely questioned whether you and he had been friends once, and he replied that you had. I knew the time frame fit these drafts perfectly, so I puzzled it out and now you have confirmed."

"I've confirmed only that the old earl was mistaken, sir."

"Of course. Perhaps these missing documents contain some other young lady's name, some other gently bred miss from Richington who had been courted by Nigel Webberly seven years ago."

Even Meg had to admit that the chances of that were basically nil. During his last summer in residence at the Downs, Nigel had shown no special attentions to anyone besides her. If the earl at the time drew up documents in anticipation of a child, he would have suspected no one but her. Her name would appear on those papers and no one would believe there were no grounds whatsoever for his concern.

“No, you are right, Mr. Perkins. There can be no other conclusion than the one you have drawn. I fear we simply must find those documents.”

"And that is where I am at a loss. Can you think of any place they might be?"

"I should think they'd be here, in this chaos somewhere."

"I've been through everything, Miss Farrow, to no avail. Are you certain the earl never confided in you, suggested where something of great value might be?"

"No, truly he didn't. Why would you expect that he might?"

"You were his friend. I thought perhaps on his death bed he would want to spare you the scandal of those papers being found. He might have indicated where he wanted you to look for them."

"No, I'm sorry. On his death bed he was mostly worried for the care of Bartholomew. I don't believe these documents crossed his mind, although..."

"Although?"

"The last few days of his life his mind was quite jumbled, I'm afraid. He'd been so healthy all along and then... well, he seemed to fade away suddenly."

"Death comes to every man in its own way."

"Papa and I visited frequently, there at the end, and I'm sorry to say the earl did speak wildly."

"And what did he say? Can you recall?"

"He mourned his sons who he lost, and he... well, he spoke of his grandson."

"Nigel Webberly, his heir."

"No, the elder one. Web, he called him. He was quite confused. It seemed as if he'd forgotten the poor man was dead."

"But he *is* dead."

"Yes, I remember when word came to the earl two years ago. He seemed almost inconsolable for some time. The poor man... so much tragedy. No wonder he was not quite himself at the end."

"Yes, no wonder. But did he say anything else? Anything about where he would hide something?"

"No, nothing like that. He grieved for his family and he worried for Bartholomew."

"You are certain?"

"Believe me, Mr. Perkins, no one is more eager to find these documents than I am. If I had any inkling of some secret place the earl hid them, I would tell you."

Mr. Perkins studied her, then nodded his head. "I believe you, Miss Farrow."

"But what of any other staff? What of the servants? Surely they must know who the earl corresponds with. After all, they would post the letters for him."

"The old steward who worked for the earl at the time is an invalid who can barely remember his name, and the servants claim to know nothing. Indeed, they seem to be the most ill-informed servants of any estate in England."

Odd, she'd thought the earl's servants seemed to be quite devoted to their master and to tending his needs. Of course it was to their credit, though, that they did not poke their noses into his personal life or his legal matters. She simply had to admit there was nothing more she could do.

"Thank you for having me here, Mr. Perkins. Short of spending hours digging though all this muddle, I'm afraid I am worthless to our cause."

"No, I appreciate your help, Miss Farrow. I'm sure if you had any idea where else to look you would tell me."

"Of course. And I appreciate your efforts to solve my dilemma. Do you mind if I look over these drafts one more time?"

"By all means, Miss Farrow. If you'll excuse me for just a moment, I need to tend something. I'll return shortly."

She excused him and turned back to the papers. None of them were in the earl's hand, as far as she could tell, but all of them were dated seven years ago, the very month that Nigel left Richington to marry his heiress. It was obvious what the earl had thought of Meg and she was distraught at the realization.

Had she really been such a cake? Had she really dangled after Nigel in so obvious a manner? If it had been easy for the old earl to think such things of her, who else in town had felt the same? How mortifying to realize it now, all these years later. She must have been quite the topic of gossip.

And what would happen now with Nigel's return? People, of course, would be watching. Would they expect her to throw herself at him, as they apparently assumed she had then? Well, that would not happen.

She was an adult now. She was beyond girlish whims.

She would be immune to whatever charms Nigel still had. She could not even remember what they were now.

Had his eyes been blue like the sky? She'd seen much bluer eyes than his, certainly. And his smile, did it dazzle every time she came into the room? No, she'd seen far more dazzling smiles since then. Had his shoulders been sturdy and broad, boasting power and confidence with every breath that he took? She could not even remember Nigel's shoulders at all. Certainly they'd been nothing like..

Oh, good heavens. She'd been comparing her memories of Nigel to Mr. Shirley! Well, that would never do. True, she was no longer infatuated with Nigel Webberly, but at least he was a gentleman. Mr. Shirley was nothing more than a parrot trainer! And not a very good one at that.

He merely had beautiful blue eyes, a dazzling smile, and shoulders that made her go weak in the knees. Oh, but those were strong characteristics, indeed. She needed to get herself firmly under control where that man was concerned or risk being the topic of village gossip again.

She turned her focus onto searching the office—for anything of interest to distract her—and vowed to ignore Mr. Shirley even harder than ever when she got home. Apparently not all of her was as mature and beyond the touch of girlish infatuation as she'd hoped, after all. But certainly she did not have to give in to it!

"I'll not fall into such fancy again," she said to a vacantly staring deer head displayed on the wall. "I learned my lesson seven years ago and I'll not be repeating it."

She was likely imagining things, but it seemed that the deer rolled his eyes.

Chapter 8

Max could see her plainly from his hiding place. He was getting a cramp in his leg, however, from crouching so long. Indeed, he'd been considerably smaller and more flexible when he and his cousin had made use of this crumbling old chimney to spy on their grandfather while he worked in his study. He'd never been doing anything of interest, but they'd been so proud of themselves for their stealth and cleverness. In reality, Grandfather had probably known all along what they were up to. Max had to smile now at those memories.

His smile faded quickly, though. Things were entirely different now. Those carefree, peaceful times he had known here in childhood were gone. Everything was changed.

He could not see the whole study from where he spied, but he could see enough. The room was in utter disarray—Grandfather would never have left it this way. Had Mr. Perkins destroyed it? Someone had, certainly. Papers were jumbled everywhere, drawers were pulled out... even the vulgar old ship's figurehead of a buxom maiden that had hung on the wall over Grandfather's desk was now gone.

Clearly someone had not been merely rearranging. A concerted search had been conducted and Max doubted it was merely for those incriminating papers for Miss Farrow.

Not that he himself wouldn't have liked to get his hands on them.

So, that's what her business with the steward was about. She was not shagging him, she was using him to save herself from public scandal should those documents come to light. She *had* been shagging Nigel.

At least, that's what it seemed those documents would reveal. Clearly Grandfather believed it, too. Given the warm reception Max had seen on her face at the reception of Nigel's correspondence, all the evidence seemed to concur. Grandfather likely had good reason to think Nigel's bastard child might be on the way. He'd done the honorable thing, drawing up papers to see to the welfare of the child, even as cowardly Nigel had run off to marry for money.

Poor Miss Farrow. Max should probably not feel so charitable toward her, knowing the truth of her character now, but it was exactly that truth that touched his compassionate side. She'd been young and impressionable. Nigel had used her abominably then abandoned her. The fact that Miss Farrow managed to hold her head high and go on with her life after that was a testament to her strength of will. Max could not fault that.

She'd not been lying and conspiring with Mr. Perkins to find Grandfather's treasure, she was trying to salvage what she could of her reputation. It was no more sordid than that. Clearly if she had been privy to any secrets from his grandfather, she would have revealed them now. Her desperation was obvious.

Also obvious was her declaration to avoid falling prey to Nigel again. Yes, Max had heard that statement loud and clear. He doubted the deer head on the wall had paid it much mind, but Max certainly had. He respected Miss Farrow all the more for it.

He considered leaving now, heading back to the posting

house to await Miss Farrow's return and to pretend he had been there this whole time, when voices below him ended all thoughts of removal. Voiced he recognized.

The chimney where he huddled served several rooms. He had positioned himself in an upstairs chamber, leering into the ancient—and filthy—opening just enough to see through the tiny slit of chink between bricks that allowed an astute spy to see into the study below. However, the chimney also served the small anteroom just off of the study. It was there that the voices were emanating.

He could not see into the anteroom from here, nor could someone in the study hear the voices from there. The thick walls of the manor would deaden the sound down below, but the hollow flue running between rooms provided a perfect conduit for the voices to travel up here. He listened carefully.

"She claims to know nothing," the first voice spoke in a tense, quiet whisper. It was the Perkins fellow.

"Did you ask the right questions?" the other voice inquired.

Max strained to hear it. A man. Did he know the voice?

"I asked everything that I could. If she truly doesn't know about it, I don't want to tell her," Perkins snapped back. "I'm inclined to believe her. She doesn't know anything."

"She came out here readily enough, didn't she? She must know something."

"No. She's worried her little dalliance with you will come to light, that's why she's here."

The second speaker laughed. *Hellfire*. Max knew that laugh. Nigel Webberly, the new Earl of Glenwick.

"If she's worried about that, she must have a much better recollection of things than I do. That chit was cold as December, laced up tight as a drum and locked together at the knees. I assure you, Perkins, she's got nothing to worry about for her precious reputation. There's no way she could believe that rubbish about my grandfather thinking I'd got her with child. It would have taken the angel Gabriel to make that happen, I'm afraid."

"She seems to believe it."

"Well, she doesn't," Nigel insisted. "No, if she's here now it's because she knows about the treasure."

"Everyone knows about the treasure."

"No, everyone has *heard* about the treasure but my damn grandfather told us all it was a myth, just a legend. No one believes that it's real."

"Whoever sent that letter to the old earl knows it's real," Perkins pointed out.

"And you went and showed it to her! If she didn't know about it before, she does now, damn your eyes."

"I smudged out the date. She thinks that letter was referring to your grandfather's suspicions about her possible condition. I told her the mention of *treasure* was nothing more than a euphemism. She has no idea what it really meant."

"Or so she let you believe. Maybe she knows who that X is and now she'll go warn him we're onto things. What did you find out about the parrot? How does he figure into this?

"I'm not sure," Perkins replied. "But they've hired a trainer for it."

"A what? Who?"

"I don't know. He seems harmless, though."

"Damn them all. Do you suppose they've learned anything from the bird?"

"They've learned to keep their fingers away from its beak, I suppose. The creature's a menace. I'd say if they'd have gotten anything useful out of it, they'd have done away with it already."

"I need to know what they know."

"And that's why you're going to put the girl into your pocket again," Perkins said. "Isn't that what you said? Make her your friend until you know what she knows?"

Nigel laughed again, a low, dusky rasp that didn't sound pleasant at all. "Indeed, I said that. Been sending her letters, you know. She's going to think I've dreamed of nothing but her virtuous countenance for all these past years. She'll be swooning for me when I gallantly present myself to her tomorrow. Who knows, maybe by now that chain around her knees has loosened up a bit."

"She's a decent woman," Perkins said sharply. "You intend to seduce her?"

"I intend to get what's mine. And don't think you ought to go growing a conscience now, Perkins. Your hands are as dirty as mine in this matter. The title, the treasure and very ripe Miss Farrow belong to me and I *will* have them. If you don't want to end up swinging on a rope, I suggest you make yourself useful."

Perkins muttered something Max couldn't make out. Perhaps the man simply swore under his breath, or perhaps the rage pounding through Max's body was drowning everything out. By God, all the horrors that had hounded him, that he'd tried to tell himself were impossible, were laid out undeniably before him.

The Glenwick treasure *was* real, Nigel *had* murdered their grandfather, and Mr. Perkins had his hands on that last letter from X. It was just a matter of time before Nigel realized the handwriting was Max's, and no doubt that date had been smudged only after he and Perkins had seen it. The worst of it all, Miss Farrow was innocent and being pulled into something that truly might ruin her. Permanently.

Of course she'd found nothing of interest in the mess that was Lord Glenwick's study. She did look around a bit, but things had not only been disorganized, she had the impression someone had truly ransacked it. Of course Mr. Perkins had been looking for things, but he was certainly not the type to toss things haphazardly into corners and dump out drawers. Surely the old earl would never have left it that way. So who had?

Her whole experience at Glenwick Downs had been odd, to say the least. Perhaps it was just her conscience that pricked, but she had the distinct feeling the whole time she was there someone had been watching her. And the way Mr. Perkins had talked, she expected to find much more information available to her when she arrived. Instead, it was only those few undamning draft copies and that one letter signed only by "X". None of that could really cause her much worry. Her name was on none of it.

Of course she appreciated Mr. Perkin's overblown concern for her, but it had been unnecessary. When he returned from his errand she thanked him, but made her excuse

and hurried out to Papa's gig. It wasn't until she was halfway down the lane that she recalled none of those papers had actually been destroyed while she was there. Hadn't that been a main purpose of her visit? Hopefully Mr. Perkins would tend to that for her before the new earl arrived tomorrow.

It was a relief to know that her name was not actually in those papers, but it would be embarrassing to think Nigel might see them. Not traumatic, though, she was happy to realize as she searched her own heart. There was nothing there that might indicate she had done anything to cause the old earl to fall into his erroneous assumption. And if Nigel did decide to hold her accountable, there was nothing she could do about that.

It was remarkably freeing to realize she truly did not care one way or the other what Nigel Webberly thought about her. She honestly felt no remaining attraction for him whatsoever. How amazing to realize that!

It would be good to have Nigel returned just because they were old friends, but for no other reason than that. Perhaps, as Mr. Perkins suggested, Nigel would ask for his grandfather's parrot back and Meg's house could become peaceful again. And with Bartholomew gone, Mr. Shirley would be gone, too. She would be perfectly happy to watch him leave.

He'd walk away, taking those blue eyes, dazzling smile and broad, manly shoulders with him. He'd walk right out of their house and out of their lives and she could practically picture it already: his long legs and self-assured gait... the way he might turn his head back to catch one final look at her... the burning regret she might see in those deep azure eyes... the adorable creases at the corners of his lips when she began running after him...

Oh, good heavens! Any more of this and she was going to require medical intervention. What was wrong with her? She would *not* run after the parrot trainer. Ever.

Determined to think no more of Mr. Shirley than was absolutely necessary—and more and more it was becoming painfully necessary—she slapped the reins on the old horse. The sun was just a tiny red glow on the horizon, shadows stretched long over the road. She had just enough time to stop at Miss Bent's house to say a quick hello then go back to the posting house to retrieve the broad shoulders. Er, Mr. Shirley.

Max had managed to keep track of her carriage from the moment it left Glenwick Downs. The sun was very nearly gone so he had ample shadows to hide in, creeping out the same secret way he'd crept into the manor, then staying low, unseen behind the lush plantings and rolling landscape until he could follow the road, hidden in the brush of the creek bed.

Poor Miss Farrow had no clue that his damn cousin was already returned, or that the vile man had some rather unsavory plans for her. Indeed, Max was firmly convinced that Miss Farrow was, in fact, innocent of all his suspicions. Well, most of them.

She may have not given Nigel any particular liberties with her body, but she'd obviously given him her heart. Judging by Miss Farrow's determination to lie her way over to Glenwick Downs and hunt through those old papers, she must know that her behavior seven years ago would be enough to give everyone reason to think Grandfather's concerns must have had some foundation. She'd be labeled guilty whether she'd done anything wrong or not.

Damn, but this new understanding made Max's already piqued interest in Miss Farrow all that much stronger. And something else—he felt an annoying need to protect her. As if he wanted that additional burden just now! Nigel would be showing his face around town as early as tomorrow and he'd be most unhappy to find Max here, alive and still breathing. If Max had any sense, he'd take himself back to London and let the authorities deal with this mess. Surely he had enough detail to raise official suspicion by now, plus he was content that Miss Farrow and her father were not involved in any of it.

He should let the courts go about the work of finding

proof to convict Nigel, and that damn, slimy steward along with him. All Max needed to do was present himself as the true heir and call for Nigel to be slapped in chains. Hell, that ought to cure Miss Farrow of any *tendre* she still felt for the man. She would do well to forget Nigel and set her sights toward someone more deserving of her esteem. Someone with a legitimate claim to a title, perhaps.

As if he could pass for someone like that just now, though. He slunk down into the brush as her carriage rattled by. He'd encountered some nettles along the way and his hands stung from the contact. His clothes were coated in leaves and grass and soot from the old chimney. He could only imagine what his face must look like. Oh yes, he was a fine gentleman indeed. He doubted he could even pass for a parrot trainer right now.

Good thing she could not see him. She concentrated on the road before her, guiding the carriage with a firm hand, clearly eager to be about her business and clearly deeply in thought. The last rays of sunlight were golden and cast a warm glow over her features. They were good features, too. Max took advantage of his position to stare, appreciating her form, the graceful movements of her hands, the light breeze tossing a stray curl that dangled at her cheek.

Yes, he could readily see what Nigel might find to interest him in the woman. She was easy on the eyes. She'd been close to their grandfather, as well. Did she possess information that Nigel was hunting? Could she even, unknowingly, have been given clues that might lead them to Grandfather's treasure? Max could not rule out the possibility. He didn't want to rule it out, either. To give up on that possibility would mean he had no further reason to study Miss Farrow. And he intended to continue that as long as he could.

For now, though, she was rounding the next bend. He

would have to hurry if he meant to be waiting at the posting house when she arrived there to get him. Unless, of course, she did not intend to go back there directly.

He crossed the road silently behind her, darting behind a long hedgerow. He had a suspicion and hoped he would not turn out to be wrong. Letting her get farther ahead of him might be problematic if she did, indeed, arrive at the inn to find him gone. How could he explain his absence and his disheveled state without giving away that he knew what she'd been up to?

But as he watched, his suspicions proved to be justified. Instead of continuing on, she pulled the gig into the yard of a small cottage that sat near to the road. Max smiled. He should never have doubted. The woman was honest to a fault. This must be Miss Bent's house. Miss Farrow was visiting her elderly friend, after all.

He crept up behind the house and fully intended to lurk outside a window, just for the amusement of eavesdropping and seeing more of Miss Farrow when she was not intentionally ignoring him or purposefully making herself as unpleasant as possible. However, when Miss Farrow was let into the home by a round little woman, a fluffy white dog came out into the yard to yap incessantly in his direction. He had to leave, disappearing beyond the low stone wall that flanked the cottage and making tracks toward an apple orchard nearby.

It was an easy walk to the posting house from there. He kept out of view from the road and remain undetected, arriving in time to use water from the pump to right his mussed clothing and wash his stinging hands. The little red welts were beginning to fade. He retrieved his small writing box that he'd left hidden behind a pile of timber stacked just out of view from the road and found a safe place to wait.

Just as Miss Farrow, he hadn't completely lied about his need to come here today. He had indeed posted a letter and was glad when the innkeeper assured him it had gone out in the last post. He could expect to have a certain friend of his arrive here in Richington tomorrow. Then the fun would begin.

He made himself comfortable on a bench outside the posting house and opened his writing box. Why look, he even had ink on his fingers, just in case Miss Farrow should have reason to question his alibi. Lord knew he was going to question hers.

Chapter 9

Miss Bent was overly glad to see Meg. Chester, her little dog, seemed rather more interested in whatever rabbit must have been hopping about Miss Bent's back garden, but he settled down eventually. It was good to see that other people had trouble with their pets, too, at times. Perhaps Bartholomew wasn't such a freak of nature, after all.

Then again, Chester didn't screech out a full dozen verses to "Roll Your Leg Over" every blessed day.

Meg kept her visit as brief as possible, but of course Miss Bent had much to say. Her widowed niece generally lived with her but was currently away at her sister's home in London. Miss Bent was quite happy to share each and every detail from each and every letter she'd received from her during her absence. As Meg discovered, the niece was exceptionally prolific. Fortunately the niece promised her visit to London would end soon and she'd return home to Richington so Meg would likely be spared another recitation of the letters.

Finally she said her good-byes. The sun had fully set, but she knew the roads well and was not worried about traveling such a short distance after dark. Besides, she'd be meeting Mr. Shirley soon. Of course she shouldn't be quite as pleased to think of reuniting with him as she was, but she worked to convince herself it was simply relief that she was feeling. Her scheme had worked as planned and soon she would be done with these lies and deception.

And should she have any worries about traveling alone after dark, she'd soon have Mr. Shirley with his broad shoulders to protect her. Although, her sensible side warned her that this was most likely the very thing she most needed protection *from*. While Mr. Shirley had only ever behaved in the most respectable way toward her, she was beginning to wonder if she ought to be worried for her own respectable behavior. The involuntary thoughts she kept having of the man were not respectable at all!

But now there he was, waiting for her, waving as if he were nearly as happy to see her as she was to see him. Despite the shadows of the posting house yard she could see that his smile lighted his eyes. And what kind, expressive eyes they were, too. Even after sharing her home with the man for nearly a week she'd not quite gotten used to their earnest blue intensity.

She would have to school herself carefully to keep from showing that she appreciated—very much—that these expressive blue eyes were fastened clearly on her. By no means did she approve of her unwelcome attraction for the man; she certainly was not about to let him catch wind of it. He'd be gone in just a few days, after all. She had no eagerness to allow him to take even the tiniest bit of her heart with him.

"Did you have a productive visit?" he asked as he swung himself easily up into her little gig.

"Er, yes, Thank you." *Good gracious, how can someone so large move so gracefully?*

"And your elderly friend is well?"

"She is, thank you." *And you are looking very well, too.*

"And her little dog?"

“He is well, also." *How sweet of you to ask after her dog. But wait...*

"Er, how did you know she has a dog?”

He shrugged, his smile not fading though he hadn’t looked at her once since climbing into the carriage with her. “She’s an older woman who lives alone, I gather. It stands to reason she must have a dog. Or sixteen cats, perhaps.”

“A dog. His name is Chester. He’s usually quite well behaved, but tonight he seemed intent on barking after some invisible rabbits out in the garden.”

“Ah, those invisible rabbits. Wiley creatures, I’ve heard. Best to use care around them.”

“Well, he was quite proud of himself for chasing them off." *And if you don't stop being so charming this very instant, I'm likely to drive us into the ditch.*

"I'm just happy someone was there to defend you," he said and finally turned one of those dazzling smiled directly on her.

Don't drive into the ditch. Don't drive into the ditch.

"As I told you and Papa it would be, my journey was purely uneventful. Miss Bent and I ended up having a lovely little visit and now I am safely on my way home.”

“Little visit? You were gone well over an hour, I think. It makes me wonder what you would consider a long visit.”

How kind of you to worry for me!

Or was he suspicious? She glanced at him, afraid she might find a brooding, glowering man just waiting to accuse her of all manner of things. She found, however, that he was still smiling. Her insides fluttered.

“I… I’m sorry if I kept you waiting overly long, sir,” she said.

“I am teasing you, Miss Farrow. Of course I did not mind waiting. After all, it was my notion to begin with, wasn't it? I had my letters to write."

Thank heavens! She hoped her sigh of relief wasn't too obvious.

"And did you get all your letters drafted and sent off?"

He nodded. "I did, thank you. It would appear a most successful evening for both of us."

"Er, yes, I suppose it has been."

"Your father will be happy to hear of it. I'm sure Miss Bent will tell him how glad she was to have you stop by."

"Er, yes, I suppose she will."

"Such altruism must make you very much like a saint, I should think."

"That's overstating it a bit, sir. I merely visited a friend, nothing more especially saintly about that."

"What? You put yourself to great trouble, Miss Farrow. You left the security of home and hearth to travel into the fading light for no greater purpose than to bring comfort and happy conversation to a lonely soul. Isn't that what you did?"

Now she gritted her teeth. If he had any idea how such praises grated inside her! It was all she could do not to unburden her conscience here and now. But she was strong. She took it all with a wan smile and a weak nod.

"Thank you, sir, but I am sure you credit me too much."

She made the mistake of glancing at him again. This time his eyes were indeed boring into her and she was certain they held some deeper meaning that was tantalizingly out of her reach. What did the man have going on in his head? The way he gazed at her was… she had no words for the heat she felt, nor the way her breath suddenly left her.

"No, Miss Farrow," he said, slow and soft. "Until tonight, I fear I did not credit you enough. But now I see there is much more to you than I thought."

She barely managed to squeak out a thank you. He grinned, appearing overly happy to have offered his praise. She felt a bit queasy accepting it, knowing how undeserved it really was.

"Such altruism is indeed rare," he said, rambling on to make her misery even worse. "I dare say, after your gracious outing tonight you will sleep easy, Miss Farrow."

Drat. Until now she had thought her meeting with Mr. Perkins would leave her at ease and let her sleep without worry, but now this unearned admiration from Mr. Shirley stood to undo all of that. He thought she was selfless and kind, when really her motives had been purely conceit. If not for her need to protect herself, Miss Bent would have gone completely uncared for this evening.

Mr. Shirley was beaming in raptures, thinking kind thoughts toward her that she could not allow. What made it even more unbearable was the fact that she found she truly wanted him to think all this of her—and more. She was already wondering which gown she should wear down to breakfast tomorrow. Would he prefer seeing her in the yellow, or the lavender with the fine lace?

Drat such thoughts! Her vanity and self-interest were disgusting. When had she become so shallow and petty? Such pride did not even deserve the good favor of a simple parrot trainer. She ought to be fully ashamed of herself.

She wasn't, though. She was already picturing how to wear her hair with the lavender gown and praying Mr. Shirley would find the effect fetching. What a giddy sap she was! Whatever would come of such thoughts?

Indeed, though, the thoughts were persistent and try as she might, she could in no way banish them. Mr. Shirley had taken up firm residence in her imagination and no manner of guilty conscience or common sense could seem to roust him. No, she would not sleep easy tonight. Not at all.

Max had noted that Miss Farrow was distinctly uneasy by the time they arrived back at the parsonage. He was sure he could detect a thick layer of ice forming over her words and she was perceivably short with him. Her father expressed relief that they'd returned before the sky got any darker, and she was cheerful enough toward him, but her words were few and she excused herself for her chamber as quickly as possible.

Quite obviously her visit to Glenwick Downs had upset her. Max could well understand that, but he'd rather hoped that since it appeared her search had turned up little that might prove discrediting her attitude would be one of jovial liberation. Clearly the outcome of her visit was proving otherwise. He worried perhaps he knew why.

She must still care for Nigel. Clearly whatever transpired in the past was not entirely resolved, despite her words to the contrary. He would definitely have to keep an eye on things to be certain his blackguard cousin didn't hurt her. Again.

In the meanwhile, he'd do well to make certain none of his concerns were detectable to his hosts. It was time to put himself whole-heartedly into training Bartholomew. Or more accurately, decoding him. He was more convinced than ever that the bird held some sort of key, and it would seem Nigel believed the same.

He made his polite good-nights to Mr. Farrow, then went up to his room. Bartholomew waited on his well-worn perch, poking his head out from under his wing and then fluffing his feathers when Max entered the room.

"Sleeping as if you've no care in the world," Max said, tossing his coat over the bedstead. "Lazy bird."

"*Give your old pole a twist, lad,*" the bird quipped.

Max snarled at him. "Go twist your own pole. I've got bigger problems."

Ridiculous creature. He'd recited that same phrase all morning long, over and over. It was to the point Max would have welcomed if he'd at least recited the rest of the vulgar rhyme that went with it.

Oh yes, Max knew all of the rhymes, even though Bartholomew seemed to repeat only certain phrases. The rhymes were contained in a book. Grandfather's book.

He'd been rather surprised when the book arrived with what turned out to be Grandfather's final letter to him. Grandfather had never been known to be a lover of great literature and frankly, neither was Max. But this book he knew—he'd stolen glances at it hundreds of times as a boy. And what boy wouldn't have poured over that volume? Nothing of any virtue at all could be found within the pages.

Grandfather's book came from pirates. Or so he had said. It had sailed around the world, entertaining all who dared open its pages. Max had most certainly dared.

The mismatched pages within the book—some of them handwritten, some in print—were indeed verse, but nothing that could be confused with Shakespeare or Byron. They were transcriptions of bawdy sea shanties. The book had been in the Glenwick collection for years and apparently Grandfather felt the need to pass it on to Max. How unfortunate that he'd obviously also shared it with Bartholomew.

"*Climb on my pole. Climb on my pole.*"

Ugh, the demmed creature was still at it. Max sighed, and reached—once again—for the Bible he kept close at hand now. For all the good that it did. Oh, certainly he himself must in some way be prospering from these repetitive readings, but the flood of gentle inspiration clearly had little effect on the bird. He took a deep breath and let the book fall open to the familiar twenty-third psalm.

"*The Lord is my shepherd,*" he read, making eye contact and praying this time his words would sink in. "*I shall not want*."

"*You'll want what she's got*," the bird interrupted. "*Just visit dear Dot*."

Another damn rhyme. Max recognized that one from Grandfather's book, as well. He growled in frustration and tossed the Bible down on the bed.

"I'm sure my father would disapprove of your treatment of God's word," a stern feminine voice spoke from the doorway.

Damn. He'd left the door open a bit and Miss Farrow had just caught him pitching the Holy Bible as if it were nothing more than a cricket ball. He was lucky she spoke up before she'd had opportunity to watch him strangle a helpless parrot, as well. Although, he had a feeling her father wouldn't be so very disapproving of that.

"Miss Farrow! Er, I was just having another go at convincing Bartholomew to replace his current vocal repertoire with something a bit more inspirational."

"Not having much luck, I take it."

"No. Not so much."

He assumed at this point she'd simply roll her nut-brown eyes at his incompetence and walk away, but she did not. She did, in fact, walk right in over his threshold and stand delightfully close to him as she studied the offending bird. Bartholomew cocked his yellow head, squinted his orange eyes, and studied her right back.

"Perhaps he does not like Scripture?" she suggested.

"I am quite inclined to believe that is the case."

"Have you any other material? Perhaps he might like something else."

"I've tried several volumes of your father's sermons, some improving lessons, and even a bit of The Ladies Monthly Museum."

"He would not learn from it?"

"Rejected my every word."

Now her eyes settled on something across the room and she darted over to the little night table to pick it up. He did not see immediately what it was or, by God, he'd have found some way to stop her. Too late, she turned to him with a book open in her hands.

"But here is a collection of poetry! Perhaps he might like something from this."

The air vacated Max's lungs and he couldn't even croak out a warning before she started reading aloud from a randomly chosen verse. And random fate was cruel. She chose a particularly meaningful verse. Worse, she was a fast reader. She was halfway through the verse before the particular meaning of it struck her.

"*A vicar and lass fell down into a hole*," she read. "*Said he, 'I've a mind for a tussle and roll. Since we're trapped in a well, nearly halfway to hell…'* What on earth…? Oh! But this isn't poetry, it's… Oh, heavens!"

Apparently Bartholomew could not stand to let the rhyme go unfinished, so he completed it for her. "*Perhaps you should climb on my pole*."

"Er, yes. Not exactly poetry," Max said.

He should probably begin packing his belongings right now. Miss Farrow's expression was a worrisome blend of shock and disgust. Max was ready to pull the book from her hands, to rescue her from its offensive content, but she surprised him by retaining it. Her expression shifted from distress to something more in the neighborhood of curiosity as she flipped through the pages.

"The whole book is that way, one rhyme after another," she noted. "And some pages are not print; they are handwritten and bound with the others. What is this book, Mr. Shirley?"

"It is.. I mean, I came by it when… that is, I found it. Yes, it is a collection I found."

She frowned. "Not in *our* house, you didn't."

"No, I found it elsewhere and didn't realize what it was."

"But then how did Bartholomew become familiar with it?"

"I… er, I believe it to be a collection of sea shanties and bawdy songs. Very likely they are widely known among low peoples, which must be where Bartholomew learned his patterns."

She cocked a dubious eyebrow at him. "Are you saying the Earl of Glenwick was a low person?"

"Certainly not. But surely the earl is not the one who taught this bird. You told me yourself Bartholomew had owners prior to him."

"Yes, that's true. He lived aboard ship for many years, raised by sailors on a merchant line. The earl had some investments in shipping, I believe, and somehow that is how the bird came to eventually be in his possession."

A brief yet accurate summation. Max nodded, as if taking in the information for the first time. Primarily, though, he was digesting the fact that Miss Farrow was still skimming through pages in the book, stopping here and there to read over a passage more than once. As he was familiar with most of those passages himself, he could barely contain his amazement at her calm demeanor.

What an enigma this miss was turning out to be! Was she the virtuous vicar's daughter she appeared, or was there something simmering beneath the surface, after all? How on earth could she not be blushing and balking or swooning, even, as she read through those crude rhymes? At a few of them Max himself had not been able to hold back an uncomfortable snigger.

"You know, Mr. Shirley, I am noticing something in this collection," she said, as primly as ever.

"Er, you are?"

"Yes. Bartholomew seems to speak some of these lines over and other, yet never in connection with any of the other lines from the same rhyme."

"I suppose that is true…"

"Well, I wonder at that."

"You wonder at *that*?"

Truly? Of all the things implied and quite plainly described in those rhymes, *that* is what she was wondering at?

"Why would he not recite several lines from the same rhyme? Presumably he repeats what he hears. Why should he not repeat the whole rhyme? Why only parts of it? Who recites rhymes without any of the rhyming?"

"He's an animal, Miss Farrow. He has no notion of rhyme or reason. Certain things stick in his little brain and certain things do not, I suppose."

She did not seem to accept that as an adequate answer. She did, however, keep turning pages in the book. He was becoming most uncomfortable with that. How could he explain this to her father should he find them like this, alone in Max's bedroom with Miss Farrow deep in a very inappropriate volume of filth!

"I suppose you are right," she said at last, and finally pressed the book shut. "Perhaps it is just a matter of patience. With all of your efforts at training, surely eventually he will have more on his mind than corruption."

Max wondered how long it would be before he could get his own mind onto something other than corruption. By the devil, Miss Farrow's wide-eyed interest in that book was doing the most unexpected things to his imagination. And the rest of him, too. He could barely recall what a parrot was just now, let alone think how to train one.

"I should go," she said, and reached to hand the book back to him.

He took it. When her skin brushed his it was like the woman had been made of flame. He pulled the book back more abruptly than intended, but it was purely for self-defense. Prolonged nearness to Miss Farrow was proving ducedly bad for his system.

She didn't wait for his reply—which was a good thing since he wasn't exactly prepared to give one—but turned on her heel and left. The door shut behind her as she glided away on the swish of crisp muslin and the scent of fresh lavender. Max drew in a long, deep breath, refusing to exhale until the room spun around him. By God, what was wrong with him?

"*You'll want what she's got,*" Bartholomew squawked out another blasted line from another blasted rhyme.

Max threw the cursed book at him. Of course he hadn't really aimed well, and of course Bartholomew flapped his wings and rose up into the air long enough to be safe from the book if it had happened to have gone near him, but the action felt good. Max needed some sort of outlet for whatever it was that had built up inside him. There was no way he'd stop to examine it any further.

Max glared at the bird. "Perhaps Grandfather thought your outbursts were endearing, but I don't find it so very precious."

"*More precious than gold. More precious than gold,*" Bartholomew recited, settling back onto his perch.

Max snarled at him, but decided that line was at least fairly innocuous. It was unfathomable why the bird chose the phrases he chose. Could he have truly heard each and every one of those rhymes so often that all of them were stuck in his brain, just waiting for some innocent word to bring them to recall? If Grandfather had thought he was perpetuating some sort of joke by reinforcing the bird's knowledge, Max wasn't finding it so very funny now.

Bartholomew was supposed to be providing something more useful than the bawdy commentary Max had discovered so far. Grandfather's last letter had alluded quite clearly. Bartholomew held the clue—even Nigel was aware of it. But what that clue was, Max couldn't guess. He was determined as hell to get it out of him, though.

He simply had to get his mind off of Miss Farrow long enough to do it. Damn, but that was proving a difficult task. He'd found her attractive, of course, and her petty deceptions toyed with his imagination, but now that he'd seen her digest that book with more interest than shock he could barely contain his curiosity of her. What else might not shock her, or send her away? The possibilities were tantalizing. Miss Farrow with her prim exterior and her secretive ways fairly screamed out to be decoded.

Not until he had more important matters in hand, though. Grandfather's final letter, his hints about Bartholomew, Nigel's cagey schemes—all that must be decoded first. Once the truth was known and matters of the estate were all settled, then perhaps Max could focus his attentions onto Miss Farrow. Provided she didn't succumb to whatever Nigel had planned for her.

"I hope to hell I find the key to this soon," he muttered aloud, stooping to pick up the book from the floor where it landed.

"*The heart is the key,*" Bartholomew croaked.

"I'll thank you to leave my heart out of it," Max said. As if either he or Bartholomew actually had any say in the matter.

Chapter 10

Meg woke up early the following morning. Rather, she slept only fitfully at best so she was glad to see the sunrise when she could legitimately get out of bed and occupy herself with something other than thoughts of Mr. Shirley and her own guilty conscience. Papa would have noticed if she'd begun polishing the handrail or sweeping out the fireplace at three o'clock in the morning and he might have asked why she wasn't abed.

Even if she told him she was nervous for Nigel—er, the new earl's visit today, it would have been a lie. Her scattered thoughts last night had hardly been focused on Nigel. Indeed, her mind turned and fretted, but it had all be centered on Mr. Shirley.

Drat him, with those unmentionable shoulders and distracting blue eyes. Why could he not have arrived here an old hunchback with false teeth and dull, uninteresting conversation? Why had fate made him a handsome, witty bachelor with a ready smile and a good sense of humor?

Oh, and that book! Heavens, she should never have looked at it. Worse, having seen it, she should never have read it! And read it, and turned pages to read it some more. What could she have been thinking? Mr. Shirley must assume her the most shocking of hoydens, a most scandalous tart, reading such things and not swooning or at least condemning them outright.

Instead, it had been all she could do not to laugh aloud, to take actual enjoyment from the clever phrases, the tawdry teasing of each bawdy line her eyes fell on. What could have come over her to make her react that way? Certainly she did not make a habit of it, partaking of other such low entertainments. Never!

Why, she'd spent years priding herself on her virtue. Now to have stood there in front of Mr. Shirley and read such things as she'd seen in that book! Heavens. How could she ever redeem herself?

By pretending it never happened and scrubbing harder at the smudges on her stair rail, of course. So she did, then leaned back to take a look at her handiwork. Drat. It was not perfect.

"Missed a spot," she grumbled, attacking the bottom-most newel with nearly religious fervor.

"*Dear Dot marks the spot! Dear Dot marks the spot!*"

It was Bartholomew, swooping down the stairway. Meg ducked low, the bird's tail feathers brushing her head as he dipped, then soared up to land on the railing knob she had just painstakingly polished. She held back a rather harsh rebuke barely in time to notice Mr. Shirley watching her from the top of the stairs. Good gracious, but he looked remarkable in the morning, his coat perfectly pressed and his cravat tied just right.

Perhaps the man had been a valet in some previous life. Or had been served by one, maybe. But that was a ridiculous notion, of course. Mr. Shirley was a parrot trainer, a nobody. He was most certainly *not* a gentleman with a valet. Still, for a nobody-parrot-trainer, he was the most gentlemanly one she'd ever laid eyes on.

"Sorry about that," he said, stepping down toward her. "Bartholomew was getting agitated so I thought he could do with some fresh air for a while."

She scrambled to stand up from her seat on the lowest step and straightened her attire. My, but he was tall, standing a few steps above her and gazing down. And those shoulders… heavens, but she was going to have to stop staring at his shoulders! Shifting her gaze up to his face was no better, though. Now she had to contend with a sculpted jaw, winsome expression, and those dratted blue eyes.

"Fresh air. Yes. Good idea," she babbled.

"Perhaps you would like some as well?" he asked. "Surely the banister is polished enough for a visit from the king, let alone a lowly earl."

So he thought Glenwick's expected arrival later today was her reason for the obsessive polishing? That was good. She'd much rather have him believe that than to hold any inkling her restless behavior might be in some way due to him.

But to accompany him for some fresh air… that would mean she'd have to prolong her exposure to his eyes and those shoulders...

"I'm not sure I can spare the time.

"Nonsense. Come out to the garden with me, Miss Farrow."

He was gazing down at her and she was gazing up at him. Not only were his eyes so very blue, but now she noticed the most entrancing violet rings around his pupils. It seemed she could fall right into those eyes, divulge all of her secrets to them. Why yes… yes, she would go out to the garden with him… or anywhere else he asked her to go...

Good gracious, what was she thinking? Of course she would not go anywhere with him. He was here to train the parrot, nothing more. She needed to keep her mind firmly on that fact, not find herself helpless and distracted by the man's features. She would *not* fall into his eyes, divulge any secrets, or follow him out to the garden.

Then again, she couldn't very well stand here forever, could she? And whether she went with him for fresh air or not, she'd have to move off of the staircase to allow him to pass by. It took another moment before her feet agreed to move and she was able to tear her eyes off of his. He stepped down off the stairs and he came to stand beside her.

He held out his arm. "Come. The sunshine looked quite pleasant outside my window."

Her resolve crumbled and she took his arm. He was solid and warm and far more pleasant than sunshine had ever been, at least so far as she could recall just now. Her insides went to jelly at his nearness. How on earth could she possibly feel like this over a simple parrot trainer?

He led the way through the house, Bartholomew flapping his way along with them, diving from high places to low and swooping repeatedly close to Meg's head. She tried to ignore him—which wasn't all that difficult to do given the fact Mr. Shirley insisted on smiling at her—and by the time they reached the rear door of the house she'd very nearly forgotten there even was such a thing as Bartholomew.

Until the bird slammed into her in his hurry to whoosh out into the open air. Drat the annoying creature! If only she had half a worry he might fly away forever, but no, she did not. Bartholomew had been out in the garden with her plenty of times and never once had he felt compelled to leave. Stupid animal.

Fortunately, the sunshine and fresh air did feel remarkably good on her skin as she stepped out into it. Her bad mood was wiped away despite how tense she had been up to this point. Not that she could fully relax, though. Indeed not; Mr. Shirley was right there at her side, ushering her quite kindly and making her jelly turn to jitters.

"A visit to your charming garden is just what is needed," the gentleman said, breathing in the outdoors so that his already impressive chest expanded and pulled the crisp fabric of his coat tight against him.

Bartholomew settled onto a post and proceeded to ruin the morning quiet. "*Go visit Dear Dot. Go visit Dear Dot.*"

Meg frowned. "I have no idea who this Dot person is, but he seems to want to visit her overly often."

"Yes, so I've noticed. I assumed she might be a family friend of yours."

"Not of mine," Meg assured him. "And as far as I know, not of the old earl's either. It's truly amazing that he will spout off the same words and phrases, day after day, as if these are the things he's heard repeatedly, yet never once did I know the old earl to speak such things, or anyone else I've ever known the bird to be in contact with."

"He must have learned it all from the sailors."

"But that was years ago! Why hasn't he happened to pick up anything more recently? Do you suppose there is something wrong with him?"

He seemed to seriously consider this suggestion. She did, too, quite frankly. It was clearly the only conclusion to draw; Bartholomew was defective. They were all just wasting Mr. Shirley's valuable time and he'd be much better off to go train some other, more deserving, parrot somewhere.

It was a very depressing thought. She almost bounced with glee when the gentleman disregarded it.

"No, I don't think that's the trouble. I think it is more likely Bartholomew is simply clinging to those things that give him comfort, considering he's lost his very dear master. Perhaps these phrases remind him of happier times."

"But surely then he would be repeating the things his old master often said, not these other phrases."

"Yes, I suppose that does put a twist on my logic."

"*Give your old pole a twist, lad*!" Bartholomew squawked.

"See?" Meg pointed out. "He is clearly aware of what is being said around him. Why should our casual conversation only trigger the basest of his memories?"

"But he has no concept of that," Mr. Shirley said, though he watched the bird pensively. "He does not know what is base and what is polite. He merely knows what he has heard repeatedly."

"But so long ago."

"Unless…"

And now he stopped speaking and was taken over completely by his pensive observations. Meg watched, waiting for him to complete his thought, but he did not. She ran the conversation over in her mind, wondering what concept had captured his thoughts. Was he re-evaluating his statement that Bartholomew was not defective, or was he perhaps wondering if there had been some influence they were unaware of, some other person who may have interacted with the bird and reinforced these bawdy sayings?

If she hadn't known for a fact the bird spoke this way long before Mr. Shirley had arrived, she would have accused him of reading aloud from that awful book she'd found in his room. Several of the passages she'd read there were every bit as colorful as the ones Bartholomew spouted off upon occasion. Indeed, several of them were very similar to what Bartholomew routinely said.

Very similar, as a matter of fact. How odd! What an

amazing coincidence that Mr. Shirley had shown up here with a book containing some of the very songs and rhyme patterns that Bartholomew had been taught years and years ago aboard ship. It was just a bit too amazing, actually.

The bird screeched on, repeating that dreadful line about twisting a pole. Meg wished to God she had no idea what it could mean. She cleared her throat and tried to seem unaffected.

"I've heard him recite that line before," she commented. "And now recently I've read it."

"Read it?"

"In your book. Last night."

Was she imagining, or did the man's complexion go pale? Perhaps even a bit pink at his neck, just above the lily-white of his cravat.

"In my book?"

"Yes, the one you claim to have little familiarity with, yet you left it sitting out quite prominently."

"Oh. Yes… that book. Well, as I said, it's very likely that is a compendium of bawdy songs that would have been common on ships such as the ones Bartholomew may have been raised on."

"Yes, it would seem that is likely. What is unlikely, though, is that you should just happen to have such a book at the very moment you take up training our troubled bird. Did you, perhaps, have some notion of where he had gotten his habits?"

"Er, yes. Perhaps I did."

"Then do you have some sort of second sight, sir, or had you been in contact with someone who might have known our situation?"

He seemed at a loss to answer this. She would have really liked to hear his answer, too, but unfortunately Mrs. Cooper came rushing out into the garden just at that very moment.

"He's here! He's come already!" she said in a fluster of nerves.

"What is it? Who's here?" Meg asked.

"His lordship, the new earl!" the housekeeper replied. "I had no idea he would come so early. What gentleman comes so early? I thought I'd have hours yet to prepare! Oh, heavens, come inside, Miss Shirley. Your father isn't even back yet from morning prayer and I've got to get tea on."

Nigel was here? Gracious, it was hardly visiting hours. What could have brought him? The man wasn't even expected into town until later. Why should he be here so early? Unless, perhaps his journey had been shorter than anticipated and he stopped by church on first arriving. Yes, he may have wanted to visit his grandfather's grave and perhaps he saw Papa there. But if he was here and Papa was not… well, she couldn't imagine what he might be about.

Quickly she dusted her hands on her apron and removed it, wishing she'd had on something other than a faded dress suitable only for house cleaning. And her hair! Oh heavens, but her hair must look a fright. Without even thinking she dashed a hand up to pat her cheeks, hoping there might be some rosy color to them.

"You look lovely, as always," Mr. Shirley said.

She was suddenly frozen. He had called her lovely! Her breath caught at the sound of the words rolling so tenderly, earnestly off his tongue. Oh, but of course he was merely being kind, saying what she would want to help calm her nerves. Surely he meant nothing by it.

Still, she could not look at him lest he realize how deeply it affected her. Their lowly parrot trainer thought she was lovely and her soul danced at the thought of it.

Good heavens, she'd best get hold of herself quickly—the new Earl of Glenwick waited in her parlor and she needed to greet him.

She'd much rather send him off to the devil and ask Mr. Shirley to repeat himself several more times. He'd called her lovely! If only she didn't wish so very desperately that he'd meant it.

"*A lovely young lass named Dear Dot…*" Bartholomew uttered.

Oh, good lord. What would the new earl say about *this*? How dreadful that Meg's first order of business with him after all these years would have to focus on Bartholomew's perpetual problem. She couldn't very well send him back off to Glenwick without informing the earl just what he was in for.

Her concern must have been evident on her face. Mr. Shirley placed his hand on her arm and spoke low in her ear.

"Don't worry. I'll keep Bartholomew out of sight. And earshot."

She glanced up at him and once again found it impossible to breath. His smile, his eyes, the gentle, comforting tone of his voice… why again did she have to leave him just now? Oh yes. Nigel was here.

"Thank you. That would be much appreciated."

"Hurry, Miss," Mrs. Cooper urged. "We can't keep him waiting! Lord knows what he's come for."

Meg pulled her eyes off Mr. Shirley and started back into the house. "Perhaps he's come for his bird."

Mrs. Cooper clucked her tongue. "Well, he'll no doubt be regretting that, then."

"Yes, perhaps he won't be in such a hurry to take him."

Which would mean they'd have reason to keep Mr. Shirley on. By all means, she'd have to inform Nigel just how dreadful his grandfather's parrot had gotten. Clearly the best thing for all of them would be to continue his training. Preferably here, in the parsonage. That would be the easiest for everyone and, well, it might also give Mr. Shirley a chance to call her lovely again.

Max watched her hurry off with the housekeeper, a bundle of nerves and blushes that he had no doubt Nigel would find hugely attractive. Damn the usurping blackguard! What was he up to, toying with a decent female like this? Hadn't he already assured himself through his scheming steward that she knew nothing useful regarding their grandfather's supposed treasure? Max had half a mind to march himself into the good vicar's parlor and give his cousin a life-altering facer.

Of course he did not, though. He made himself remain in the garden, tucked safely behind the house, hidden by rose bushes and hedgerows and undetected by Nigel. He would not ruin things now by charging in there prematurely. He would, however, keep a close eye on Miss Farrow. It was painfully obvious she was not over her apparent infatuation with the clod-faced lout. Max would make it his priority to see that she was not ill used or mistreated in any way.

He did not relish being the one to break her heart by presenting the truth about Nigel, but he sure as hell wouldn't let her fall deeper in love with the scoundrel. She'd need to know sooner rather than later and he'd try to make it as painless as possible. And then he'd present a ready shoulder for her to cry on.

Currently, however, his shoulder was serving as a perch. Bartholomew left the post he'd been gnawing at and came to rest on Max's coat. He could fairly hear the bird's clawed toes snagging and tearing at the fabric.

"Oh, so now you think you are free to climb all over me?" he asked, digging in his pocket to find a few of the morsels he'd tucked in there for the creature.

"*Climb on my pole*!" Bartholomew replied, repeating the phrase until finally Max was able to distract him with his thumb.

By God, the bird was incorrigible. The least little thing seemed to trigger his outbursts. How was anyone ever to retrain him when he seemed so utterly untrainable? Perhaps it would be easier to train every human in the village which words to avoid in hopes of eliminating any of the prompts that usually sent the bird into bawdy banter.

The thought hadn't been intended as anything to seriously consider, yet even as the words passed through his mind Max found himself pondering them. Could it really be possible to identify phrases in particular that set Bartholomew into chatter? He hadn't considered this, but perhaps he ought to. Sometimes it seemed the bird railed on for no reason, but other times there was clearly some impetus, something spoken that resonated with the bird and moved him to speech. What were these things?

"Climb all over me," he said aloud, testing his theory.

"*Climb on my pole. Climb on my pole*," the bird responded as if by rote, despite the fact he was working at detaching Max's thumb.

Well, clearly the trigger there was obvious. Max used the word climb, and that produced a response. Bartholomew knew that word and reacted. But what sort of phrase was that for him to have learned? Why not, "Climb up the rigging!" or "Climb down in the hold," or any other more common phrase that he'd have been likely to hear over and over aboard a ship. Why only these bawdy phrases?

"Climb on my pole," he said, watching the bird for response.

"*Give your old pole a twist, lad.*"

So, the word pole appeared in multiple phrases. Not really a surprise, given the tone of the bird's repertoire, but again, why should it be that phrase and not hundreds of others he had to have heard year after year? The more he thought of it, the more he was convinced something more was at play here, some reason the bird said what he said and would not be swayed.

"What the devil is your fascination with twisting poles, anyway?" Max asked him.

He really hadn't expected an answer, but the bird piped up eagerly.

"*Rub her down, twist your pole!*"

Well, that was just nonsense from another rhyme, of course, and he would have easily ignored it, except that something suddenly struck him. Those two phrases together that way… he'd seen it recently. Yes, he was sure of it. In that book but...oh, hell and damnation. Could it really be so very simple? He stared at the bird and the bird stared at him.

"Bartholomew, it's time you and I had a little discussion."

Bartholomew simply cocked his head and blinked one bright, orange eye. Apparently he had no response for that. Just as well. Max had a fair notion he knew what the bird *would* have a response for.

"Come on. Let's go take a look at something."

Offering the bird something actually edible to work at as he clung to his human perch, Max let himself back into the house. There was a narrow servant's stair close at hand so that there was no need for him to use the one in the main part of the small home, risking an encounter with Miss

Farrow and her guest. It was tempting to aim that direction and interrupt whatever smarmy attempt Nigel was making at winning yet more of Miss Farrow's favor, but for now Max forced himself to focus on the bird.

He could not shake the feeling that the solution to all of this lay close at hand. Up the stairs they went, ducking silently into Max's room. Bartholomew chattered as the door brushed past him, Max shutting it tightly. There, on the table near the bed, sat the object he was beginning to realize was much more than it seemed.

The damned book of bawdy poetry. He took it up and scanned a few pages, finally finding the one he was searching for. Ah, there it was. The handwritten rhyme he'd recalled.

A lovely young lass named Dear Dot
Likes to boast of her grand treasure spot.
Rub her down, twist your pole,
Find her sweet hidey-hole,
And make free with whatever she's got.

By all accounts, it was vile; nothing more than a verse for adolescent boys to snigger at. Max proudly did not snigger. He read through it again, making a mental note of the various phrases he was certain he'd heard Bartholomew utter more than once. To be sure about this, he decided to read aloud for the bird.

"*A lovely young lass named Dear Dot,*" he began.

Bartholomew cocked his yellow head and blinked. Max continued.

"*Likes to boast of her grand treasure spot.*"

Bartholomew blinked again. Then he proceeded to continue the rhyme.

"*Rub her down, twist your pole; Find her sweet hidey-*

hole,"

"*And make free with whatever she's got,*" Max finished in perfect unison with the bird.

Ah ha! So that was a rhyme from the book, and Bartholomew knew parts of it he didn't often spout out. What else was locked in that parrot brain, accessible only with the right inducement? It appeared payment was required to find out. Bartholomew reached his foot out, scratching against Max's face and clearly demanding some recompense for his labors.

Very well. Max could certainly play this game. He gave the bird another treat—a stale piece of bread this time—then placed him back on his rag-wrapped perch. Flipping to another page in the book, Max began reading.

Last Saturday night young Nancy lay a-sleeping
And into her bedroom young Johnny went a-creeping

He waited, but Bartholomew did not join in. Even as Max read through the familiar and repetitive chorus of *fol-the-riddle-i-do*, it was as if the creature had never so much as heard the rhyme—any of it. So Max moved onto another.

Now you bishops and deacons, priests, curates and vicars…
Know that Nottingham Ale, it's the best of all liquors…

No reaction again. How could Bartholomew not know any of these? Max had heard them again and again as a lad off at school, with his mates on a binge, and surely aboard ship on his journeys to and from the Americas. Not all of the rhymes in the book were well known to him, of course, but why on earth should it be that Bartholomew had not picked up even the most common among them?

Damn. He thought he'd come on the source of the bird's inspiration, but it seemed apparently not. Whatever had provided Bartholomew's education, it seemed the book was not it. Max would have to come up with some other method of getting to the root for his obsession.

He stepped back to study the bird who stood effortlessly on one twiggy foot as he used the other to hold the hard piece of crust. His sharp, hook-like beak chiseled at it and tiny crumbs fell like powder onto the floor, to join the gathering pile of feathers, gravel, dust and other undesirable refuse. Honestly, whoever decided a bird was an exceptional pet had never met this one.

Still, Max had to admit being with Bartholomew again after all these years was like rejoining and old friend. Indeed, filthy and objectionable or not, Bartholomew *was* an old friend. There was no way Max was going to let Nigel get his fool hands on him. He'd simply have to find a way to keep that blackguard away from the bird and from Miss Farrow until such time as he felt it was safe to reveal himself.

With Nigel dropping in for visits here and traipsing about town calling himself the new earl, that was going to prove harder and harder to do. Max had best get busy solving his riddle if he didn't want circumstances to play his hand for him. Grandfather's letter had indicated Bartholomew knew something of the hidden treasure, so Max needed to get back to the business of figuring out if that was true, or if Grandfather had been off his cockloft.

It seemed Max would not be doing that now. A knock at the door interrupted his thoughts. Bartholomew dropped his bread crust and complained by making repeated door-knocking sounds. Max gritted his teeth and went to see if perhaps Mrs. Cooper was come to beg him to go rescue

Miss Farrow from the lecherous grasp of Nigel.

But it was not Mrs. Cooper. It was Miss Farrow herself, safely out of any lecherous grasp and appearing fully unmolested. For now.

As he opened the door she batted huge eyes at him and chewed her lip in the most fetching way. “Er, may I speak with you?” she asked.

“Of course. Certainly. Come in,” Max replied a bit too eagerly, realizing he still held the book in one hand and hiding it behind his back.

She slipped past him into the room and stood there, wringing her skirts in her hands so that the fabric bunched and gathered tightly against her. That also was most fetching, though Max tried for decency’s sake not to notice. He was not very successful.

“I have just spoken with the new Glenwick,” she began.

“He is gone already?” He should not sound so very happy about that, he knew, yet it was impossible not to be.

“Yes. He only just now got into town and must be on his way to the estate to oversee things there. He merely wanted to stop and give regards to my father.”

The ruddy liar. He'd been in town since at least yesterday. What game was he playing now? Max imagined how pleasant it would be to rip Nigel's arms off, but kept his expression bland.

“I see. What a shame he did not wish to linger. Surely your father will be home soon and would have enjoyed seeing him.”

Not nearly as much as I would enjoy strangling him.

“I’m sure we are much honored that he took time to visit at all," she said with far more benevolence than the scoundrel deserved. "There will be other opportunities to reacquaint ourselves, of course.”

“Of course. So… why do you seem upset, if I may be

so bold as to notice your obvious agitation, Miss Farrow?"

She dropped her bunches of skirt, taking a deep breath and schooling her face. It did little to relieve the tension he could still see around her eyes, at her lips. Damn his fool cousin for leaving her in such a state!

"I… yes, I suppose I am a bit out of sorts. It's just… well, he said…"

"He said what?" By God, Max would make sure that he'd never say it again.

"He said that… oh, I hate to even think it."

"If he was in any way inappropriate, or unpleasant with you, Miss Farrow—"

"No, nothing like that. He was… well, he told me his intentions."

"Intentions? Good lord, isn't it a bit soon for that?"

"His intentions for Bartholomew," she clarified.

"Oh. Of course. And what are they?"

Her wide eyes fairly glistened with tears and Max had to struggle to keep from putting his hands on her to comfort her. At least, that's what he hoped he'd be doing with his hands. His conscience felt the tiniest niggle of concern that he might possible have just a bit more than comfort on his mind right now.

She was practically weeping when she found her voice to speak.

"The new earl says Bartholomew is to be put down!"

Chapter 11

"But he cannot do that," Max protested. "I thought the old earl made it clear he wished for your father to keep him?"

"Yes, that was our understanding, but Nigel… er, the new earl says the bird is a part of the estate and should have gone to him."

"Then why by heaven's name should he want to have him put down?"

"He feels that since the bird is… well, he worries Bartholomew's behavior might reflect poorly on the family name."

"A silly parrot is going to tarnish his fine family name?"

"I know. I tried to convince him he was worried for nothing, be he is quite sensitive about this. It is his place to be concerned about such things, after all. He is the last of his line. So much hangs on him to preserve family honor."

Max nearly snorted aloud at her mention of that imaginary item. As if Nigel had—or cared about—family honor! Indeed, this only added to his burden to find his incriminating proof quickly. More than ever he needed to unlock the secrets that Bartholomew had pent up in his feathery head.

"Does this heartless young earl expect you to wring the

bird's neck for him, or will he sent for the poor thing later?"

She cringed at his words. "He suggests Bartholomew be readied for return to him as early as tomorrow. And…"

"And led to the gallows? Or does he plan to borrow from the French and employ Madame Guillotine?"

"Don't joke about such things! Heavens, I hate to think of it. He said he will give Bartholomew a chance. If he does not show signs of being rehabilitated by the time we deliver him tomorrow, the earl will be forced to put him down."

"*Forced*? I don't see anyone forcing him to do this, do you?"

"I'm trying to see this as he does. He truly believes it is the only way to protect his family name."

"To drag his family name through mud as pet murderers, you mean. Surely you've no intention of giving the bird to him."

"What else can I do? I can't very well hold his bird hostage here, can I?"

"What would your father tell you to do?"

She frowned. "He would probably say we must turn the other cheek, to give unto Caesar what is Caesar's and let fate do what it will."

"And what do *you* want to do?"

"I want you to stay! That is, I want you to continue the training, to complete Bartholomew's correction and *then* allow the earl to take him back if he wants him, when there would be no need to be embarrassed for the things that he says."

"So you don't think he's a hopeless case and that the earl should put him out of his misery?"

"Of course not! Only a heartless fiend would be so unmerciful."

Well, he certainly was pleased to hear her speak this way of his cousin. She had a good head on her shoulders. Perhaps she was not likely to be swayed by the coldblooded snake after all. He wondered what his chances of swaying her were.

"You speak rather harshly of your friend the new earl," he said, taking half a step closer.

"It has been a number of years since he and I were acquainted," she replied, not retreating at his nearness.

So he took another step. testing the waters. "Still, he did feel the need to stop here on his very first day in town."

"Only to discuss the business of the bird."

"Only that? I must admit, Miss Farrow, that is a rather thin reason. After a journey of any duration, that a man should feel compelled to stop for a visit before reaching his home speaks that he must have a very strong motive for it. Are you certain it was the bird that was foremost on his mind… and not a certain young woman?"

She blushed. "I… you are mistaken in that, sir. He was here only on business."

"For a man such as that, business can always wait. It seems to me that perhaps *you* are his business, Miss Farrow. Have you always wanted an earl of your own?"

"Heavens, sir! You misunderstand my opinion of him."

"Do I? It certainly explains all your nerves and your color."

"There is nothing remarkable of my color, sir. If you please, we're discussing Bartholomew, not his earl."

"*Your* earl, you mean."

"He is not *my* earl! Who have you been talking to? I swear I have no interest in the man."

"You've not fancied yourself mistress of Glenwick Downs?"

"No, of course not."

"You'd do it justice, you know."

"Don't be ridiculous. What do you know of the place?"

"Er, I know that you'd be a remarkable Lady Glenwick."

Now her blushes were practically scarlet. He thought she might slap him, in fact, though he remained just where he was, well within arm's reach.

"Stop teasing me, sir. I've not set my cap for the man, nor has he any designs upon me. It's Bartholomew we should both be concerned for just now."

"I'd rather concern myself with you."

And now he was very close to her. He could see the rise and fall of her chest, her breaths coming in quick little gasps, yet she did not back away. Her eyes were huge and round when she blinked at him. He wondered what would happen if he touched her. Would she welcome it? Shove him away? Be unaffected entirely? He decided to find out, giving a gentle brush of her velvet cheek with his thumb.

Another chest rise, another little gasp.

"You had a spot of dust," he lied.

"*Dear Dot marks the spot*!" Bartholomew cackled.

Damn that bird! The moment was ruined. Miss Farrow came to her senses and stepped back, safely away from whatever Max might have been planning to do next.

"I can't imagine why he continues to repeat that," she said quickly. "What unusual rhymes he must have heard aboard ship."

"It isn't from a rhyme," Max said, then wondered if he ought to have kept silent. He would never want to give Miss Farrow the impression he was particularly well-versed in such things. Then again, he was sure it was true. He could not recall any lines he had ever heard or had read that contained that particular phrase.

She seemed doubtful of his expertise. "Surely you are

not very familiar with every song or bawdy lyric employed by common sailors, sir?"

"Er… no, happily, I am not." *Not all of them, anyway.* "What I mean to say, I've noted that Bartholomew's other common phrases seem to be found within that volume of, er, poetry that you discovered last night. This phrase does not appear to be among them."

"And you feel this is significant?"

"It just… it's merely something I observed."

He couldn't very well tell her the book came from his grandfather and he believed somehow it was related to a hidden treasure that only Bartholomew supposedly knew about but that had gotten the old man murdered, could he? Of course not, even as much as he was convinced she could be trusted with knowledge of such things. It was for her own good he kept quiet, though. Miss Farrow should be protected from such unpleasantness, not dragged into it.

"How have you observed it?" she asked.

Again, he was helpless against her gaze. He had to give her some sort of explanation quickly or, by the devil, he was likely to fall under her spell and confess all.

"I… that is, it would seem… I believe that if most of the phrases the bird utters can be found in this book, then perhaps there are other phrases—less offensive phrases—from it that he is equally familiar with."

Yes, this was as good an explanation as any. He took a deep breath, tore his eyes from her earnest expression, and lied as if his life depended on it.

"I think you will agree that it appears Bible verses are entirely foreign to him. This likely explains why we've had no luck at all getting him to recite them rather than his usual fare. So, if it is rhymes from this book he has come to know, then it might stand to reason there are some—however few—less offensive phrases in it that he already knows. I was hoping to simply refresh his mind of them and perhaps he will be content reciting those, rather than the more colorful ones."

By God, he was proud of himself. What a perfectly logical explanation! Rubbish, of course, but quite clever. He might have even believed it himself, if he didn't already know better. Now all he could do was hope Miss Farrow might be equally gullible.

"So that is why you've been studying these horrible rhymes?" she asked.

"Yes. Though I hate them, I have suffered in silence for the sake of the bird."

"How noble of you."

He wasn't completely sure he didn't detect a fine layer of sarcasm behind her words. But her eyes were still huge, and trusting, and warm, so he decided he must have imagined it. She believed him and he thrilled at the notion. She trusted him; he'd won her over. It was a feeling of triumph he rather enjoyed.

"So what is your plan?" she asked after a moment.

"My plan?"

"Have you found the phrases you think might refresh Bartholomew?"

"Well, of course it all takes time…"

"But he doesn't have time! Here, let me see that book."

She practically ripped it from his hands. It was all he could do to keep from pulling it back. What was she doing, corrupting herself with such material? Didn't she worry what it might do to her immortal soul? Worse, didn't she know what it might do to *him*, watching her read through what he knew she must be reading?

"Here's something," she said, pulling open a passage and studying it. "This does not seem so bad. It's a song, I believe, though I don't know the tune."

She started reading aloud.

"*A lonely old sailor forlorn and distressed, Forever alone on his island way West.*" She paused to glance over at Bartholomew, who simply stared back had her. So she continued. "*I never will go, to stay is the best. I'll guard with my life the old man's chest.*"

At that last line, the bird ruffed up his feathers. He cocked his head toward her, though, as if something in her words was familiar. She glanced at Max, gave a shrug, then continued. He wished she wouldn't. Whether Bartholomew knew the rhyme or not, Max did.

"*No wenching or ale, he would not take his rest; Year after year, his cock all repressed.*" Now she winced, the word having escaped her lips before she realized what she was saying. "Forgive me. I was already reading ahead past the chorus."

"I'm not certain this is a good idea..."

But she had already gone back to reading.

"*A buxom young maiden of soft, flaxen tress, Called the sailor one night for to come be her guest.*"

Again she cringed, the context of the story becoming clear. Max thought to step in here, to stop the reading, but she forged bravely ahead. This time, however, she was not alone. At the last line of the stanza, Bartholomew joined in with her.

"*I never will go, to stay is the best. I'll guard with my life the old man's chest.*"

She beamed up at Max now.

"Did you hear that? He does know this verse! And I've never heard him speak that line before!"

"*I'll guard with my life the old man's chest,*" Max said, repeating it.

Could it be there was meaning here beyond merely the obvious? He could not help but think so. *The old man's chest…* what could that mean besides what it seemed to mean? Grandfather really *did* have a treasure and he really *did* put Bartholomew over to guard it. By God, the bird *did* know something.

Max had to admit he was rather intrigued by their efforts here—and not just for the most obvious, inappropriate reasons. Miss Farrow seemed excited by their progress, as well. Unfortunately, her interest seemed to be mostly for the damned book.

"Here, let me continue: *But the maiden was greedy to see herself blessed, she appeared there before him in a state of undress*!"

"I don't know that you ought to keep on with—"

She ignored him and kept on. "*I never will go, to stay is the best. I'll guard with my life the old man's chest.*"

As predicted, Bartholomew recited the chorus again with her. And now he left his perch to fly toward them, landing on the nearby bedpost and gazing expectantly up at Miss Farrow. It seemed he expected reward for reciting that one particular line.

Max forced himself to take his mind off the situation, to forget that a beautiful young woman was reading bawdy verse in his presence with considerably more enthusiasm than he would have ever expected, and focused on Bartholomew. Clearly the bird knew the verse, yet he kept silent as she read on. When she got to that one repetitive line, he was right on cue with her.

Indeed, he knew the verse well. Someone, for some reason, had drilled this into the bird's tiny little brain. But how? And perhaps more importantly, why? It didn't make sense. Grandfather's letter had indicated that Bartholomew knew the whereabouts of the Glenwick fortune. So far all it seemed the bird knew was how to offend.

"He certainly does know the contents of this book,"

Miss Farrow said.

Indeed, her suspicion was evident. Max would have to come up with some better explanation for how the book got into his possession, and how the bird was so familiar with it. He rather wished he knew the truth of that last part himself.

"It is a book of very common bawdy songs."

"Does he know them all?"

She turned to another page and began reading. She paused at the repetitive refrain, but Bartholomew remained silent. She continued, this time getting all the way through to the end. Still the bird made no sound.

"It would appear he doesn't know this one."

"No, it would appear not."

"Is it less common than the others?"

"Er, no, I'm sorry to say it is not. I daresay most boys know it front to back by the age of thirteen."

"I see. Then what about this one?"

And she flipped some pages and started on another. It was the same story—she read, and Bartholomew did nothing more than preen his green feathers. Max forced himself to ignore the suggestive words tripping over Miss Farrow's perfectly pink lips and concentrated instead on the bird's actions. It was clear this rhyme—like so many others—meant nothing to him.

When Miss Farrow turned to another page and began reading there, however, the change in the bird was immediate. He left off his grooming, cocked his head, and refolded his wings. He sat rapt, listening carefully like a trained actor awaiting his time on the stage. It was most fascinating and Max knew beyond all doubt that there had to be some reason to this madness.

"*When your fortune has long since been missed, lad, And your coffers have long since been pissed, lad,*" the prim miss enunciated eloquently. *"Then go visit Dear Dot, 'Cause you'll want what she's got, You need just give your old pole a twist, lad.*"

This time not only did Bartholomew join in for the last part of the rhyme, but he accompanied her quite loudly on the whole second portion. It was the first time Max had heard him put all of those lines together, though he realized he'd heard pieces of them repeated separately on multiple occasions. It seemed this was apparently one of the bird's favorites.

He also realized—and felt rather foolish that he'd not noticed it before—that Dot was mentioned by name. He'd previously assumed that "Dot marks the spot" was some sort of term for a sailor's mark, a dot rather than the more typical X. He should have noticed the connection before now. Perhaps Dot did indeed mark the spot, but instead of it being some mysterious code, Dot was a person.

"This is most interesting," Miss Farrow declared.

"Indeed it is," he replied, although he suspected he might be finding it just a bit more interesting than she was. For the wrong reasons, of course.

"There's most definitely a pattern. Have you not noticed it?"

"A pattern? Well, yes… he seems to know some of the rhymes and is oblivious to others."

"Exactly! But the ones he knows… where did they come from? They are not like the others."

"What do you mean?"

He'd already acknowledged the verses Bartholomew favored were hardly well-known in other settings. Why was the girl leafing through pages as if she expected to find the answer there, spelled out before her?

"I mean, where did these pages come from? They are not printed like the others—they are written by hand, yet bound in the book with the others."

Max shrugged. "I don't know. I assumed all the pages were taken from other collections and compiled here by my… by whomever felt he needed a compilation of this detritus."

"But why is it only the handwritten pages that Bartholomew seems to understand?"

Max had no answer for her. He moved around to her side, looking over her shoulder to see that, indeed, the words that Bartholomew had just quoted along with her were written in the same long, scrawling hand that several of the other pages were written. Of course Max had noted them before, but it had never struck him that only the handwritten pages were the ones familiar to the bird.

"Are you certain of this?" he asked.

"I believe so. I read several of these others and Bartholomew ignored me. It was not until I turned to this page that he seemed to have something to say. And these others," she turned through the pages again. "See? Here is one that he knows, and here is another…"

"By Jupiter, it appears you are correct, Miss Farrow. He recites from only the handwritten rhymes, not the printed ones."

"What do you suppose it means?"

He had a very good idea what it meant—that somehow Grandfather had taught the bird these particular phrases and then hid them in plain sight here in this book. Obviously this was the very bit of information he had been searching for; *this* was the code to the hidden Glenwick treasure. Max simply needed to decipher it all.

To do that, however, he needed to get Miss Farrow off the track she had so thankfully been following.

"Er, I suppose these were the favorite rhymes of someone the bird had once been close to."

"But that would be the old Earl of Glenwick, and how on earth should he have knowledge of these?"

"They must be more common than we assumed, that's all."

"But why only the handwritten ones? It makes no sense."

Clearly she would not be easily dissuaded from contemplation of this. He could hardly blame her, it was quite a tantalizing puzzle and she was a clever woman. Surely she would want to understand, to reason this out. And she would reason it out, would realize the only explanation for how he came to possess the book. She'd likely think him a thief and a villain. Then he'd have no choice but to unmask himself.

He could not allow that! It was too soon. If word of his identity went out prematurely, the treasure might be lost forever and Nigel would get away with murder. Even worse, Miss Farrow would feel sorry for Nigel and hate Max for deceiving them. That would be losing a treasure indeed. He simply needed more time.

Meg stared at the book, forcing herself to overlook the bawdy content and focus only on what it must mean—how could Mr. Shirley's book contain these obscure passages that Bartholomew seemed to know so very well? If she did not know better, she would have to assume he'd been the one to teach the bird, but of course that couldn't be. Some of these phrases she'd heard the bird utter as long as she'd known him, and Mr. Shirley with his book had turned up less than a week ago.

There had to be an explanation. How could the bird know these things if they only existed in this book? Unless… this was not the first time Mr. Shirley encountered the bird. She had not thought of that, but perhaps she should have. Bartholomew had taken to the man almost immediately, hadn't he? She'd never known him to be particularly friendly with strangers. And there was still the matter of the man's missing references, wasn't there?

Indeed, all this required investigation. She glanced up at him to find him eyeing her worriedly.

"Tell me again how you came upon this book?" she asked. "I believe you said that you found it. Where, exactly, did you find it?"

He appeared very worried now, indeed. He fumbled a bit, his words sluggish and overly careful. "Well, I found it… that is, I could see it was an unusual book but I really gave it no mind and knew little of it until you so kindly pointed out the bird's familiarity with it."

"Yes, so you've indicated. But *where* did you find it?"

"I… er, where?"

"Yes. Where?"

She waited for him to answer. Really, why should this be such a difficult question? Could he not recall where he came upon this book? More likely he knew exactly how he found it and was hesitant to explain. Why, though? Was the story so very shocking—she could hardly imagine it would be any worse than the rhymes they'd already been reading together—or did he have some more nefarious reason to keep the information from her?

What was really going on here? She had so many questions! Who was this parrot trainer and why did he have so very many secrets? Was the thrill of electric reaction that coursed down her spine as she met his eyes nothing more than her pesky response to those dratted wide shoulders of his, or were her instincts warning her against him?

She jumped when Papa cleared his throat from the doorway behind her.

“Mrs. Cooper informed me of his lordship’s decision regarding the parrot,” he said. "I take it you and Mr. Shirley are planning what to do about that?"

“Yes, Papa,” Meg answered, closing the book silently and praying to God her father did not ask about it. “We are both hoping to convince him to change his mind.”

"I doubt there's little hope of that," Papa replied. "Poor bird. Seems his wicked ways are coming home to roost, as they say."

"That's dreadful, Papa. You can't really agree with his lordship that the best thing to do is to destroy poor Bartholomew? Where is your mercy?"

"Oh, of course I don't believe it, pet. But the new earl does have a claim, and the bird is his to do with as he sees fit."

"The old earl wanted Bartholomew to come to us, Papa," she protested. "Surely that means something. He went to his grave expecting us to keep the bird safe. How can we betray our old friend with such an injustice?"

"Such words!" Papa said, eying her. "How very unlike you. I should think you'd be pleased to have an end to our struggles, to know that life will finally return to sober normalcy."

She realized he ought to be right. *Sober normalcy.* Isn't that what she wanted? Indeed, she thought she had wanted that these past years with her heart locked up tightly and nothing allowed to upset her carefully crafted tedium. Until very recently she had been well pleased with herself for it, too. But now... to realize peace would only be regained by Bartholomew's death and Mr. Shirley's departure... how could she be in any way pleased with that?

She couldn't. She hated the very notion of it and wanted

to say so. She had half a mind to order Nigel to abide by his grandfather's wishes and to inform everyone in town that he'd been a heartless bounder seven years ago and clearly still was. Heavens, but she might even admit that despite everything she knew to be wholesome and proper, she found some of Bartholomew's rhymes highly amusing. Especially now that Mr. Shirley supplied her that book.

"I do hope you come to your senses quickly about this, Meg," Papa went on, deflating her. "His lordship is highly respected in town and you must think of his sensibilities. He cannot allow such a silly thing as a bird to upset his standing."

And there it was. The burden she'd carried for seven years now—her standing. The reason she had let her own neighbors whisper behind her back and assume even the worst of her. She didn't dare speak up, not even to save a life. She'd be labeled and condemned all over again—the jilted little ninny who had tried to reach beyond her station.

The old emotions washed over her and compressed her insides like a vice. Anything she said against Nigel would be dismissed, would be considered proof of her past indiscretion. She could not let herself suffer that humiliation again. Ever.

"Perhaps you're right, Papa. The old earl put nothing in writing that he wanted Bartholomew to come to us, so I suppose the new earl does have a legitimate claim."

She drew in a slow breath and tried to keep calm. It did not help that she was so acutely aware of Mr. Shirley's presence, his disapproving gaze.

"That's a sensible attitude," Papa said. "Perhaps when you are out driving with his lordship this afternoon you might find out when he intends to retrieve the bird."

Meg felt Mr. Shirley's inquisitive eyes on her. Indeed, she'd not mentioned to him that she'd agreed to go driving with the new earl. Not that it was any of his business, of course, but he'd very likely have an opinion on the matter. No doubt he'd think her quite the hypocrite, claiming to worry for Bartholomew while at the same time planning for a pleasant outing in his lordship's new Phaeton. Not that it really be would pleasant, considering how nervous she was about it. Still, it did seem a bit like fraternizing with the enemy.

"I will make certain to raise the topic, Papa," she said, pretending not to hear the dubious snort that emanated from Mr. Shirley.

Chapter 12

"Driving with the earl?" Mr. Shirley asked, as she suspected he might when he found her alone in the drawing room some time after noon.

"He invited me, yes."

"How kind of him."

Oh, but sarcasm was dripping from the man's voice. She supposed she ought to have expected it. She'd left with Papa after their discussion earlier and she'd known he was frustrated with her willingness to capitulate on the subject of relinquishing the bird. Indeed, she was frustrated, too, at the thought of it, but he simply did now know all the details of her situation.

"The new earl was often in our company during his youth," she said, as if that might explain everything. "He is a longstanding family friend and an invitation is perfectly acceptable."

"I've no doubt it is. You accepted right away."

"I should have delayed? And what would that accomplish?"

"It might show him he isn't quite as important as he seems to think he is."

"He's the earl now. That's fairly important."

"It's still no excuse for him to get everything he wants around here."

"He only just arrived here. What on earth has he gotten that isn't already his?"

"*Already his*? Is that what you are, Miss Farrow? Already his?"

"Certainly not! What on earth could make you suggest such a thing?"

"He told you he wants to destroy your pet, so you put on your best bonnet and are ready to hop up into his carriage. Forgive me if I assume that—"

"You should not assume, sir. No one should."

"Then perhaps you should not be so willing to comply with this so-called earl."

"You'd have me be rude to him?"

"I'd have you say *No* to him."

"I... it's merely a carriage ride, sir."

"Is it?"

"He's been gone several years and simply wants to get reacquainted with the area."

"As if that's *all* he wants to get reacquainted with."

"I'm not certain I approve of your tone."

"But you do approve of this earl's dashing new conveyance, of course."

"I don't know anything about his conveyance."

"You can bet it's something purse-proud and sparkish."

"I have no interest in a man simply because of the carriage he drives."

"I never claimed that you did."

She scowled at him. He'd not needed to make any sort of claim; the very tone of his voice made it for him. Oh yes, she saw the insolent sneer that just barely tipped the corner of his lip, the almost-roll of his eyes. The nerve of him to judge her for this!

And how infuriating that she was even the least bit concerned what he thought of her.

"You make more than enough claims, sir."

He shook his head. He was close enough that she could feel the warm breath that he released slowly as his hand came up to brush her cheek. She was frozen in place when his eyes locked onto hers, the intensity of his gaze holding her captive.

"I don't make nearly enough of them, Miss Farrow."

Oh, but there was that liquid warmth that bubbled up inside her again and seemed to drain the strength right out of her body. The heat radiating from him... the smoky timbre of his voice... the sizzling impact of his tender caress... it all made her legs tremble and her head spin. Not that she was about to complain!

Indeed not. She pressed herself closer to him. The bubbling warmth threatened to turn into raging lava when he wrapped his arms around her held her as if he had every right to do so. Perhaps he did, at that. She felt remarkably comfortable in this intimate posture.

She studied his face to see if he felt something similar. His eyes were dark and his jaw set firmly. His lips moved as if to speak, but instead he merely smiled down at her. He seemed far more controlled than she felt, all that bubbling and lava making it extremely difficult for her to think straight. But he was fully possessed of all his faculties. Hers as well, it seemed, when he wrapped her tighter and brought his lips down to press against hers.

Was this a kiss? Good heavens, but it appeared that it was! So many years had passed since the few awkward attempts with Nigel, she'd come to believe she didn't care for kisses. But this... she rather liked this. Kissing Mr. Shirley was clearly something she had been wanting to do. That notion had not fully dawned on her until just now, but as the man's firm, heated hands slid tight around her and his lips lingered with rising fervor, she quite eagerly kissed him back.

His body was solid beneath her fingertips as she ran them over his arms, reaching up to very nearly hang upon his neck. His dark hair grew well beyond his collar and it was tempting to desperately run her hands through it. But that would distract from the kiss and, really, she wanted nothing to pull her focus away from that wonder. She clung to him and relished his taste, his scent, his very potent being.

The room around her ceased to exist and all that mattered was pulling herself closer to him, touching him and letting the waves of warm awareness roll her under their influence. Mr. Shirley was a master at what he did to her. Who would ever have thought such a thing from a mere parrot trainer?

A parrot trainer... good heavens, she was kissing their parrot trainer! And she was kissing him in a manner that could only be called wanton and gratuitous. What must the man think of her? Gracious, what would anyone think if they were to find them here like this? What if Papa came by, or if Nigel... Oh dear! Nigel would be here any minute!

She pried her hands off of him and shoved herself away.

"No! We can't."

The world seemed to whirl circles around her and she was forced to grab the nearest wall to keep herself upright. Mr. Shirley, however, appeared singularly unaffected. Only the hint of a knowing smile on his beautiful face gave any indication that he'd even noticed their kiss.

"I would say it appears that we can, Miss Farrow," he said smugly.

"But... oh no, but we shouldn't! Please, Mr. Shirley, you must forgive me."

"For *that*? Absolutely not."

"I don't know what I was thinking!"

"I have a fair notion what you were thinking."

"Well, I shouldn't have been."

"No, probably not. But I'm so glad you were. Come, my dear, let me help you think more on the subject."

He moved toward her so she staggered back, keeping as much air as possible between them. Any more kisses from this man and there was no telling what might happen. She needed to clear her head, to make herself think straight.

"No!"

"Ah, so you can use that word. I'm very happy to hear it. May I suggest you use it frequently when your companion arrives for your little outing today?"

She nearly panicked at the reminder. "He's expected any moment. Please, Mr. Shirley, don't make mention of... of what has happened here."

Now his smug smile went away, replaced by a darkening frown. "Yes, I suppose you would prefer to keep this particular thing from him."

"From everyone!"

"Of course. I am, after all, nothing more than a lowly parrot trainer."

"What? Oh, but that isn't it..."

"Isn't it? I'm not nearly so grand as your earl."

"He isn't *my* earl."

"No, he most certainly isn't. Don't let his honeyed words or elegant demeanor make you think otherwise."

"Why would you say that? Have you met the man?"

"I know his type."

"So you are an expert on parrots *and* the aristocracy, are you?"

"You ought not trust him, Miss Farrow."

"Believe me, Mr. Shirley. I, better than most, know that."

It was too much. She should not have confided in him—no doubt he would infer all manner of things from her words. Some of them might even be true.

"Then make an excuse. Tell him you cannot go with him today."

"But that would be a lie and I abhor lies, Mr. Shirley."

"Yes, I'm sure that you do. I've no right to instruct you how to live your life."

"No, you don't."

"You will accept my friendly warning, though? He isn't all that he seems. Be careful, Miss Farrow."

"I'm always careful, Mr. Shirley." And then her cheeks went hot as she had to correct herself. "Well, almost always."

She wanted to look away from him, since it was only too obvious just how un-careful she'd been not five minutes ago, but she couldn't. His blue eyes had captured hers and she was held there, backed up against the wall, still flushed from his kisses. He moved closer and her breath stopped in her chest, held there by invisible force. The pounding of her heart nearly deafened her.

He reached for her hand and brought it up to his lips. Her knees went all weak again and she wondered if it would be careful to grab him about the neck again and pull herself into his arms. She didn't, though. She struggled to breathe as he spoke softly over her hand, his eyes never leaving hers.

"I'll never let him hurt you again."

What had he said? Dear gracious, but it seemed he knew what had happened. But he couldn't. How could he? And yet what else could his words mean?

Now it was even harder not to cast herself into him and pray for more of his kisses. He knew the truth yet he didn't condemn her! Parrot trainer or not, this man was more than exceptional.

A sound from outside caught her attention. She glanced over, and saw the gleaming black carriage just outside their home. It was Nigel... the new Earl of Glenwick. He'd arrived for her, just as expected. She could make out his form, adjusting his hat and descending from one of the highest Phaetons she'd ever seen. The idea of climbing up into that—with him—filled her with sudden terror.

It must have shown on her face.

"You can still claim a headache," Mr. Shirley whispered.

Indeed, she very nearly agreed with him. But no, that would serve no useful purpose. This was something she must face and she knew what to do.

She pulled her hand back from Mr. Shirley and slid away from him.

"I will go with the earl," she announced and hoped it was honest disappointment she thought she saw in his expression. "And I'll plead for Bartholomew. Surely as an old friend, the earl can't ignore my appeal, can he?"

Now his disappointment was coupled with an inelegant snort. "I daresay he cannot. Your appeal is undeniable, Miss Farrow."

A giddy delight welled up in her now. How silly, to find herself girlishly effected by such flattery. She could not help it, though. She'd somehow become hopelessly infatuated with this parrot trainer and the mere fact that he smiled at her nearly caused her to swoon. What a ninny she was!

At least, though, she had no worries of falling under the sway of Nigel's old charm. The very thought of it was laughable now. As she watched him move from his carriage toward their house the panes in the glass made him appear small and distorted. How had she ever found anything of him attractive?

She was glad she resisted the urge—once again—to throw herself into Mr. Shirley's strong arms. Mrs. Cooper appeared in the doorway and cleared her throat just then.

"It seems his lordship has arrived," she announced.

"I'll receive him in here," Meg replied.

Mr. Shirley appeared uncomfortable. "I suppose I'll take my leave."

"Would you care to meet the new earl?" she asked, wishing he would accept, and perhaps even insinuate himself into their outing.

He declined. "No, I think your fine earl would care little for me. I'll go tend to the bird."

Nodding to her and then to Mrs. Cooper, he let himself out of the room. It almost appeared to Meg as if he rushed, but surely that was imagination. What reason could Mr. Shirley possibly have to hurry off, avoiding someone he'd never once met? She attributed it to some sense of inferiority on his part and promised herself she would set him straight on that later. He may not have a fine title or high-perch Phaeton, but Mr. Shirley was far more the gentleman than Nigel Webberly had ever been. If he did not believe that now, she'd find a way to convince him. First, though, she must rescue Bartholomew.

A knock sounded at the front door. It was hollow, insistent. Mr. Shirley's footsteps had disappeared up the nearby stairs and Mrs. Cooper raised an eyebrow, waiting for instruction from Meg.

She waited a long moment before giving it. The knock sounded again. Meg took a deep breath and picked up her gloves.

"Very well. You may let him in, Mrs. Cooper."

"She's going driving with the blackguard," Max grumbled.

He stalked back and forth in his room, pausing to glare out the window and snarl as Nigel's carriage jounced down the street, Miss Farrow perched tenuously on the bench and clearly at Nigel's mercy. What could she be thinking, to go off with him like this? Did she really care for him that much, even knowing that he was heartless enough to rip Bartholomew from their home with the intent of destroying him? He couldn't believe that of her.

No, Miss Farrow had a conscience, she cared for what was right. Perhaps some tender feelings for Nigel still lingered in her, but he was certain it had not been Nigel she was thinking of when he kissed her. When she kissed *him*.

By God, she *had* kissed him—had kissed him quite well. He was not likely to forget it any time soon, either. He only wished he could forget that she'd likely kissed Nigel in similar manner sometime in the past. It was entirely possible the ruddy fool expected the same from her today, too.

Well, surely she'd not succumb to any advances Nigel might make. Miss Farrow cared for propriety. She was well aware Nigel's wife was barely cold in the grave—surely she'd rebuff any overtures he might make. The man ought to be in full mourning, not out touring the countryside with an unchaperoned lady.

While Max... well, he ought to be figuring out the bloody mystery he had at hand instead of worrying over a woman who saw him as nothing more than a parrot trainer with a penchant for unseemly poetry. He dragged himself away from the window and went back to the papers he had strewn over his bed. Bartholomew squawked from his perch and stretched his wings as if he might fly.

"No, I don't need you on my head, or mucking about

with my papers," Max informed him. "You just stay there in your spot."

"Dear Dot marks the spot," Bartholomew responded.

No less than four times.

Max ran his hands through his hair and bit back some unholy words. "Stop it! What the hell does that mean, anyway, 'Dear Dot marks the spot?'"

As if in sensible reply, the bird simply said, "*You'll want what she's got.*"

Max was about to give in to some unholy words but suddenly the bird's phrase linked with some little memory inside his brain. *Dot*. A woman's name... short for Dorothy, as he recalled. Why should that seem suddenly familiar to him?

He didn't know anyone named Dorothy, as far as he knew. He kept getting a fuzzy image in his mind, a distant memory of someone, though. A woman... yes, a woman with red hair. How did he know her?

He couldn't picture her face, no matter how hard he tried. All he could recall was long, waving red hair and, well, a rather remarkable bosom. Yes, that part was not so very fuzzy in his recollection.

But how on earth could he have a memory like that? Surely he'd not been on such intimate terms with a woman and then completely forget her face or anything else about her? Indeed, he'd not lived the life of a monk, but still... he was a gentleman. Surely he was not cad enough to play so fast with a woman and then entirely forget her.

For the life of him he could not place her. She was nothing more than a vague, red-headed, big bosomed figure in his murky memory. It was almost as if she had not been real; yet not a fantasy, either. For certain any fantasy woman of his invention would be shaped in a manner more closely resembling reality. She'd be shaped like Miss

Farrow, for instance. This Dorothy person... well, she was almost grotesque in his mind. He could see her quite plainly now: weathered skin, clumsy, bulbous, breasts barely hidden behind indecently clinging fabric, a vacant stare from a face he couldn't quite place... By God, what on earth could he have done with the woman to be so well acquainted with her?

Bartholomew ruffled his feathers, croaking and cackling insensibly as he preened on his perch. And then suddenly the image in Max's memory became clear. He remembered the woman.

"*Dorothy Rose*."

He breathed the name slowly, allowing the sound of it to hang in the air and his mind's eye to see her completely.

Yes, he did know her well. He'd admired her for years, gazed in awe-struck wonder at her. More than once he'd even climbed up onto his grandfather's desk in order to touch her. That had seemed forbidden fruit to a young lad of ten and after all these years such foolishness had been nearly forgotten.

Not entirely, though. Dorothy Rose still held a place in his heart. He could hardly believe he didn't recall her at once. He had no doubt Bartholomew recalled her. His separation from her, actually, might be some part of an explanation for his unpleasant attitude of late. In all of Max's memories, Bartholomew and Dorothy Rose had been together. She had been the bird's security, his foundation, his place of refuge.

Literally. Max had been more than a little relieved to remember that Dorothy Rose was not, in fact, a real woman. She was the decrepit wooden figurehead from one of Max's less-than-noble ancestor's ships. Bartholomew insisted on using the bawdy thing as his perch as she hung year after year over the desk in Grandfather's office. Over time, Bartholomew had left so many claw marks and refuse on her head that at least once a year Grandfather had been forced to repaint the old girl.

And he had called her Dot. She'd been part of the family for years, proudly displayed as if there was no shame at all in the scandalous rumors of a Glenwick who'd gone to sea, devoting himself for a time to all the depravity of piracy before bringing home a stolen bride and forever tainting the Glenwick name. Max had found her entrancing and exotic. His parents had been appalled at the very thought of her existence. Neither of them shared his grandfather's fascination with the old figurehead, or for the secret family history. If not for the gossip of servants, Max may have never heard of the terrible things his great-grandfather had supposedly done, roving the seas on a mission to pillage and plunder.

What coincidence, then, that the subject of one of Grandfather's vulgar rhymes should share the same name. Or was it? Perhaps he should take another look at that book. He went to the bed, brushing papers aside until he found it. He flipped pages to the first handwritten sheet bound there.

A lovely young lass named Dear Dot
Likes to boast of her grand treasure spot.
Rub her down, twist your pole,
Find her sweet hidey-hole,
And make free with whatever she's got.

It did indeed mention Dot, but the rhyme was nothing but pure rubbish. Catchy and titillating, but rubbish. Why should this be the sort of thing Bartholomew heard often enough to build his vocabulary around? Clearly Grandfather had become obsessed with these rhymes in his later years. Max supposed that, at least, made sense. It was only natural for a lonely widower to find his thoughts drifting in a certain direction.

Which of course reminded him just where Nigel might be drifting even now as he carted Miss Farrow off along some secluded country lane surrounded by rustic beauty and no one to offer interruption. Damn that ruddy blackguard! Max should never have allowed Miss Farrow to go off with him. He should have found some way to disrupt her plans.

Hell, he could still disrupt them. At this point, perhaps the woman would welcome any distraction that might call off Nigel's obviously intended onslaught. Max would be a fool to trust the rogue to behave himself with such a tempting companion as Miss Farrow. The least Max could do was to keep an eye on things, make sure Miss Farrow was safe. He might not have to reveal himself just yet.

But he would if it meant rescuing her. Bartholomew's training and all studies of the rhymes in his book could wait. Miss Farrow was his utmost priority now and he was already kicking himself for letting her walk out the door.

He bundled his papers and hid them with the book. Bartholomew had a big pile of seed and a fresh dish of water at hand, so there was no reason on earth not to leave him to squawk and to preen on his own. Max grabbed up his coat and headed out.

On foot he would have very little hope of catching up to Nigel's smart rig, but fortunately he would not be on foot. He would not be alone, either. It was time to pay a visit to the local inn and call on a friend.

Chapter 13

The warm, fresh air felt good on Meg's face, but she wished Nigel... er, Lord Glenwick... wouldn't drive so fast. It was taking both hands to hang onto the bench for dear life, leaving no hands to hang onto her bonnet for dear life and she feared she was getting a bit too much warm, fresh air. She'd likely be blotchy and freckled by the time they returned home. *If* they returned home, which was beginning to feel doubtful.

"Please, my lord, I'm afraid you didn't hear me when I asked you to drive a bit more slowly," she said, practically yelling over the clattering hooves of the horses and the carriage jouncing over the rutted lane.

"And I'm afraid you didn't hear me when I asked you to dispense with the ruddy formality, Meg. Surely we have been more to each other than 'my lord' and 'Miss Farrow'."

"You know I have always valued our friendship, but... Gracious! The road takes quite a curve ahead."

"The best Corinthians in Town have declared this carriage a prime goer. Fear not, my dear Meg. Just sit closer and hold onto me, if you're afraid."

Heavens, but she was sure she'd much rather take her chances tumbling out of the carriage. What had gotten into the earl? He was suddenly behaving as if what passed between them those many years ago had been everything his grandfather seemed to suspect. She was beginning to think it had been stupendously unwise of her to come riding alone with him like this. Whatever did the man have on his mind?

"Ah, here it is, just up around the bend."

If they didn't topple completely over as he took the bend at reckless speed, perhaps she would find out what he was referring to. She gave up on protecting her face and saved her person, clinging to the bench and holding her breath until—miraculously—they did not overturn and die. She whispered a silent prayer and glanced around. There was nothing to signify what he had been talking about.

"What is here, my lord?"

"Our picnic spot. See? That lovely old oak tree standing alone, just near that picturesque stream."

"Ah. Yes. I see a tree. And a good number of sheep. I'm not sure this is a good place for a picnic..."

"It's perfect. Don't you remember? We've been here before."

No, she was positive they had not. If she recalled, he had talked of taking her off on a picnic, and of course her girlish infatuation had assumed that could only mean he had meant to propose, but her memory was quite clear. The picnic had never happened, and neither had the proposal.

"I'm sure I would remember if we'd picnicked here before."

"Of course we did. It was right there, in the soft grass beside that old tree. I remember it clearly, although... perhaps the day did not mean quite as much to you as it did to me."

What could he be talking about? There had been no day—meaningful or otherwise. Was he teasing her, or were his memories truly this faulty? She could not feel at all comfortable when he pulled the Phaeton to a halt and turned a glowing smile her way.

"Picnic with me, Meg. The weather is perfect and I can see you are eager to get your feet back on solid ground."

Indeed, she was at that. But somehow sitting in the grass for a private picnic with Nigel did not seem quite the same things as getting her feet onto solid ground. Was her heart racing? It was. Did she have those same, silly butterflies she'd felt around him as a much younger woman?

No, she did not. Her nerves today were of a very different sort, something far less pleasant. Certainly she'd encountered those butterflies earlier when Mr. Shirley had taken her into his arms and... yes, there had been butterflies, indeed. And they were most enjoyable. This sensation she felt now... it was nothing like that. It was much more along the lines of panic.

"You hesitate, Meg," he said when he hopped out of his seat and came round to hers. "What is it? Does my new title change things between us?"

"Change things? Your title? Of course I am pleased for you, my lord, and—"

"Nigel. You must call me Nigel. I insist on it, Meg."

"Very well, Nigel. It's been over seven years since we've seen one another. I cannot think it is your new title that has changed things between us."

He drew in a deep breath and nodded, as if some great light was suddenly dawning for him. Then he put out his hand to offer assistance and smiled adoringly up at her. Years ago she would have been quite taken by the look on his face and the honeyed words on his lips.

Today she simply found him ridiculous. His flattery was trite, his posturing was vain, and what she assumed he meant to show deep feeling in his eyes simply made him look as if he'd eaten something not quite right. Compared to the image of masculine perfection that was Mr. Shirley, even Nigel's new title could not bolster Meg's opinion of him.

Compared to the parrot trainer, Nigel appeared lacking in every way. He did not have the fine cut of his jaw that Mr. Shirley had, and his shoulders were considerably less broad than his, and even though the color of his eyes was somehow similar to Mr. Shirley's, something was lacking there, too. Mr. Shirley's eyes pulled her into them, inviting her to share in some great adventure, to walk through a gateway for which only he held the keys. They were deep and endless and full of hidden mystery she longed to understand.

Nigel's eyes... well, there was little mystery there. She had no doubt she fully understood what she saw behind them. The man's shallowness gave it all away. He'd toyed with her until his heiress had come along, and now that he was free again he was hoping to toy with her some more. Much of Nigel Webberly was an enigma to her, but certainly not that part. What she did not understand, however, was how she could have ever thought him worthy of her fondness in the first place.

Well, she supposed youth was filled with foolishness and he had been hers. Not any more, though. If Nigel thought her still a simpleton to be played with at his leisure, he would end up disappointed.

But not before she bartered for Bartholomew's life. Indeed, she might just find a way to make use of this man's vanity after all. She took in her own deep breath and smiled back at him.

"Very well, Nigel, I will accept your offer to dine *al fresco* today."

He had the good sense to appear grateful, bowing slightly then taking her hand to help her alight. She would have to be on her highest guard with him, she knew, but the man was, after all, a gentleman. He might think to play fast with her, but she was too well connected for him to attempt anything truly imprudent. He thought he could lure her into caring for him again, but he would never stoop to attempting to force any affection. She could handle this man.

She hoped.

Max found his way to the local inn quickly. He was unexpected and was half worried when he rapped at the door to the private room that his man might not be there. His fears were relieved, though, when Hugh Baxter opened the door.

"Webberly! I had no idea you'd be coming today," the man said in his slow, American accent.

Max hushed him immediately. A quick glance assured him no one was about in the corridor to have heard, but he ushered himself into the room and shut the door securely, just to be safe. If there was any way he could yet salvage their plan...

"Although since we're on this side of the pond, I suppose I ought to start calling you Lord Glenwick now," Hugh mused, his American sensibilities dreadfully unimpressed with Max's pedigree.

"No time for that. I've had rather an emergency come up," Max explained quickly. "I need your help, Hugh."

"Of course, man. What can I do?"

"We'll have to go after Nigel now."

"Now? But I thought you wanted to wait until we were sure there was enough proof?"

"He's planning to take possession of Bartholomew. Obviously he knows the bird is the key to all this."

"Which obviously means he still doesn't have his hands on that treasure."

Max wished that was all he needed to worry about Nigel getting his hands on. He wasn't sure just how desperate he wanted Hugh to know he was right now, though. In his last correspondence with Hugh, he still held Miss Farrow under suspicion. To deny all that now might lead Hugh to question just what had altered Max's impressions of her.

It would be dashed embarrassing to admit he'd gone soft for her brown eyes and the pretty way she stood on her tip-toes when Max kissed her. He wasn't sure, actually, how he would explain to Hugh he'd been convinced the Farrow's were allies in this battle. No doubt whatever he said, Hugh would see through his words and make some snide remark about Max turning into a sap.

Hugh was sharp. Max appreciated that about him. They'd met years ago when Max's mother had taken him to live in Boston with his brand new step-father. Hugh was the son of his step-father's business partner; a rough and tumble kid who didn't care the first thing about Max being the heir to some fancy English lord. They'd been like brothers ever since.

To remain close to his mother, Max had gone to school in America. A dozen years now he'd lived a full ocean away from his homeland. At first when he began noticing strangers following him, prowlers darting about outside his windows at night, and other mysterious happenings, he ignored it. He wrote to his Grandfather faithfully and never mentioned any of it.

When he was nearly run down in the street by a carriage that appeared and then disappeared without explanation, he began to get a bit suspicious. When someone he barely knew started asking after the legend of the so-called Glenwick Pirate Treasure, he became more than a bit suspicious. The acquaintance disappeared, but the odd occurrences did not.

Max enlisted Hugh at that point. Hugh was not like the friends Max had had growing up in England. Hugh was well-educated and intelligent, but his father was a self-made man. Hugh had grown up in the seedier parts of Boston. A heart, Hugh was a thug.

He knew how to get information, and he did. Hugh was able to warn Max that his cousin Nigel had been making interesting inquiries into Max's life: what his patterns were, who his friends were, where he went on a daily basis. Max scheduled a journey home to England to investigate, and that was when someone attacked him aboard ship.

Hugh had been close at hand, though. Together they over-powered the attacker and when the man tried to escape, he went overboard. By the time he was fished out, the body was unrecognizable and Hugh suggested Max take advantage of the situation. Word of his death began circulating.

Only a select few knew the truth. It had taken months for Max to get word to his grandfather, and he would always regret that the poor man mourned him as long as he had. For two years now he'd been playing dead, secretly collecting tips and clues that would tie his cousin to his attempted murder—and now to the successful demise of their Grandfather. He should have known that anyone who would be low enough to try murdering him would surely not stop before getting that dear old man out of the way.

Nigel wanted the title. He wanted the treasure, too. He thought he'd removed Max from inheriting, so of course Grandfather had been the next stumbling block for his goal. Max should have seen that coming. He just never imagined Nigel could be truly capable of....

And now he'd allowed Miss Farrow to go off driving with him. He ought to have his head examined.

"So what is the move now?" Hugh asked, pouring them both a good stiff whiskey.

"I still don't have all the proof that we'll need, but we've got to do something. He's gone driving today. With *her*."

"*Her*?"

"Miss Farrow."

"The pretty young vicar's daughter? She's one of your top suspects."

"I was wrong."

"Oh? But she's got her cap for Nigel, doesn't she?"

"No! She can't stand the blackguard."

"Then why is she driving with him?"

"For Bartholomew. She says she's going to convince Nigel to save the bird's life, but I'm afraid she's got no idea what my cousin is fully capable of."

Hugh chuckled, downing his drink. "Or maybe she's got more than an idea. Word in town says she and the new earl were once awfully chummy. Maybe she sees this as her chance to finally get a title for herself."

"She isn't like that!"

Hugh paused over pouring a second drink and his eyebrows went up.

"You know she isn't like that because you've been living in her house for a week, or because you *want* her not to be like that?"

"She *isn't* like that, and have a care what you are implying, Hugh. The important thing now is to find her and make sure my ruddy cousin doesn't enjoy his afternoon."

"Without tipping him off to your presence, I suppose."

"Exactly."

Hugh shook his head and rolled his eyes, but he had the good sense not to say anything he might end up regretting.

"Fine. Tell me where they went and I'll go take care of things for you."

"I'm going, too."

Now he laughed out loud. "Of course you are. That's the sensible thing to do at this point."

Max tried not to be angry. This was Hugh, after all. He could trust him with his life—and Miss Farrow's life, too. He'd formulated a plan on his way here, and he knew without doubt Hugh would go along. No matter how foolhardy it was.

"It's the only thing to do at this point," he said, tossing back the whiskey Hugh handed him and getting to business. "Now where's that bag you carry, with the masks and what not?"

"Masks? It's the middle of the day, Max. What exactly do you plan to do with those?"

"Highwaymen don't always wait for the dead of night. What better way to distract a criminal than by presenting him with another criminal?"

"I believe you've lost your mind."

"Where's the bag?"

"Under the bed. I'd like to just say, though, that I'm not in favor of whatever you've got planned."

"You don't even know what I've got planned."

"I can guess, and I don't like it."

"Fine. Noted. Now go get the carriage ready. They headed north out of town and there's no telling what Nigel might be about by now."

"Oh, I think you've got a fair idea what he's about."

Max clenched his fists. Yes, by God, he was afraid Hugh was right. He had more than a fair idea what Nigel was about. The same damned thing he himself would have been about if he'd been lucky enough to cart Miss Farrow off for a drive through the quiet, lonely countryside.

"Just see that you hurry, man."

"You are even more lovely now than that day five years ago when we sat here under this tree," the earl of Glenwick said.

"Seven years ago," Meg corrected. "And we never sat under this tree."

The summer breeze rustled through the branches above them, bees bumbled from clover to clover in the quiet meadow around, the nearby stream babbled a delicate cadence, and birds trilled lovingly to their mates. It was the perfect day for a romantic picnic and this gentleman was outdoing himself with flattery and pretty words. Meg tried not to be sick.

"I remember it like it was yesterday," Nigel cooed with all the warmth and sincerity of a reptile.

"I'm sure your memory is clearer than mine," she said, having given up on convincing him the truth of what happened. "I had no idea you felt such deep sentiment and emotion, Nigel."

"I have always felt things very deeply for you, Meg. They never diminished over the years."

"Even when you left to get married?"

He lowered his head and gave a mournful sigh. "Even then, I'm ashamed to admit. I was forced by my station to marry where expected. I only wish things had been different."

"They've worked out well for you now, I suppose," she couldn't help adding. "You've become earl."

"Yes, though the only joy that it brings me is the knowledge that finally, at long last, I am free to give my heart where it wills."

"Joy that comes at the expense of your poor wife, of

course."

"God rest her poor soul. I came to care for her, I assure you, but she was not an easy woman to abide. She had none of the gentle virtue you possess, Meg. She was cold and unfeeling—I was forever a stranger to her, no matter how I tried. You've no idea how lonely I've been these past years, Meg. Not a day has gone by that I haven't missed everything about you."

"And thought longingly of our picnic, apparently."

"Every day! Please don't think me too forward... but being with you again, here, like this... it's my dearest dream coming true."

"Even when you left to marry someone else you were dreaming of me?"

"Yes, Meg. Please don't think less of me for it. Let your heart speak for my honor and say you understand."

Oh, she understood very well. Far better than he could guess, given the cow's eyes he was making and the hopeful little smirk at the corner of his mouth. He thought she was ready to swoon for him here and now. Could he be so very stupid? Well, what better time to make this work in her favor?

"Your heart is so tender!" she said, letting out the sorrowing sigh she was sure he expected. "Oh, you dear man. I had no idea you'd been so lost."

"Yes. Yes, I have been. Lost and lonely for you, Meg. Tender only for you."

"That's sweet. If only your heart could be so tender for poor, poor Bartholomew."

"Er, what?"

"It's so sad that you feel he must be destroyed."

"But you admitted he's caused chaos in your home, brought scandal onto your father."

"Yes, he has done all that."

"And you've been reduced to hiring a stranger to come live in your home, make free with your generous hospitality, all to no avail. Surely you see that a creature such as that cannot go on. You can't truly feel sorry for the beast?"

"But he was your grandfather's. Have you no sentiment toward him for that? The old earl loved him dearly despite all his flaws. He told me time and again that bird was his treasure."

"Yes, yes, but... wait, treasure? What do you know of a treasure?"

"That's how much he loved the silly bird."

"And he used that exact word? The bird was a *treasure*?"

"His treasure, he'd say."

"What else would he say? What did he tell you?"

Now he was leaning in close to her, his eyes losing the dark languor that had filled them and going bright, piercing the air between them. She instinctively pulled back. He must have noticed her reaction. Immediately his expression softened, his voice went low and his smile returned.

"I had no idea you were so close to my grandfather. Of course you must tell me everything of his last years. I regret I was away, not here at the end."

"He... he missed you, too. He loved you all the way to the end."

He nodded, his expression clouded and unreadable. Was this grief? Or something darker? Why did the skin on her back suddenly tingle and every instinct within her scream out that something was not right, that she should find some excuse to leave now?

But she'd not yet got him to discuss Bartholomew. How could she give up her one chance to convince him, to gain a reprieve for the bird? She'd best steel her reserve and give one more try.

"And he hoped Bartholomew would stay at the parsonage. With my father and me."

His expression grew cold now.

"My grandfather said that? I had no idea there'd been so much discussion on the topic. He wished to bestow his best treasure on the lowly town vicar, did he? How kindhearted of him."

The glint in his eye and the edge to his voice sounded anything but kindhearted. She pulled back even farther from him, scooting to the very edge of the blanket he'd laid out for their picnic. To her dismay he followed, looming over her as he rose up onto his knees.

"What else did he leave you, Meg? Did he give you the book?"

"Book? He didn't give me a book. Maybe my father... he has a large collection of sermons bound nicely."

"It's not that kind of book. It's not a nice book at all, Meg. It was a collection of tawdry, vulgar songs and rhymes passed down from my great-grandfather, the pirate."

Good heavens! The *book*! There was no doubt in her mind he was speaking of the book she had found in Mr. Shriley's room. But how could he have it? What on earth was going on here?

"You know the book, don't you?" the earl spat out at her. "I see it in your eyes! Tell me where it is. What have you found in it?"

"I... it's just a book as you said, a collection of very rude poems and rhymes. Song lyrics, perhaps, for the sorts of songs pirates might sing."

Now his arms shot out and he grabbed her by the shoulders. "Where is it? Where did you put it?"

"I didn't put it anywhere, sir. And please, you're hurting

me."

"Tell me where it is. Where did you see it?"

Her mind was a muddle. What should she say? He seemed about ready to shake her and she was quite terrified of him now. It almost appeared he had murder in his eyes. If she gave the wrong answer there was no telling what he might do.

But what was the right answer? What on earth was so special about that horrible book? And what could it mean that Mr. Shirley had shown up at her door with it claiming he'd arrived to help train their parrot? He must be in on some horrible scheme. And... oh good heavens, but she'd let herself kiss the man. And liked it!

Nothing made sense to her and she tried desperately to think straight.

"I... I don't know where it is."

"Where did you see it?"

"I'm not quite certain. Why are you hurting me? Please, let me go, my lord."

"Tell me! Where was the book?"

"I can't recall! I didn't pay attention. I think it was in—"

The crack of a pistol suddenly rang through the air. The flock of sheep grazing nearby scattered, crying out in distress as they ran. Nigel released Meg, dropping her onto the ground as he spun round to find the source of the noise. She could see past him now and nearly cried out in her own distress.

Two figures approached, appearing from the thicket that grew alongside the stream. Two men, both clad head to toe in black. They wore masks.

Dear gracious... highwaymen!

Chapter 14

These were real, murderous, terrifying highwaymen! Here, just outside her own little village! She'd never heard of such a thing, not here, and certainly not in broad daylight. They must be bold indeed if they came at them now, brandishing pistols in the bright afternoon, so close to the roadway.

Not that there appeared to be any traffic there. Unfortunately, she and Nigel had been painfully alone. Now they were painfully *un*alone and at the mercy of these well-armed criminals. She scrambled up to her feet, tripping on her skirts and being completely unassisted by her previously attentive companion.

"What is the meaning of this?" Nigel demanded.

"Stand and deliver!" one of the men said.

"Do you mean to take our lunch?" Nigel asked. "I've nothing else to give you, it's just me and the girl."

Meg frowned at him. That sounded surprisingly as if he were offering her up in his place. Well! She rather hoped the highwaymen would shoot him dead. Except, of course that that was hardly a Christian attitude. Besides, if Nigel were dead she'd be left alone with the ruffians. That would not be her first choice.

Perhaps, though, if they wounded Nigel they might be distracted to look through his pockets and she could run off and escape...

"We've heard otherwise about you," the man responded, waving two still-loaded weapons. "We hear you've got a treasure."

What? Now *they* were talking of treasure. What on earth was going on? First Nigel perked his ears at that word treasure, now these men. How unfair that she should be dragged into this even as completely ignorant as she was.

"I don't know what you're talking about," Nigel said.

She wished he'd be a little less antagonistic toward them. The first highwayman was a giant, the very epitome of one accustomed to violent behavior. His accent was strange, American perhaps. He held his guns steady, both pointed securely toward Nigel. The second highwayman was less burly and more elegant. He only maintained one unspent pistol, but he looked every bit as menacing as his partner. Between the two of them, Meg's plan of escape was feeling less and less hopeful. That second highwayman, in particular, had his eyes pinned directly on her.

Good heavens, was her face going hot at his stare? Indeed she must be desperate for male attention. Once she got out of this mess, she'd best go directly home and lock herself away in her room, safe from Nigel and parrot trainers and even highwaymen, apparently.

"You know what we're talking about," the burly man said, snarling at Nigel. "Now where is it?"

Nigel's eyes darted back and forth. Meg could see him trying to formulate a plan. He was standing next to her, the blanket and all their picnic supplies crumpled under their feet. The highwaymen were coming nearer and instinct drove her to step closer to Nigel. For all the good that would do. If one of these horrid men happened to shoot a pistol again, Nigel would likely dive behind her for protection.

"Give us the treasure and we might let you live, Webberly," the brute insisted when Nigel made no reply to him.

"I am the Earl of Glenwick!" Nigel corrected, a matter Meg felt seemed rather petty just now.

"Not if you're dead, you're not."

Nigel seemed to consider that. In a flash of sudden movement, he grabbed Meg by the shoulders and nearly tossed her directly at the highwaymen. She was caught so off guard that she tumbled to the ground, crashing into the legs of the larger highwayman and crumbling into a heap at his feet. He staggered and her ears nearly shattered at the sound of more pistol fire. She buried her head under her arms, praying some miracle might happen and she might get out of this.

There was shouting and rustling around her. When she dared peep out, Nigel was running away, back toward his Phaeton. Both highwaymen still hovered over her, but the elegant one muttered something to the other and she felt his boot shift beside her.

"I'll get him, sir," the larger one said, stepping over Meg as she cowered again.

"Don't kill him," his partner replied in flawless gentleman's English. "In fact, let him think he's escaped. Just give chase for effect."

The burly one grumbled at that, but Meg heard his heavy boot steps racing away. This left her alone and at the mercy of the other one. She trembled as he crouched beside her, touching her. His hand gently pressed at her cheek as he pushed her disheveled hair aside to, apparently, view his trophy.

She would not give him the satisfaction of seeing her cowardice. Plucking up a backbone that was otherwise numb from fear she pushed up onto her elbow to glare daggers at him. His blue, blue eyes glared back through two holes in his mask. Aside from the fact that he was very likely about to put a bullet in her head, the man appeared completely dashing.

"I will not give in to you, sir," she said as boldly as she could. "If you want compliance, you might as well kill me now."

Instead of insult or violence, he beamed a broad smile at her. "Never, Miss Farrow. Not in a million years."

He knew her name! But how could he... wait, she knew that voice... those eyes... Good gracious, this wild, pillaging highwayman was none other than her mild-mannered parrot trainer!

"Mr. Shirley!"

He pulled off his mask to reveal that face, that masterful jaw line, that unruly dark hair... oh, but she was happy to see him. Considering she expected to be faced with a monster he was truly the most beautiful sight she could ever imagine. Even had she not expected a monster, he was quite a beautiful sight.

"Are you well? Did he harm you?" he asked, glancing over her. "You haven't been shot, have you?"

"No, I'm quite fine, as far as I can tell."

"Thank heavens," he said. "When I saw him leering over you that way, I feared I had come too late. Forgive me."

"Forgive you? I thought I was about to be murdered. I'm overjoyed to see you!"

She wasn't sure if he pulled her into his arms, or if she literally launched herself at him, but in the end it did not matter. She was pulled up tightly against him and it was the most wondrous place to be. Despite his dark clothing, the pistol he'd been brandishing just a moment ago, and the fact that she had no idea what was really going on, she was quite convinced she could spend the rest of her life quite content here in Mr. Shirley's arms.

If Shirley was really his name. A modicum of good sense came back to her and she reminded herself she knew nothing at all about this man. Well, other than that he made her knees weak and her heart beat an unseemly rhythm. Those, of course, were not necessarily traits to well recommend a man. Or a lady, for that matter.

She pushed herself away.

"But wait... I don't even know who you are."

"You do know me, Meg," he replied. "I'm this man, the man who would do anything to keep you safe."

"You're a highwayman?"

"Er, no."

"Thank heavens for that, but... I have a strong suspicion you aren't a parrot trainer either, are you?"

"No, I'm not really that, I'm afraid."

"And your name isn't Shirley, I daresay."

"No. It isn't."

"Then what is your name?"

He sighed, shifting from his position on one knee to sit beside her on the blanket. This pistol dangled harmlessly from his hand.

"I can't tell you that just now. I'm sorry."

"And all this business about treasure?" she asked. "Can you tell me about that?"

"No. I wish that I could."

"How you knew of Papa's advertisement for a trainer?"

"A lucky coincidence."

"And what of that book? Nigel—the earl—is looking for it. How did you come by it?"

"I'm sorry, Meg, but I simply can't tell you these things."

"What *can* you tell me, then?"

"Very little, I'm afraid. It's for your own good."

"Well, please don't tell me you have a wife and children waiting for you somewhere!"

"No, that I can tell you. I am entirely a bachelor, at this point. Beyond that, I'm afraid you'll just have to trust me."

"You've been living in my home under false pretenses, you go around dressed as a robber, and you shoot pistols at noblemen. Why on earth would I not trust you?"

"Why indeed?" he said, grinning as if they shared some private joke together.

Perhaps they did. They way he looked at her made her face go hot again. The full rest of her, too. She lowered her eyes and hoped he would not realize what a little ninny she was, feeling this way over him for no good reason whatsoever. Of course she would trust him. Apparently she was helpless not to.

He stood, reaching a hand down to assist her.

"Here, let me get you home. There's no telling what panic will ensue if Nigel goes to your father and informs him you've been abducted by highwaymen. I would hate to allow your father to feel that sort of worry."

"Yes, poor Papa! He'd be very concerned."

She let Mr. Shirley—or whoever he was—help her to her feet. She let him brush imaginary dust off her, too. She was rather disappointed that was all he required her to let him do, as a matter of fact.

"I promise, as soon as it is safe I will answer all of your questions," he said when she made the mistake of meeting his gaze.

The tenderness and sincerity in his voice would not allow her to doubt him. Not that she was trying very hard. She wanted more than anything to believe what he said, to trust that there was noble purpose to all his deception and lies.

Especially the bit about him not having any wife or children tucked away somewhere.

It took everything Max had not to sweep her into his arms and kiss her right there. After all, they were alone, her voice was still breathy from the nerves of her recent scare, and the blush that crept over her cheeks whenever she looked at him made him think maybe she would not rebuff his attentions.

Could it be she might care for him? He had no reason to expect it of her, of course. He'd be quite a cad, indeed, if he pressed for her affections now, when she knew him only as a liar and possible criminal. Still, when she look at him... he thought perhaps he could hope.

Hell. He would do more than hope.

He ignored his good sense and he pulled her into an embrace. A good, solid embrace that let her know he meant business. She didn't scream or push away, so he went right on ahead and he kissed her.

Her lips were tender and soft, then greedy and hungry. She kissed him back, just the way he hoped she would. She tasted as warm as the sunshine and as sweet as the clover scenting the air. All his good intentions faded away as the only thing he could think of was making a full meal out of clover and sunshine, and making Meg Farrow his once and for all.

"Ahem."

It was Hugh announcing his return. By God, the man's timing was dreadful. Or perfect, Max supposed, considering he'd been about to forget he was a gentleman. Miss Farrow was spared. She stepped away quickly, righting her clothes and keeping her eyes fixed on the ground.

Hugh had brought up their carriage. They'd left it out of sight just around the far bend, behind a thicket. Fortunately things had worked out as planned and Nigel hadn't spotted it to be able to connect them to the inn, where they had hired the carriage. So far there was still hope Max's plan might work out.

"I suppose we should get the young lady home safely?" Hugh asked.

"Yes. But I'm afraid our time is running out. Nigel knows we are after him so he'd bound to take action."

"But you said the book holds the key. If he doesn't have that..."

"He might still figure it out if he gets his hands on Bartholomew."

Miss Farrow was listening eagerly and he realized that, despite how much he hoped to keep her out of all this, their only hope of success at this point required her assistance. Would she do it? Would she help him even though he'd been unable to give her any reason to trust?

"Because Bartholomew recites certain lines from that book," she said, proving she was every bit as clever as she looked. "Those are all clues to a treasure, aren't they?"

"I wish that I could tell you, but—"

"I know, I know. It's for my own good. Very well, don't tell me about it. Just tell me what I can do to help."

"I can't ask you to help me," he said, though of course he hoped she would insist.

"Then don't ask me to help you. Tell me how I can help Bartholomew. If Nigel takes him, we all know what will happen."

"No doubt he's on his way there right now," Max said. "So, here is what we must do. I hate to involve you, Miss Farrow, but—"

"I'm already involved."

"So you are."

He knew what had to be done. He'd make it as safe for her as possible, but there was no way to know what extremes Nigel would go to. When pushed into a corner, they could all expect him to react badly. Max could only hope Miss Farrow was safely out of the picture before it got to that point. They just needed one more thing, one last bit of proof that could put Nigel out of commission forever.

"Into the carriage," he said, ushering her toward it and helping her inside. "We'll drop you as close to home as we dare without being seen, and you're to tell everyone the highwaymen set you free when they learned your father is vicar."

"Why would they do that?"

Max shrugged. "Perhaps they are criminals with a conscience."

"More likely they realized they'd get no hefty ransom for me," she suggested.

Hugh chuckled, shutting the door on them and hopping up into the box to slap the horses into motion. The carriage lurched and Max put his hand on Miss Farrow to steady her. It was not really necessary, but instinctive. She was something of great value. He *would* find a way to protect her.

Chapter 15

Meg left the two gentlemen at the edge of town, just out of sight of passers-by. They stopped the carriage behind a stand of evergreens, against the far wall of the cemetery. From here she could dash home safely while the gentlemen would be unremarkable in their return to the inn where, apparently, Mr. Shirley's accomplice was staying.

Mr. Shirley had at first insisted he should accompany her all the way to the parsonage, but she begged him not to do so. He was still dressed as a highwayman, after all, and if someone should see them there was no telling what trouble might ensue. The earl had had plenty of time to return to Richington and begin telling his story to anyone who would listen. By now he was probably already delivering the bad news to Papa and calling for the magistrate. Until Mr. Shirley and Mr. Baxter were changed into their proper attire and returned where they belonged, they were in danger.

Mr. Shirley gave in to her insistence and she left them, creeping out of the carriage unseen and ducking through the cemetery. From there she simply trotted around the church, ran up the parsonage steps, and threw open the front door with great drama.

Papa was just inside the drawing room, pacing back and forth and ranting to whoever might listen. His listeners at this moment happened to be Mrs. Cooper, Mr. Barrelson—who was the local magistrate—along with some apparent assistant of his, and an artificially worried-looking Nigel.

They all turned and gaped when Meg burst into the room. Nigel especially.

"Meg! You're alive!" Papa cried out, swinging his arms wide and scooping her into them.

"Yes... I'm fine Papa," she said, her voice muffled into his chest.

He held her away from him, looking her over and turning her first one way then another. If she hadn't been injured before, she might possibly be now, the way he was manhandling her. It was quite endearing, though. She did her best to reassure him, though, and save herself from further bruising.

"Really, I'm fine Papa. I'm fine!"

"But Glenwick said you'd been taken by highwaymen!"

Taken was rather an odd word, considering the last Nigel saw of her she'd not been removed anywhere and he'd been the one who changed location—running away like a frightened little girl.

She didn't question him, though. Mr. Shirley had a plan and she had her part to play.

"I was, Papa," she said, and made a good show of smiling in gratitude toward cowardly Nigel. "The poor earl, I thought for a certain they were going to kill him. He's lucky to be alive now!"

Indeed, that part was true. Mr. Shirley's attitude regarding the man indicated he had good reason to wish him dead. Given Nigel's recent behavior toward Meg, she was tempted to feel the same way.

"But you... somehow you escaped!" the earl stammered.

"A miracle, indeed," Papa said. "Glenwick told us it

was a whole pack of them, blood-thirsty and heavily armed."

"Er... I counted only two," she said and gave Nigel a glare that warned him he'd best not think she'd forgotten his actions.

"How fortunate that is all you encountered," Nigel said, glaring right back. "No telling how many of them waited aside in the thicket, with all manner of depravity on their minds."

Papa shuddered noticeably. "Thank the lord you escaped, Meg!"

"I didn't escape," she said, letting Papa steady her but directing her words toward the very interested magistrate. "They let me go."

"They let you go?" Papa questioned. "The Lord had His hand on you."

Mr. Barrelson nodded and contemplated her claim, but the earl seemed a bit less willing to credit divine intervention. Or her accuracy.

"Those cutthroats simply let you go?" he asked. "Why would they do that?"

"I could scarcely believe it myself," she said and produced a tremulous sigh. "Oh, but I was quite overwhelmed with terror, as you can imagine. They hauled me into their carriage and said I was their prisoner, that they would hold me for ransom. I thought for a certain I'd never see you again, Papa, and I wept over that fact. When they heard me say that you are the vicar... well, apparently that changed their minds. They set me free and I came running back home."

Papa went on in raptures of God's goodness, but Nigel seemed fixated on the more mundane.

"Those two violent criminals set you free because your father is a man of the cloth?"

"I'm assuming it's more about the size of a ransom they could expect to get for me."

"I'd have given everything I own to get you back here, Meg. You know that," Papa said.

Mrs. Cooper dabbed at her eyes. Mr. Barrelson smiled kindly while his assistant sharpened the tip of the pencil he'd been using to make notes on a paper he held folded in his hand. Nigel still glared. Meg chose to ignore him.

"Fortunately, I'm safe and sound, Papa," she said. "There's nothing further to worry about. I'm sure those scoundrels are well away from here now."

But Mr. Barrelson wasn't so quick to dismiss this. "They can't have gotten too very far, Miss Farrow. I'll have some men set out to search for them. Can you say which direction they were heading, or what sort of conveyance they used?"

"Er, I'm afraid I wasn't paying much attention to detail, sir," she answered quickly. "They were simply two frightening men in black masks and their carriage was... it was old and quite worn, I believe. At least, that's what I recall."

Drat, but she really was no good at this sort of thing. All her life she'd prided herself on being honest. Now to suddenly try and create such a falsehood! It was most taxing, to say the least. Mr. Shirley needed it, though, so she'd do her best. Despite how sick it made her feel at her stomach.

"And did they leave the area going east, or going west?" the magistrate asked.

"East," she replied, then wondered if perhaps that would help Mr. Shirley or not. "Or perhaps it was west. No wait... perhaps they were heading for Portsmouth! Yes, I am certain I heard them say Portsmouth."

"South? They're heading *south*, you believe?"

"Yes. That's what they said."

"But that would have sent them right back through the village," Nigel protested. "Surely they would have been seen. Where did you say that they let you out of their carriage?"

Oh, botheration. She truly was no good at this at all. She'd have to give up altogether and rely on pure feminine hysteria. If that couldn't detract attention from the hunt for the so-called highwaymen, she had no idea what would.gg

"I can hardly recall it, my lord," she whined, letting her voice rise in pitch as she continued. "I assure you, I wish that I could give our magistrate the answers he needs. But I've been so distraught... this has been a horrible ordeal for me and my nerves are quite frayed. I can barely keep my balance, let alone recall details to help aid in the search. I'm quite ashamed at my weakness, truly! I fear I am useless to you all."

"Now, now, my pet," Papa said, gently tightening his arm around her and patting her shoulder. "Of course you're not useless. The earl has only the highest regard for you, isn't that true, Glenwick?"

"Of course," Nigel replied as sweetly as syrup. "I would never mean to cause Miss Farrow distress. It's understandable she would be at all ends over this."

"It was dreadful—every moment of it!" she agreed and hoped he understood that included her time spent with him. "I hope to heaven those horrible men truly are gone off to Plymouth."

"I thought you said Portsmouth," Mr. Barrelson noted.

Drat. "Oh, er, yes. One or the other."

"You mean you can't really be sure where they were headed?"

"All I cared was that they were letting me go," she declared, with a hand to her forehead for effect. "I wanted only to be rid of them."

"And so you are," Papa said. "I, for one, am most thankful."

Mrs. Cooper dabbed at her eyes again and added a sniffle this time.

Mr. Barrelson nodded, apparently won over by the tears and the sighing. "I thank you, Miss Farrow. You've done well to share what you could with me. I'll do my best to locate these ruffians and see they meet justice."

"Thank you so much, sir," she replied. "I wish I could be of more help."

"You've helped all you could, miss."

The magistrate patted the same shoulder Papa had been patting. Meg began to feel somewhat like a pet cat. Nigel's sneer said he didn't much care for cats.

"It's most remarkable that you're here to help us at all," Nigel said. "What luck these highwaymen have no stomach for vicars' daughters."

Oh, what a vile, dreadful man he was. She forced a sweet smile for him.

"Yes, isn't it lucky things worked out the way that they did?"

And she did not simply mean regarding her so-called escape from the highwaymen. Her escape from a misplaced infatuation was far, far more lucky.

"I'll be on my way, then," Mr. Barrelson said, collecting his hat and his assistant. "I shall put men out directly to hunt for these renegades."

Mrs. Cooper bustled about, ushering the men out and making a fuss over everything in the room. Papa went along, too, spouting off gratitude over the magistrate's attention to detail and wishing him safety in his task ahead. Meg was alone in the drawing room with Nigel. He seemed much more pleased about that than she was.

"I have underestimated you, my dear," he said, slinking toward her like the weasel he was. "I never thought you to be so very clever."

"Clever, sir? In our acquaintance seven years ago I'm quite sure I never gave any indication of being that. Certainly I was a terrible judge of good character."

"All the more reason I'm impressed with you now. You had me quite fooled, you know. Until the moment you came through that door I had no idea you were in league with those criminals."

"*I*? In league with *them*, sir? If you're attempting to fun with me, I can't say that I like it."

"I'm not the one playing games here," he growled. "Give me the bird and the book and tell me what you've learned from them."

"I have no idea what you mean, sir."

She could tell it was killing him that her father and the magistrate were so near, speaking just in the entrance way outside the door. If not for that, she had no doubt he would have struck her. Whatever secrets he felt he could get from that book or from Bartholomew, he was clearly desperate to get them. This treasure they were all after must be very dear, indeed.

"You told your friends where to find us, didn't you? You lured me into a trap."

"That's just absurd. Move away from me, sir. Your breathing offends me and I am done with this discussion now."

"Then give me the bird and the book and I'll leave."

"No. I told you I haven't got the book, and the bird will stay here to finish his training."

He narrowed his eyes and glared at her. If not for Papa coming back into the room at that moment she would have been very afraid indeed. Even with him there, she could not abide the wild look that came over Nigel's once handsome face.

"You've even hired a parrot trainer to assist with that, haven't you?" he sneered.

"Yes. I told you about that."

She stepped away from the angry earl and tried to pretend all was well, but she could see on Papa's face that he detected something amiss in Glenwick's malevolent smile.

"Is something the matter?" Papa asked.

"Yes," Nigel announced. "I believe I've located our highwaymen. One of them, at least."

Mrs. Cooper gasped from the doorway.

"What?" Papa said with a frown. "Where is he? Shall I call back the magistrate?"

"You should," Nigel said.

Mrs. Cooper scurried back to the front door. Meg could hear her calling from the front steps. No doubt the magistrate would be back here in a matter of moments. Heavens, had Nigel really figured things out? She couldn't guess how—she herself didn't even fully understand any of it.

"You should call down your alleged parrot trainer, too," Nigel declared. "But be careful—he's most likely armed."

"What are you saying?" Papa asked. "You think Mr. Shirley is one of these highwaymen?"

"I do, sir. I believe he has corrupted your daughter and swayed her to do his bidding."

"That ridiculous," Papa said. "Meg doesn't even like the fellow. She merely tolerates him for me."

"Then call him down here," Nigel said. "Prove to me that he's where he should be right now and that he's not involved in this attempt on my person today."

"But Meg was the one who was abducted—" Papa

began, only to be interrupted by Mr. Barrelson and his assistant rushing back into the room.

"What is it? Have you recalled some clue of some sort?"

"Better," Nigel informed him. "I've concluded who these highwaymen are. One of them has been living in this very house!"

Papa huffed at the notion. "Nonsense! He claims the man I've hired to train our fool parrot is a blood-thirsty highwayman."

Mr. Barrelson seemed to be willing to consider this, though. He looked toward Papa and asked, "Is he?"

"Of course not," Papa replied, then turned to Meg. "Is he?"

"No! I'd certainly have recognized him. Most definitely not Mr. Shirley."

"Then produce him!" Nigel demanded. "Call him into this room so we can see that he's here and not somewhere else. He is here, isn't he?"

Now Meg was worried. Of course Mr. Shirley wasn't here. He was returning the carriage and changing his clothes. This was dreadful! The magistrate would have no choice but to consider Nigel's accusations. It was his duty and, after all, Nigel was the earl. Poor Mr. Shirley would be hunted down and not able to produce any proof that he wasn't a highwayman!

"Of course he's here," Papa said, moving out of the room toward the stairway. "He's been up in his room working with Bartholomew all afternoon."

"But he told me he might be going out for a walk, Papa," Meg called after him quickly.

It was a stupid, desperate attempt that only caused Nigel to sneer at her all the more.

"So you know he is not here, Miss Farrow? And how

could that be, since you were out driving with me until those highwaymen interrupted our day?"

"I... I know Mr. Shirley's habits. He often takes walks."

"I thought your father said you didn't care for the fellow."

"That doesn't mean I'm not aware of when he does or does not take walks," she snapped back at him. "I simply meant to offer a reasonable explanation for why he isn't here. If, in fact, he isn't here."

"You meant to give him an alibi," Nigel said.

"Mr. Shirley doesn't need an alibi. He isn't your highwayman."

Nigel arched his eyebrows. "Ah, but is he *your* highwayman, Miss Farrow?"

"He's nobody's highwayman," she replied. "He isn't a highwayman at all. He's nothing more than a parrot trainer!"

Even as she spoke the words she knew they were not true. Max Shirley was so much more than a parrot trainer. She didn't know what he was, exactly, and to be fair, she had only his word that he was not a highwayman, but in her heart she was convinced he was something more than she knew. If only she could hope it was something that would not land him in jail.

"That's what you say about him," Nigel grumbled. "I'd rather hear him speak for himself."

Papa marched to the foot of the stairs. "That should be simple enough." He cleared his throat and called in a loud voice. "Mr. Shirley! Are you up there, man?"

Meg felt her heart drop down to her toes. He was about to be found out. If he was smart, he would already be heading far away from Richington. If he were not... he'd be arrested at the inn and end up in jail. Either way she had to accept he'd be gone from her life. The worse of it all, he'd be taking her heart away with him.

"You should come back to the inn with me," Hugh said.

"No. She'll need me at the parsonage," Max replied, already scanning the quiet lane to make sure no one would see him leave the carriage.

"But your clothes—"

"Will be fine," he assured his friend.

They had clothes in the carriage and once Miss Farrow was gone he and Hugh changed their black shirts for a white ones. He'd changed quickly so he was all at odds, his shirt tucked haphazardly and his attempt at an elegant knot utterly failing, but at least no one would take him for a highwayman.

"Get yourself back to the inn," he ordered, knowing Hugh could be trusted to comply perfectly. "My man in London has promised the information we need should be in official hands by tonight. Wait there for confirmation of that."

"Very well. You're certain you don't need me with you?"

"Not until later. I don't know what accusations my cousin will be making or how many men he'll send out to hunt for us. We must give him no reason to find us."

"I'll make short work of any man who does," Hugh assured him.

"I'd prefer that you not make any widows," Max admonished. "My hope is to eventually be on good terms with the residents of Richington."

Hugh chuckled, then cocked his head in the direction Miss Farrow had just gone.

"One little resident in particular, I gather."

"I don't dare consider hoping in that quarter until all

this is over," he replied, but of course they both knew it was a bluff. He did hope already. He hoped a good deal.

Straightening his coat, he hopped out of the carriage and reassured himself no one was around. He gave a last string of advice to Hugh, then vaulted the cemetery wall and darted between stones, keeping to shadows and corners as he made his way behind the church and toward the gardens at the rear of the parsonage. Perhaps today would be a perfect time to make use of the trellis Mrs. Cooper kept secure at the back corner, going up to the roof just below Max's bedroom window.

Since his arrival here he'd often thought that might provide a handy means of clandestine escape, but now it seemed he might wish to try the route in reverse. He caught a glimpse of Nigel's gaudy Phaeton waiting in front of the house. It seemed a very good idea to avoid running into the man in the drawing room just now. True, there had been years and years since their last meeting, but he had no doubt Nigel would recognize him. Just as Max had known the face of that murderous bastard the moment he'd seen him.

Chapter 16

The little group at the foot of the stairs waited in silence. Papa called again.

"Mr. Shirley, are you there, sir?"

Meg was about to insist that the man's absence meant nothing at all. She even toyed with the wild notion of announcing that she had planned an assignation with him and he was off preparing for that. Oh, but she had to do something to save him!

Nigel was already half gloating as seconds ticked by with no sound from above. She wanted to slap the smug grun right off his face. How dare he attack her as he had on their picnic and now come into her house, accusing her of all manner of wickedness. If she thought anyone would believe her, she'd tell them just what sort of man their new earl had proven himself to be.

Her inward struggle was interrupted, though, by a voice from upstairs.

"I'm sorry, Mr. Farrow. Were you calling for me?"

By heavens, it was Mr. Shirley! She could scarcely believe it, but this was his voice. She had no idea how it could be, yet it was. He was here, in this house, calling to them from his very own room.

A quick glance at Nigel gave her the satisfaction of seeing that not only was he every bit as shocked as she was, he was also heartily disappointed.

"Are you available, Mr. Shirley? Some gentlemen would very much like a word with you down here," Papa called.

But now Mr. Shirley's reply wasn't so encouraging. He was decidedly hesitant.

"Er, I'm afraid I'm rather in the midst of something just now..."

Nigel fairly crowed in triumph. "Ha! What on earth could the man be in the midst of that he cannot come down to us? I tell you, he's hiding something!"

"Perhaps he's having some trouble with the bird just now," Papa suggested. "He is a very disagreeable bird at times, as we all know."

"I don't even hear the bird. How do we know he hasn't abducted it, or done away with it?"

Even the magistrate's face showed that Nigel's words sounded a bit crazy. But he was a man bent on his duty, so he sighed and turned once again to Papa.

"Perhaps if you'd allow me, I could go up to the man's room and ascertain once and for all if his lordship's concerns are well grounded?"

Papa shrugged. "I've no objection, though I have no idea what you think you will find."

"Search for his mask, and his weapons!" Nigel ordered. "You'll find them, no doubt. And the bird—"

Nigel was still ranting as the magistrate put his foot on the bottom tread to begin his upward climb when a figure appeared at the top of the stairs. A loud squawk from Bartholomew drew their attention up to him. Yes, it was Mr. Shirley, alive and well! Bartholomew clung to his shoulder.

And what a fine shoulder it was. Meg could see it quite plainly. The man was in his shirtsleeves only, and his crisp linen shirt was thoroughly wet. She could see the shape and the musculature of his shoulder almost as if he had no shirt at all, and she very much liked the looks of it. It looked perfect, as a matter of fact. Everything about him looked perfect as he stood there, tall and bold, looming over them from the height of the staircase.

The only thing odd was the fact that his head was covered. The man wore a towel wrapped round his head, obscuring most of his face. That did somewhat detract from the masterful image he portrayed. That, and the fact that Bartholomew began reciting the most vile line from the most vile rhyme in his vocabulary.

"Forgive me," Mr. Shirley said when he had calmed the bird by presenting him with a finger to gnaw on. "I'm afraid Bartholomew bestowed an unexpected gift onto my head and I was compelled to wash my hair. My coat suffered, as well, and I was working on saving it."

"There, you see?" Papa said, beaming with pride. "My parrot trainer."

Meg could fell that she was beaming, too.

"*This*? This vagabond is what you claim to be your parrot trainer?" Nigel said, not even attempting to hide his disgust. "You cannot possibly tell me he's done one bit of good for that bird."

"Oh yes, he's actually made great strides," Papa said in defense. "Bartholomew used to be completely unbearable. Now he's just barely insufferable."

"But... this man can't be..."

"He is," Papa said. "An excellent parrot trainer. *Not* a highwayman."

Nigel sputtered and Mr. Barrelson took to patting him on the shoulder.

"So all is well, my lord," the magistrate said. "Your fears were in vain. Don't you find that a comfort?"

"Hell no I'm not comforted," Nigel insisted. "Just look at him! That bird is not safe in this house."

"I think, sir, from the looks of things your concern would be better placed on the man. It appears that bird can take care of himself."

"Shameful," Nigel glared up at Mr. Shirley, fairly seething with rage. "It's no wonder the whole village whispers about my grandfather's bizarre love for the creature. I'll not have such a thing even associated with my name. Give me the bird now. I'll take him with me."

"But you mean to destroy him!" Meg said.

"Then there'll be no need for your trainer, will there?"

A new wave of panic washed over Meg. She turned to the magistrate and prayed he might be able to help.

"Please sir, isn't there something we can do? The old earl loved this bird. He knew we would care for him; that's why on his deathbed he gave him to Papa. I could never forgive myself if I felt we failed our dear friend."

She implored with big, doleful eyes. She might have even allowed her lower lip to quiver, just a bit. The tears blurring her vision weren't false, though. Despite Bartholomew's many, many shortcomings, she truly did not want the poor thing destroyed. He was only a bird, after all. He had no idea his words were offensive, or that he should not do his business atop Mr. Shirley's head.

Mr. Barrelson glanced from her to the earl and then back again. At last he sighed and gave a final decree.

"My lord, I think in light of today's traumatic events, you would not wish to cause Miss Farrow any further discomfort. She has come to care for this bird—God alone can know why—and it would pain her to lose him this way. Perhaps it is better for all if you simply return home and continue this discussion again tomorrow, when nerves are less frayed and heads are all cooler."

"But she is in on it, I tell you! She's in league with the highwaymen."

"You cannot mean such a thing," Papa said. "My Meg is a paragon of virtue."

"But she must have told them how to find me."

"I daresay that fancy rig of yours did more to alert them to your whereabouts, sir," Mr. Barrelson said, laying an arm over Nigel's shoulders. "Now come along. My assistant will see you home, safe and sound."

"I don't need a ruddy nurse maid," Nigel grumbled.

"But you've had a rough day and you're not quite yourself," the magistrate said, inching him toward the front door. "It's understandable. None of us thinks less of you."

"Of course you should not think less of me! I'm the Earl of Glenwick, by God."

"And that's why you can trust Mr. Farrow not to breathe a word of this to anyone in the village," Mr. Barrelson went on. "Not about your unfounded accusations or about nearly letting his daughter be abducted by highwaymen."

"I tell you, she was a part of it!" Nigel's eyes had gone wild. He waved his arms and pointed up the stairs at Mr. Shirley who worked the towel over his head, drying his hair while Bartholomew screeched and pecked at his arm.

"You'll feel better in a bit, after a good meal and a rest," Papa assured him in his most clerical tone of voice.

Meg saw her opportunity. Mr. Shirley's plan would play out as intended, after all. The man had told her he'd been looking for a way to get into Glenwick Downs when Nigel was gone, and here was her chance to allow him to do that.

"A meal is an excellent idea, Papa. We should invite his lordship back here for dinner, so he knows we are all still friends and there are no hard feelings."

"Capital idea, Meg!" Papa declared.

"There, you see now, sir?" the magistrate said. "All will be well. Let's get you home for a clean-up and maybe a stiff drink, then you can come back around for dinner and things will be normal again."

"Things are not normal!" Nigel went on protesting. "I tell you, that man is not who he claims and a scheme is afoot here. The parrot is the very key to it!"

It was in vain, though. He could have been ranting about unicorns and little folk for all the sense he was making. Papa and Mr. Barrelson helped him out the door, the assistant went to ready the Phaeton, and Mrs. Cooper followed them out, tossing off instructions about what time to expect dinner tonight and to ask Nigel for a list of his favorite foods.

Meg barely caught his peevish reply and was quite certain the substance he mentioned would *not* be considered food.

She peered around the doorframe to watch the action outside. A creak from the stairway behind her drew her attention inside and she turned. Mr. Shirley was descending the steps, moving toward her. She could see his blue eyes now and they sparkled. Her knees went predictably weak so she hung onto the doorframe.

Bartholomew flew off onto the stair rail and proceeded to natter on about twisting one's pole and viewing things from behind again. Meg hardly heard him. Mr. Shirley had her full focus.

"I'm sorry I was very nearly late to this party," he said.

"I was afraid you were about to be found out," she confessed.

He moved closer still. "I would never wish to make you afraid."

The only thing she was afraid of right now was that

she'd not be able to keep her hands off the man and that Papa would find her making a cake of herself in his arms. She held onto that doorframe and refused to budge from it. There was much to be sorted out yet before she could do anything foolish like profess her love for this man she knew nothing about.

But his gaze was every bit as powerful as an embrace. For a long, silent moment he held her there, his eyes locked onto hers and all manner of unspoken things passing between them. She was well out of breath by the time Papa came marching back up the front steps.

"I say, our poor Glenwick has been quite badly affected," he said as he breezed past Meg into the entrance way.

"That was the earl?" Mr. Shirley asked.

"Yes, and I'm sorry to say you did not see him at his best. I'm afraid he and Meg were accosted by highwaymen today and he is not taking it well."

Mr. Shirley's eyes went huge and his astonishment seemed real. "Highwaymen? Good God, Miss Farrow, are you quite well? I've heard dreadful things about those sorts of scoundrels."

Her cheeks heated instantly and she couldn't meet his eyes.

"I'm fine, Mr. Shirley. Thank you."

For a moment more she felt his gaze linger on her, then he cleared his throat.

"If there's nothing more you need from me, sir," he said to Papa. "Perhaps I should go back upstairs and dress myself properly."

"By all means, Mr. Shirley. I'm sorry to have bothered you and hope you were not too distressed by his lordship's behavior."

Mr. Shirley shrugged and put his arm out for

Bartholomew. The bird hopped onto it readily and accepted the crumb of biscuit the man pulled out of his pocket. For the first time, Meg could see that Mr. Shirley had indeed made some positive headway in the bird's behavior. For this brief, pleasant moment Bartholomew was not cursing or squawking or attempting to dismember any of them.

"I suppose the nobility must be allowed some measure of eccentricity," Mr. Shirley acknowledged with an indulgent shrug. "I've heard they often do unpredictable things."

Papa agreed. "Indeed. Who can make sense of it? Perhaps we should be glad for our lower stations in life."

"Or perhaps we simply need different nobility."

"Well, it'll take more than a talent for parrot training to accomplish that," Papa said with a chuckle. "Have you had your fill of the earl, or will you be joining us for dinner tonight, Mr. Shirley?"

He looked surprised at having been invited, but masked that quickly. "I'm sorry, sir. I'm afraid I have plans. A friend is on the way into Richington from London. He's bringing something and I'm expecting to meet him tonight."

Papa seemed very interested in this. "A friend? Bringing a gift for you, perhaps?"

"No, sir, for you. He'll have those references you asked for."

Now Meg had to mask her own surprise. She'd all but given up hope for any references on Mr. Shirley. Could it be? There actually were such things? Perhaps the man was something respectable, after all. She could have danced for joy at that thought of it. How much easier life would be if she found herself in love with a decent, honorable man instead of a sham and a cheat.

Mr. Shirley started up the stairs, the view of his broad

shoulders from behind was almost as awe inspiring as the view she had seen from the front. She shouldn't have been staring, but she was. Two steps up, he turned and gave her a smile.

"With luck, all of your questions will have answers tonight."

She smiled back at him. *With luck.* Yes, she supposed they were going to need a lot of it. After all, she had a lot of questions.

Max waited, hidden behind decorative plantings and shadows from the setting sun. He let a full five minutes pass after watching Nigel's bright Phaeton leave Glenwick grounds before he whispered to his companion.

"We go in through the back."

The same entrance Max used on his last secret venture into the house would be the one they'd use this time, so he expected no difficulty. At least, he hoped for no difficulty.

"What about the steward?" Hugh asked quietly.

"His master is out. I expect that particular leech will be taking advantage of his evening off to get drunk."

"I hope so. I'd never recommend your plan otherwise. We need at least two other men to make this work, you know."

"Ordinarily I'd happily bow to your vast experience and superior education on this subject, Hugh, but tonight we have no other choice."

"I hope you're right. It just seems to me you ought not have to be breaking into your own home this way."

"If Nigel had any idea I was alive and in England to be doing such a thing, he'd never allow it. He'd finish what he started in Boston."

"He'd have to get through me first," Hugh assured him.

"Perhaps he would and then we'd both be dead."

And that scenario did not hold much appeal. He would much prefer to keep living. So much easier to win Miss Farrow's affections that way.

Would his untimely demise mean anything to her? She seemed to have grown beyond her instant dislike for him, and perhaps his kisses had done something to remove a bit of her distrust, but he had little reason to tryly hold out much hope her sentiments ran any deeper for him. She knew him as nothing more than a secretive, scheming parrot trainer. The truth, when it came out, might do more to turn her against him than to create any endearment.

Women, he'd learned, were rather particular about being lied to, and he certainly had lied to her. She could hardly be expected to overlook that. A dashed shame it was, too. Any woman who could read that bawdy poetry without swooning was someone he'd very much like to know better. Any woman who could read that poetry looking as fresh and lovely as she did—AND who could melt so perfectly into his arms—was someone he fully intended to know much better.

Provided she didn't end up hating him. And provided he didn't end up dead.

"I just wish we'd had word from London by now," Hugh grumbled as they moved in the cover of shrubbery toward the looming manor house.

"My agent there assured me he'd have what we needed. He'll be there."

"We should have waited until that was certain before coming here. After dark would have been best."

"We couldn't wait until then—this is our chance. Miss Farrow didn't invite that bastard into her home for the fun of it. She knew I needed him to be gone from here so she arranged dinner. We'll just have to hope we can find what we need and get out before he returns."

"So what are we hunting, then? Treasure?"

"No. It's here, but I still have no idea where to start. Tonight we seek letters."

"Letters. We're risking our necks for some *letters*?"

"You don't have to go along with me, you know."

"I didn't follow you all the way over here from Boston to abandon your cause now," Hugh said. "If you say there are letters we need to locate, then that's what we'll do."

"Thank you. Now follow me closely. Miss Farrow's reputation depends on us accomplishing our goal undetected."

Hugh stopped dead in his tracks. "*Those* letters? That's what we're here for?"

"And anything else we can find that might implicate Nigel in my grandfather's death."

Now Hugh was glaring at him. "But you don't really expect to find anything here, do you? You don't believe your cousin is stupid enough to leave such evidence lying around."

"Let's just say I sincerely hope that he is."

"But your primary goal is to strip the place of anything that might damage Miss Farrow."

"Yes, that is a goal, I'll admit."

Hugh clucked his tongue and shook his head. "Hellfire, man, you need to keep your wits about you. Nigel means business! You're the only thing left between him and the entire Glenwick estate, and he thinks he's already rid of you. You'd better get your mind off that female and think about your future."

He was not about to tell him those two elements were not mutually exclusive of each other. Hugh did have a valid point, though. Max would have no future—with or without Miss Farrow—if Nigel was allowed to go on as he had.

Whatever their plan tonight, it had to include some way to bring down that contemptible villain.

"Very well," Hugh said after he contemplated a moment. "We'll do what we can to protect Miss Farrow. If you are convinced she did not know what your cousin was when she involved herself with him, then I suppose she doesn't need to be scandalized now."

Max could tell Hugh was not thoroughly convinced of Miss Farrow's blamelessness, but his friend would not let him down. He appreciated all Hugh had done for him and he vowed he'd make it up to him at some point. They'd find what they needed and they'd bring Nigel to justice. Then perhaps they would both find some peace.

Chapter 17

Meg fidgeted, pushing her food about her plate and trying desperately to appear interested in Papa's conversation about the village festival planned to help raise funding for the parish choir. The earl was pleasantly polite, yet she could not be at all comfortable with the glances he kept shooting her way. It seemed every time she looked up from her meal, Nigel was staring at her.

And not in a good way. It was in a way that said he'd fully meant everything he'd said and done earlier today and he was ready and willing to do them again. He was convinced she knew more than she did. How could she convince him she did not?

Worse, how on earth was she to ensure he remained here at their home for a leisurely meal when he was eating as fast as a starved pig? It was obvious the man had not come to stay. He would likely want to leave soon—she knew she certainly did—and he'd want to take Bartholomew with him. Probably he'd find some way to have private words with her, too. No doubt she would not like them.

"I hope your parrot trainer was able to gather himself together after his ordeal with Bartholomew," Nigel said when Papa had at last exhausted the festival topic.

"Oh, he was indeed. As I said, he's remarkably good

with that bird. Pity he couldn't join us tonight."

"Yes, a pity. But I suppose it would be highly irregular to invite the help to dine with us."

"Oh, but Mr. Shirley has taken most of his meals here with us since his arrival," Papa explained. "I invited him tonight, but he declined due to a friend from London he was planning to meet."

"He's gone on to London?"

"No, his friend came to Richington from there. He's staying at our local inn and Mr. Shirley was to meet with him there."

"I see," Nigel said, his food intake suddenly slowing to a crawl. "I don't suppose he told you anything about this friend, did he? Why they were meeting tonight?"

"As a matter of fact, he did mention. He said his friend was bringing his references. Seems the fellow has had a devil of a time getting copies sent on when they were lost on his travels. You will not be surprised, I'm sure, to know Meg has been quite up in arms over this. I hope finally seeing the man's credentials will make her warm a bit more toward him."

Papa chuckled at his own words. Meg felt her face burning up. Heavens, she most certainly hoped seeing Mr. Shirley's credentials did not make her feel warmer toward him. She was nearly combusting from her feelings already.

"I should think you'd both be most interested in seeing his credentials," Nigel said. "I would, as well. Of course, that's assuming he was telling the truth."

"What do you mean?"

"Well, it is possible, you know, that he's not meeting a friend. He could very well be leaving the village."

"Leaving the village?"

"Don't you think it a bit odd that there's been no sign of a friend up from London until the day I arrive and accused him?"

"I really thought nothing of it."

"Then perhaps you should," Nigel declared. "Perhaps you should wonder what really brought the man into your home, or why he is so very close to that parrot. Or your daughter."

Papa's eternal reserve and Christian charity was growing thin, Meg could tell. It was not often she watched her father struggle with the emotions of mortal men, but just now she could see that he battled back everything from anger and frustration to indignation and shock. It was, indeed, most infuriating to sit here and have the earl question their every action and insult Papa's ability to judge character. Not that Papa had actually judged Mr. Shirley accurately, but Meg was sure Nigel's suspicions were all based on motivation far more destructive than their parrot trainer's. Not that she knew Mr. Shirley's motivations, but still... Nigel was not a good man and he was being decidedly rude.

"Mr. Shirley has done nothing to make me suspect he is not all that he claims to be," Papa declared. "You, however, sir, seem intent on insult and accusation yet you can produce no tangible reason for it."

Instead of being put out by Papa's rebuke, Nigel simply smiled. "Just wait. I have a feeling you will soon have all the tangible reason in the world to regret not heeding my words. You should have given me the bird and thrown that pretender out."

"If there is tangible reason I should doubt Mr. Shirley, I should welcome it," Papa said.

"Then you'll be happy to know my steward and Mr. Barrelson are in the process of gathering it right now."

"What exactly do you mean by that, sir?"

"I mean, before this dinner is done, I expect you and

your daughter will owe me an apology." Now he turned his smug smirk off of Papa and onto Meg. "And anything else I might ask for."

"Don't be ridiculous," Papa said. "If an apology is owed, you will certainly get it. I'm quite sure, though, that neither of us owes you anything."

"And I have some particular documents drawn up by my grandfather that indicate Miss Farrow might choose to feel differently. Unless she'd like everyone in town to know about them."

The documents! Good heavens, he had them. She knew from his face he did not lie: he had the documents and he would use them against her. She would be ruined. Worse, Papa would be scandalized for her. Nigel knew she would do anything he asked rather than allow that to happen.

He had won.

"Meg, what is he talking about?" Papa asked.

"Nothing, Papa. He is playing a game with us because he's worried we'll see he is wrong about Mr. Shirley."

Nigel shrugged and went back to his beef. "Believe what you will. The evening draws on and we will soon see who is wrong and who is right, won't we? Now, don't look so sad, Miss Farrow. Eat up your dinner. You're attractive enough, but I find a woman much more enticing if she has a bit of meat on her bones."

The house was quiet as Max led Hugh inside through a dim, heavily cob-webbed corridor. Most of the rooms in this part of the house were unused, closed up over the years as Grandfather had aged and the once vibrant Glenwick line withered away. A feeling of sorrow and loss still hung over the place.

Max tried to recall the many happy years spent here,

but then his father had died suddenly and his mother claimed there were too many painful memories to visit here often. Then the family suffered the loss of Max's uncle, and then the attempts on his own life started. Then finally tragedy struck Grandfather. The house was left in a state of mourning and the staff dwindled to barely enough to keep the place standing.

But this left it easy to creep about undetected. Carefully, silently, they made their way into the large, dark-paneled room that served as an office. It was still in disarray from obvious previous searches, but Max wasn't concerned about that. If Nigel had found what he'd been seeking, the hunt would have been over and he'd not have come after Miss Farrow for the book or the parrot.

Nor would he have lured Miss Farrow into the house to search for those incriminating documents drawn up by his grandfather. If Max had not overheard the scoundrel discussing them himself he would have assumed them to be non-existent. He thought it unlike his grandfather to leave evidence that would harm Miss Farrow when clearly his intent had been to help her, but he supposed it was possible. Apparently they did exist and Nigel had wanted to be sure Miss Farrow knew of them. It was an excellent lure to get her to join in his search and to reveal any secret hiding places she might know of. Obviously Nigel had been out of luck. She had no clue of anything like that.

But he could still use the documents to hold over her head. He wanted the book and he wanted the parrot. What better way to force Miss Farrow to deliver those than to threaten her with those documents? Max had to get them into his hands before he could press things further.

But now that he was here, where should he look for them? Nigel claimed he merely knew of them but had not found them. Was that to be believed? Not likely. Nigel could not very well use them against Miss Farrow if he did not actually have them. His threats were invalid if he had not already located them.

Yes, Nigel must have had them already when he lured Miss Farrow here to help hunt. Max stared at the piles of disheveled papers and ledgers and assorted books of all sizes. The room had been thoroughly ransacked, searched top to bottom more than once. It was far worse, even, than when Miss Farrow his visited. Clearly Nigel was repeating his efforts and clearly they had not been aimed at finding those documents.

This room had been ransacked in search of the book. That was the item Nigel knew he needed yet had been unable to find. That's why he has resorted to near violence when he realized Miss Farrow knew of the book. Just as Max had realized, Nigel had, too; the book was the key to finding the treasure.

And those incriminating papers regarding Miss Farrow... the likely truth of them dawned over Max like an approaching thunderstorm. The fact that Nigel knew of their existence while Grandfather had never once mentioned them in any of his correspondence with Max could only mean one thing. They weren't real. Nigel had crafted them himself when he realized he'd need to get Bartholomew away from the vicar.

So that meant Nigel would not leave the parsonage tonight without what he wanted. He needed that book and he suspected Miss Farrow knew where it was. He would use every trick he could pull to get her to relinquish it. That could only mean one thing.

"I know where those documents are," he announced to Hugh.

"Good, because this place is a wreck."

"They're not even here," Max informed. "We've been

duped."

"What do you mean?"

"I mean we'd better get the hell out of here. It's a trap."

Before Hugh could question his meaning Max heard the unmistakable click of a pistol from the darkened doorway behind them. Boots echoed on the floor. Damn, Max had fallen right into Nigel's scheme. He raised his hands helplessly, feeling the merciless aim of the pistol on his back.

"Good evening, gentlemen," a voice said. "I see you've forgotten your masks."

Chapter 18

Dinner tasted like dust as Meg tried in vain to continue. Nigel seemed so smug, so sure of himself. What did he have planned? What could he know that they didn't?

Max was in danger—that had to be it. Somehow, even seeing the man in person and finding nothing to convict him, Nigel was still suspicious. The vicious gleam in his eye said he had no doubt that whatever he planned would succeed.

She did not like that one bit.

"Would you care for some fruit?" she asked, forcing herself to play hostess and offer the tray from the center of the table.

"Thank you, Miss Farrow," Nigel said, reaching for an orange. "Your fruit looks quite tempting. I'm surprised there is any left, as a matter of fact, after allowing that parrot trainer at your table all week."

It took everything she had not to throw the tray at him. What a monster he was! Her mouth popped open to give a snippy retort, but the loud pounding at their front door interrupted her. She glanced at Papa. He raised his eyebrows in surprise. Nigel, however, seemed to have expected the disruption.

"Are you expecting someone?" he asked.

"No, I don't believe so," Papa replied.

"Well, I am," Nigel said, dropping his uneaten orange and rising from his chair.

Meg jumped to her feet, as well. Mrs. Cooper scurried past the dining room on her way to the front door and soon they heard loud voices and the sounds of several sets of heavy feet. Meg glanced at Papa. He shrugged at her, just as confused as she was but not nearly so worried.

After all, he would have no idea that Mr. Shirley might be in danger of hanging just now.

Meg gave up the pretense of calm. She darted from the table, rushing to the entry hall where Mrs. Cooper seemed at a loss to deal with the four men who suddenly crowded their home. Meg recognized all of them.

The first two were Mr. Barrelson and Mr. Perkins, the shifty-eyed steward from Glenwick. They did not look happy. Between them, two other men stood with their hands bound: Mr. Shirley and his companion. Her heart clenched in her chest. What on earth had they been caught doing?

"Well, what do we have here?" Nigel said, coming up behind her. "Could it be someone owes me an apology?"

"I suspected there had been thieves in the area of Glenwick," Mr. Perkins said. "So I convinced Mr. Barrelson to assist me in hunting them and look what we found."

Papa followed Nigel into the hallway and was trying to make sense of the scene. "You found these men at Glenwick?"

"Not only at Glenwick, but inside, ransacking his lordship's personal study," Mr. Perkins replied. "Thieves, no doubt about it."

"It's true," Mr. Barrelson confirmed. "I saw them myself."

Papa stammered in shock. "Is this so, Mr. Shirley? You

were found inside the very house?"

"It is, sir," Mr. Shirley replied, not nearly as terrified as Meg felt for him. "My friend, Mr. Baxter, and I were inside the study."

"I told you!" Nigel fairly sang. "These are the highwaymen who fired at me, now they have broken into my home!"

"And what were you doing there?" Papa asked.

"Looking for something," Mr. Shirley replied.

For heaven's sake, didn't he realize how badly this looked for him? Meg chewed her lip, desperate to think of something to say. But what could she? They'd been caught in the very act.

"Likely looking for more things to steal from me!" Nigel said. "No doubt you are the same ruffians who broke into my home and stole from me some days ago."

Mr. Barrelson seemed taken aback by this. "You had a burglary some days ago? I have heard nothing of this."

"I did not wish to make a fuss."

"But you only just arrived in town this morning," Meg noted. "How could you have been robbed there some days ago?"

"Er, my steward informed me," Nigel said quickly. "Isn't that so, Mr. Perkins? When I arrived, you told me of the break-in and that you suspected a book had been stolen."

"Yes, of course that is true," Mr. Perkins agreed. "I did not go to the magistrate at first because I wasn't certain the earl would want such notoriety."

"No doubt these are the guilty parties," Nigel said, pointing angrily at Mr. Shirley. "This one seems to be the leader. Search his room and you will likely find my missing book. Search the whole house!"

"I beg your pardon," Papa said. "I see no reason to

search my home. Surely Mr. Shirley will tell us if he has your book hidden here."

Nigel rolled his eyes and gave a dubious snort, but Mr. Shirley appeared entirely agreeable.

"Certainly I'll tell you. I've stolen nothing from this man."

"You have my book! I know you do!"

"I have a book," Mr. Shirley admitted. "But it isn't yours."

"So you are a thief *and* a liar. Magistrate, I demand you search the house."

"No need to overturn this house as you have done to Glenwick," Mr. Shirley said, scowling at Nigel. "The book you've been looking for is upstairs in my room. You'll find it tucked under the mattress."

"Ah ha!" Nigel said.

"Very well, I will look into the matter," the magistrate said. "Mr. Farrow, if you will accompany me. The rest of you should wait in the drawing room while we get to the bottom of this. Perkins, see that these men do not escape."

"We wouldn't dream of it, sir," Mr. Shirley said.

The magistrate shook his head, confused by all of this. He led Papa up the stairs while Mr. Perkins ushered the rest of them into the drawing room. Mrs. Cooper waited in the doorway, wringing her hands and watching nervously up the stairs. Two minutes... three minutes... five minutes ticked by slowly before the men's footsteps were heard on the staircase again. By the sounds of squawking and repetitive cursing, it would appear Bartholomew was returning with them.

Nigel had taken a spot on the settee and motioned for Meg to join him, but she'd sooner have faced a roomful of savage tigers before she accepted that. She waited across the room, wracking her brain for some way to get poor Mr.

Shirley out of this mess. It seemed things were getting worse for him by the moment.

"Is this the book?" Mr. Barrelson said when he and Papa returned.

Bartholomew leaped from Papa's shoulder onto Mr. Barrelson's head. He swatted the bird away and held up the book. As expected, it was the book of rhymes. Nigel's eyes grew twice normal size and his hungry grin covered only half of his mouth.

"Let me see it," he said, leaping up off the settee and practically dragging it out of the magistrate's hand. "Yes! This is it! I told you he stole it from me. This was in my grandfather's study, kept under lock and key. The only way he could have gotten it is if he stole it himself."

Suddenly inspiration struck Meg. If the book had been the old earl's, and if Nigel hadn't actually been here to see it before it was stolen... perhaps there was a way to save Mr. Shirley, after all. All she had to do was ruin herself.

"No, he didn't steal it," she announced loudly. "I did. I stole the book."

What the devil was the lunatic woman doing? Didn't she realize what this would do to her reputation, what people would think of her if she made such asinine claims? Max simply wouldn't allow it.

He was, of course, flattered beyond measure that she would do this for him, but it was completely unnecessary. He'd best set things straight before they got even more out of hand. If only Miss Farrow would quit incriminating herself long enough for him to get a word in edgewise.

"I had seen the book once before while visiting the old earl. It, er, fascinated me," she was saying.

Her father gaped in horror and Mr. Barrelson cleared

his throat.

"You do know this is a book hardly well-suited for a lady, don't you?" the magistrate asked.

Now Miss Farrow blushed deeply. "Yes, I know what it is. They are rhymes of a very, er, evocative nature. I'm sorry, but I've read all of them."

"Why on earth would you take such a thing?" the reverend asked.

"Well..."

Her glanced darted around the room, lighting on anything but Max.

"After I met Mr. Shirley... I wanted to share it with him."

"Good gracious, Meg," her father stammered. "You shared a book like *that* with the parrot trainer?"

"I'm sorry, Papa. I should have had more restraint. Please don't be angry with him. It was never his idea."

"I told you he was taking more than just his meals here," Nigel sneered. "The little trollop has been in league with him since the start."

"That's enough, Nigel," Max demanded, drawing everyone's attention. "I'll not let anyone believe ill of Miss Farrow. Thank you, my dear, but there is no need to do this now."

"But... they must know you did not steal it!" she protested. "Tell them you aren't a criminal, that it's all a mistake."

He couldn't help but grin. What had he done to deserve this from her? Perhaps he did have much more to hope for than he'd been aware. Perhaps his revelation would not result in instant dismissal by her, after all.

"She's telling a tale in an effort to save me," he explained to the room. "Mr. Barrelson, if you will be so kind as to look in the book, I can tell you how to ascertain the true and legitimate owner of it."

"And how will you do that, sir?" Mr. Barrelson asked, reaching for Nigel and taking hold of the book. He had to tug twice to get it.

"Open toward the back and you will find a letter tucked there. Yes, that's it. Go ahead and read it."

The magistrate carefully unfolded the letter as Mr. Farrow peered over his shoulder. Nigel sent a questioning glare toward Mr. Perkins, who could do nothing but shrug. Meg watched in breathless curiosity. Concern was written into her delicate features and Max wished she'd glance at him so he could, at least, encourage her with a smile. Her grave concern for him was most heartening.

Now the magistrate's face grew into a dark, questioning frown while Mr. Farrow's went pale and he stared at Max in astonishment.

"How did you get this letter, sir?"

"It was sent to me," Max stated.

"When? When did you receive it?" the magistrate asked.

"Approximately two weeks after the date it was written. I believe you will see that noted at the top."

"But this was just days before the old earl met his end," Mr. Farrow said. "And... it is addressed to his grandson who has been dead two years at least."

"So it is."

"How then did you receive it?" the magistrate asked.

But Max didn't need to answer. He'd been watching Nigel's face and knew the moment realization struck him. His cousin's eyes went huge and a curse slipped past his lips.

"It can't be!" Nigel exhaled.

"Oh, but it is. I'm surprised you don't recognize me, cousin," Max said to him. "And after I went to all that trouble with the towel earlier."

"But you... they said..."

"You thought you succeeded, didn't you?" Max questioned. "I'm sorry to inform you that the scoundrel you hired to do away with me aboard that ship failed. He was quite inept, as a matter of fact."

Here Hugh interrupted with a low, menacing chuckle as he, apparently, relived the events of that terrible night. The man showed entirely too much glee in the recollection. Not that Max wasn't happy to have survived, but things had not ended well for the would-be assassin.

"It was his body they found," Max went on. "I merely allowed them to mistake it for mine while I determined to seek out who had plotted my demise."

"But... you can't be alive!" Nigel insisted.

"I am! And it gave me no pleasure when I realized my own cousin had been behind the attack on my life. And then poor Grandfather... how could you, Nigel? He loved us."

"No, he loved you! You were the heir. Once your father died, everything should have passed onto my father. *He* should have been next then *I* could have inherited. But no, because of *you* I was left out of everything."

Mr. Barrelson stepped in before things got out of hand. "So this is true; the parrot trainer is the rightful Earl of Glenwick?"

"And my grandfather sent me that book just before he died, with that letter indicating he feared for his life," Max said. "Now, do you think you could possibly untie our hands? The binding isn't nearly as comfortable as one might expect."

The magistrate sheepishly pulled out a small knife to quickly unfasten Max's hands. Hugh cleared his throat when it appeared the man might have been going to forget him. It felt good to be loosened, especially because the way Nigel was glaring at him made him feel he might, at some point, have the need of defending himself again. Hands would be rather useful at that point.

"But why did you not tell us this?" Mr. Farrow asked.

"I still had no proof to indict my cousin for his acts," Max explained. "As long as he was still pre-occupied with hunting the supposed Glenwick Treasure my grandfather used to tell us stories about, I thought he might make some mistakes and I could find the way to bring him to justice. It appears I was right."

"You have no proof of any of these accusations!" Nigel insisted. "I'm not even sure you are who you say you are. What proof do you have of that?"

"I'm well acquainted with the old earl's hand, and this letter is certainly genuine," Mr. Farrow said.

"And I can produce any number of reliable people who will attest to my identity," Max added. "It's no use, Nigel. I saw you making threats against Miss Farrow and I have this letter in our grandfather's own hand, doubting your trustworthiness."

"The old man didn't like me," Nigel said. "That hardly indicates I did away with him. I wasn't even here; I've been mourning my dead wife."

"And I'm sure there'll be an investigation into the circumstances of her death, as well," Max noted.

"I'll send word to the magistrate in that area," Mr. Barrelson said then turned a cold eye on Nigel. "Obviously in light of all this, my lord—er, Mr. Webberly—I'll be taking you into custody. Mr. Perkins as well, considering he was present during the time of your grandfather's death."

"I had nothing to do with it! It was all his idea!" Mr. Perkins cried.

"Shut up, you idiot," Nigel growled. "They have no

proof of anything."

At that moment, there was more pounding at the door. Mr. Farrow wrinkled his brow and looked toward Nigel, oddly enough.

"Are you expecting anyone else?" he asked.

"I'm not talking to anyone about anything," Nigel hissed and crossed his arms over his chest.

"It's a messenger for Mr. Shirley," Mrs. Cooper called from the doorway when she had gone to answer it.

Max glanced at Hugh. Perhaps fate was working on their side tonight, after all. He nodded toward Mr. Farrow.

"We've been expecting word from my man in London. Send him in, if you don't mind."

The room became yet more full as the housekeeper ushered in a tall man Max recognized from his solicitor's office. He stepped forward to greet him. The man removed his hat and bowed politely.

"Good evening, my lord. Forgive the interruption, but I was told you wanted to be notified immediately when the information you've been seeking was finally located."

"I do. Has it been?"

"Indeed, sir. My employer received word from Bow Street just this morning. He confirmed the validity, and I set off immediately to bring word."

"Excellent, Mr. Henning," Max said, then turned to face Nigel.

"I regret to inform you, cousin, that my solicitor in London has everything needed to remand you over to the courts. You'll have your fair trial, but I'm certain you will not care for the outcome of it."

"So is it safe to announce your return and your rightful claim on the title?" Mr. Henning asked. "My employer has been most distressed at keeping such a thing under his hat, as they say."

"You may inform him I no longer require his silence on the matter. Everything is in order and now that we have what we need to hold Nigel so he won't run off, there's no further need for subterfuge."

"Glad to hear it, my lord. Such a relief for all of us."

Nigel did not seem relieved. He stomped his foot and complained. "But I'm the earl! He was dead. The title is mine!"

More than once Max had held questions regarding his cousin's sanity, and now he was questioning again. The man certainly did sound a bit off.

"I was never dead, so you were never earl," he explained patiently. "The instant I learned of our grandfather's passing I went to London and corrected any misconceptions regarding my supposed demise. Your claim has been invalid from the start."

"But what about the treasure? I should inherit some of that, at least!"

"If there is any treasure I'm sure you're entitled to your share. Except for the fact that it's forfeit due to the little detail of you being a murderer."

He thought he caught Meg hiding a smile but he couldn't be sure. She was quite determined to avoid his gaze. He wished to God the room would suddenly empty and he could go to her and beg her to say she might forgive his duplicity. Not being able to read her expression in the midst of all this was hell for him.

"Well I'll never tell you what I know about the treasure," Nigel said. "Grandfather left me some clues, too, you know. He told me the treasure is real and that Bartholomew is the key."

"And you figured out the book was a part of that," Max said. "Yes, I believe we've all come to that conclusion."

"The book?" Mr. Farrow questioned. "You mean, those

old rumors of a Glenwick pirate treasure are true? And this horrid book tells where it is?"

"No, the book tells how to amuse yourself during a long sea voyage. The key phrases Bartholomew has been taught tell which passages from the book can be used as clues to find the treasure."

"I already knew that," Nigel snapped.

Mr. Farrow narrowed his eyes and glanced at his daughter. "And you knew about this, Meg?"

Now she avoided eye contact with her father as well as with Max. "Not all of it, Papa. Mr. Shirley and I recognized that Bartholomew's phrases came from certain rhymes in the book, but I had no idea it was related to any treasure."

"So you have been reading tawdry rhymes with the parrot trainer. Did you also know he was the legitimate earl?"

Now she did look at Max and he could see the anger and hurt in her eyes.

"He never actually mentioned that little bit to me."

"But he showed you his book," her father persisted.

"I thought he was using it to train the bird. I didn't realize he was merely hunting a treasure."

Her words twisted like a knife in his gut. Could she really think that's all it had been for him? That his time spent with her had been all about locating some silly treasure? He'd have to set her straight on that as quickly as possible.

"Well he can just keep on hunting that treasure," Nigel said. "There's not one area of the manor that hasn't been searched. Not a single spot."

Bartholomew—who'd been perched on his favorite cornice—seemed to think this was as good a time as any to chime in, repeating one of his favorite phrases a few times.

"Dear Dot marks the spot. Dear Dot marks the spot."

Suddenly it was clear. All the parts to the puzzle made sense. Bartholomew really *was* giving the location of the treasure. Max felt like a fool not to recognize it right away.

"Pity you've had so much contempt for Bartholomew all along," he told Nigel, tossing Bartholomew a biscuit and trying not to appear too proud of himself. "You'd have noticed something important."

"And what on earth would that be?"

"One of his favorite things seems to have gone missing."

"What are you talking about?"

"I noticed it was not on the wall in Grandfather's office. I wonder where it could be?"

"What are you talking about?"

"Dot, Nigel. I'm talking about Dot. Surely you recall her from our youth."

It took a moment for the light to dawn, but eventually Max read understanding over his vacant face.

"You mean that hideous old thing?"

"Did you have it removed?"

"Of course not. I haven't been wasting my time on decorating."

"Obviously. But if she's not there, where did she go?"

"How the hell do I know? Maybe our grandfather had a glimmer of good taste and had the thing burned."

"I doubt it. I'm fairly certain that's where the treasure is."

"That dreadful thing is the treasure?"

"Dot marks the spot," Max said, gaining a cock-eyed stare from Bartholomew. "But where is she?"

"She?" Mr. Farrow asked. "I thought you were looking for an object."

"An object who is a she. Bartholomew's favorite perch," Max explained.

Now suddenly Meg caught her breath and put her hand to her mouth. "Oh! You mean the ghastly old figurehead!"

"You're familiar with it?"

"You think that will lead to the treasure?"

"Only if we can find it," Max said. "Unfortunately, she's not in her usual place of honor on my grandfather's wall."

"No, she certainly is not," Meg agreed.

"You know where she is?"

He was almost afraid of the answer. But Meg didn't cringe at her reply. Instead she gave him a beaming smile.

"She's here, in this very house!"

Chapter 19

Meg was happier than she ought to have been. It was petty, but she had information to offer Max, information he needed and wanted. He may have only been using her for this all along, yet she was practically giddy to be able to supply it.

Pitiful, really. She should have some pride—she should refuse to help him at all, the way he had lied to them and used her for his greedy little treasure hunt. But what did she do? She smiled at him like a simpleton and gave him exactly what he was looking for.

"Upstairs, in your room," she said.

He frowned. "What? I never saw it up there."

"Good heavens, no. Let us hope no one ever saw that thing in this house," Papa said.

"Come, I'll show you," Meg added when it seemed Max wasn't quite certain he could believe them.

She threaded her way through the people cluttering the room. Nigel sneered and let his eyes roam over her as she passed by, but she made sure he knew she was ignoring him. He'd be out of her hair soon enough and not likely to bother anyone else. She'd not so much as waste her distain on him now.

Max stepped aside to let her pass and she was careful not to get too close. She knew from experience her knees and her heartbeat could not be trusted in close proximity to the man. It would be best right now if she keep all parts of her carefully under control. She would need every bit of resolve to get by when he apologized for using her in his scheme and then left to go take up his place as an earl.

What a fool he must think her! Treating him like a lowly parrot trainer when all along he was the Earl of Glenwick. At least he had the decency not to laugh in her face over it, so far. She doubted the meddlesome gossips of Richington would be so charitable toward her once they heard the whole of this story.

She led the noisy group up into the room that Mr. Shirley—er, the earl—had been using during his stay. Once inside, she pointed toward the far corner.

"There it is."

He looked confused. "But that's just Bartholomew's perch."

She went to it to show him. Her face burned involuntarily, feeling the many sets of eyes on her as she stooped to untie one of the strings they had used to bind the padding and rags all around it.

"The old earl made us promise Bartholomew would never be parted from it," Papa explained, coming to her side to help with the unwrapping. "But of course, we just couldn't have this... thing... sitting out for public view."

At that point the first strip of rags covering the figurehead's face fell away, revealing one darkly lined eye, a heavily rouged cheek, and the hint of unnaturally red hair. Bartholomew squawked loudly and leaped off of Mr. Shirley's shoulder. Drat,she meant *the earl's* shoulder. He landed with clicking toes onto the figurehead, dancing and squawking with delight at the sight of her.

More rags came off and Meg had to glance up for a moment. Her former house guest was watching, and chuckling. Not at her, though. His eyes were set on the figurehead. He grinned like a child as more and more of the offensive thing became visible.

"That's the old girl I remember," he said. "Let me help out."

He stepped over to them and aided in the unceremonious stripping. Meg found herself feeling a bit missish as their hands happened to come together just at the front of the figurehead. She hadn't meant to touch him, to make contact this way. The fact that she did so just as they uncovered the extremely buxom expanse of skin at the figurehead's bosom... quite mortifying, indeed.

"Don't let my adeptness at this make you think I'm the sort of man who goes around doing this to just everyone," he said softly.

The rest of the crowd grumbled and mumbled amongst themselves so Meg could reasonably hope his words had reached no ears but her own. She didn't quite succeed at hiding her smile. She hoped she was slightly more successful with the butterflies bursting to life inside her and the raging thrum of heartbeat in her chest. No lady should be so thrilled as she felt at helping a man undress a wooden wanton.

"So where is the treasure?" Papa asked as the last of the padding fell away and the figurehead was fully revealed.

Meg had to agree. The very last word she might choose to describe this item was "treasure" and she couldn't see how on earth any sort of treasure might be hidden anywhere in it or on it. So far all they had done was pull the covering off a thing that most definitely ought to have remained covered.

"I'm afraid now we will have to rely on the book," Mr. Shirley said.

Er... she meant *the earl*. Heavens, but when would she

ever get used to thinking of him as anything other than that?

The magistrate handed him the book and he studied it, then walked around the perch, studying that. Bartholomew climbed along the waves of carved hair billowing from the figure's head. Every now and then he would lovingly nibble at the wood and make soft, cackling sounds. It was the most calm Meg had ever seen the bird.

If she'd have known just how much he loved the ugly thing, perhaps she would have left it uncovered. Since the earl had taken it off his wall a couple years ago and mounted it on this thick pole, Meg could have perhaps found a place to keep it out of view. She could have turned the pole to face the wall, even.

The phrase snagged in her mind. *Turned the pole.* That sounded remarkably like... Good heavens, perhaps she had it figured out!

In her enthusiasm she nearly ripped the book away from *the earl* and started flipping through pages.

"Look, my lord," she exclaimed. "They aren't just clues, but they're instructions!"

Max was only too happy to let Meg grab the book from him and rummage through it. He felt warm and electric every time she read through those lewd rhymes. Not that she seemed in any way affected by them just now. She frowned and chewed her lip in the most studious fashion as she hunted through the verses, clearly seeking something specific.

"Ah, here it is," she said brightly, and began reading. *"When your fortune has long since been missed, lad,*

and your coffers have long since been.... well, I'll skip that bit...

Then go visit Dear Dot,
'Cause you'll want what she's got.
You need just give your old pole a twist, lad."

Nigel snorted. "The vicar must be so proud. What a demure little miss you are, my dear."

"Shut it, Nigel," Max warned. "She's searching for clues; nothing more."

Mr. Farrow cleared his throat loudly. "This is highly irregular. I can't say I approve of it."

"I'm sorry, Papa," Miss Farrow said. "I don't mean to distress you. But as we're all adults here, and since I have already read through this book and seen the worse that it offers, perhaps you'll allow me to continue."

The reverend sighed and gave her a nod.

"Very well, my dear. I'm sure the Lord will forgive you since there's so much at stake. I must go on record as saying, though, that familiarity with sin hardly make us immune to its consequence."

Meg nodded, all prim and proper. "Indeed. Thank you, Papa. That is an excellent point and I hope we will hear it in one of your sermons on some Sunday quite soon."

Now the older man turned his sermonizing scowl onto Max. The usually docile minister could be quite formidable when riled, it would seem. Max's collar felt decidedly tight and he resisted the urge to tug at it.

"I'd much rather pursue further discussion on the topic in more private fashion," Mr. Farrow said pointedly. "I hope his lordship will indulge me at his earliest possible moment."

And that, Max recognized, was an angry father calling him onto the carpet for what he perceived as inappropriate behavior toward his daughter. Max could hardly dispute the man, either. He *had* behaved most inappropriately toward Miss Farrow. Given his growing fondness for her, it was only by the grace of God he had not found opportunity to behave even more inappropriately.

"Of course, sir," he replied.

Miss Farrow, however, seemed oblivious to the meaning of that exchange. She was still studying the book, turning pages and making comparisons. Suddenly she looked up at Max.

"Do you still have those lists that we made of the most common of Bartholomew's phrases?"

"I do, " he replied and went to the drawer where he had stashed them.

Laying them out, he looked over Miss Farrow's delicate shoulder as she compared them to the various pages in the book. She pointed to lines here and there as a means of holding her place and before long Max could see what she was doing.

The rhymes in the handwritten pages were clues, that much he could see now. All of them pointed to the figurehead and insisted that something dear could be found by encountering it. The phrases Bartholomew uttered in particular, well those were instructions. They referneced the rhymes in the book, but beyond that they gave specific directives. All they needed to do now was follow them.

"I wonder what order we should proceed?" Miss Farrow asked, clearly at the same conclusion as he.

Max knew exactly what order he'd like to proceed, but letting his mind wander off in that direction would bring them no closer to the treasure. If there *was* a treasure. Then again, perhaps if the clues were taken from bawdy rhymes about carnal activity, Max's thoughts weren't so far off from the mark.

Perhaps in order to get to the treasure, he ought to consider the usual course.

"The bird says, 'Go visit Dear Dot.' What does one do

first when one visits a bawd?" Max asked as he stood before the figurehead and contemplated.

"Well, you've already stripped her near naked," Nigel taunted.

"Mind yourself, Webberly," the magistrate warned.

"You would knock at her door," Miss Farrow offered. "At least, that is the first thing I do when I pay a visit to anyone proper."

It sounded reasonable. Since Dear Dot did not actually have a door, Max knocked on the pole she was hanging on. It sounded as one might expect a knocked pole to sound.

Nigel groaned. "Cart me off to jail now if this is the way the rest of the evening will go."

"If you don't have anything productive to offer, keep your mouth shut," Max demanded.

But Miss Farrow was still deeply in thought. "Hmm. Bartholomew says, 'Climb on my pole'," she announced. "Knocking doesn't seem to do anything, so you don't suppose you are to climb the thing, do you?"

Well, if the lewd analogy of attaining sexual treasure held true, there would very likely be some form of climbing at some point. Max decided not to mention that just now. The woman's father was already glaring daggers at him.

"Not sure climbing it will have the hoped for result," Max said simply.

Miss Farrow nodded. "What about twisting it? Perhaps now is when you ought to give your old pole a twist?"

Nigel snorted again and the other men in the room shifted nervously. Mrs. Cooper gazed on in the doorway and Max thought he heard a slight snicker from her direction. Perhaps it would be best, after all, if the females found something else to do with their time while the men continued at this.

"I'm not sure if that means what it says," Max offered, reaching to take the book from her and end the torment of such suggestive phrases falling from her innocent lips.

"But Bartholomew says that repeatedly," she insisted, keeping the book. "And this is a pole. Why not try twisting it?"

"Very well," he sighed.

He put his hands on the pole and tried to twist, but of course nothing happened. He moved slightly to the side so he could reach around the figurehead to make a better grip. Still nothing. Miss Farrow was flipping through the book and the pages laid out before her.

"Go from behind!" she exclaimed.

"Excuse me?" Max choked loudly.

"*Thank God for the view from behind*," she recited. "That's one of Bartholomew's phrases. Try from behind it."

Nigel was not even attempting to hide his lascivious laughter. "That's right, Cousin, do as the lady asks. Try her from behind."

It took everything Max had to pretend he hadn't heard that. Keeping his mind on his business, he moved to the rear of the figurehead's stand and put his hands on it. He found he could get a much better handle on the large pole, so he gave a good twist. To his surprise, he felt it shift. The pole turned on its base, accompanied by an audible click. Clearly he'd done something.

"Something's happening!" Miss Farrow exclaimed. "Whatever you're doing, do it some more."

Now Mr. Henning was clearing his throat loudly, adding to the uncomfortable noise of Mrs. Cooper's snickers and Nigel's guffaws. Max ignored all of it and put some muscle into his twisting. The pole had stopped, though. He detected no further shifting.

"Seems you've ended too early," Nigel scoffed.

Max shot a hateful glance at him.

"Perhaps there is something more you can do," Miss Farrow suggested.

"There is *always* something more I can do," Max replied, making sure Nigel knew exactly what he meant by that.

"What other instructions are there? Surely the bird repeats more phrases than those," Mr. Farrow said.

Meg held up a paper and waved it. "*The heart is the key!* Look, carved into her bodice..."

And Max knew that was it. The heart. He reached around to feel for it, the rough outline of a heart, carved into the figure years ago. It was nearly smoothed out from layers of paint, but he could still feel it. He'd seen it from a distance, wondered at it for years, assuming some drunken sailor had carved it. Gingerly now, he pressed it.

It gave. The heart was not merely carved into the figurehead, it was actually a separate piece. With a faint click, Max felt something unlock. The heart-shaped piece came loose, protruding just slightly from the figurehead's form.

"It came undone!" Miss Farrow cried.

She was so excited, so fetching with her wide eyes, pink cheeks, and innocent enthusiasm in the face of these appalling rhymes, Max thought he just might come undone, too. Surely his heart already had.

Chapter 20

Meg watched breathlessly as the earl carefully extracted the little heart-shaped piece of wood that served as a plug for a small opening into the body of the figurehead. She was not particularly thrilled to be watching the man run his hands over the fantastically huge, round bosoms of the wood carving, but she forced herself to remember Dot was not an actual woman.

It didn't help very much. She still wanted to file the flirtatious little moue right off the tawdry tart's painted face.

"There's an opening there!" Papa declared.

"Can you feel if there's anything inside?" Meg asked.

The earl seemed oddly hesitant to poke his fingers inside, but after a long, deep breath he finally did. She watched his face, watching a smile come over him. He drew his fingers out slowly.

"There's something inside," he said.

He withdrew a small bag, just large enough to fill the palm of his hand.

"That's it?" Nigel complained, craning his neck to see. "That can't be much of a treasure."

"Perhaps our great-grandfather wasn't much of a pirate," the earl replied.

But he opened the bag and carefully tipped the contents

into his hand. It was treasure, indeed! A fortune in glittering gems of all sizes and colors made a beautiful pile. Meg had to blink her eyes a few times to really see all of it.

"Or perhaps he was ruthless," the earl added.

"Jewels!" she exclaimed.

"All unset, too," the magistrate commented. "No way to know where any of them came from."

"I'm sure they are all stolen, just the same," the earl said.

"Half of them are mine!" Nigel insisted. "Give them over. I'll buy my way out of jail."

"You don't really believe I'll do that, do you?" the earl asked.

Nigel shrugged. "You are rather a stickler for justice. Perhaps you might give me my share now in the interest of fairness."

"Perhaps first we'll determine if these stones can be considered legitimately part of the Glenwick estate or if they need to be returned to someone."

Mr. Barrelson took his turn leaning in to see the treasure. "Don't see how anyone could possibly know who to return them to. No charges were actually ever levied against your great-grandfather, as I recall. All those piracy tales could be just legend, for all we know."

"We'll see that the matter is fully investigated," the earl assured.

Meg couldn't have been prouder of him, both for figuring out how to locate the treasure as well as for being willing to verify his claim to it. He may have spent the past week lying to her face every day, but he really was an honorable man. All the more reason she should be ashamed of herself for getting caught up in the treasure hunt and being so free with those dreadful rhymes. That could not have presented her in the very best light.

But Nigel was a bit less than pleased with his cousin's actions.

"You cannot be serious. After all this, all these years of hunting that damn treasure, you're just going to try to give it away? That's shameful, it is. You're probably not even going to properly debauch the Farrow chit either, are you?"

"That's enough, Nigel," the earl growled.

"You're damn right it is. I've had enough of all of you!"

And suddenly Nigel bolted from the room. During the excitement of the treasure hunt everyone had moved in closer to see what was happening. Nigel, on the other hand, had inched closer to the door. Now he had violently shoved poor Mrs. Cooper out of the way and run off, Mr. Perkins trailing desperately after him.

Mr. Barrelson swore then sprinted out, too. Hugh gave the earl a questioning look and the earl's shrugged reply seemed all that was needed to send Hugh tearing out after them. Papa and Mr. Henning followed, with Mrs. Cooper behind them yelling for everyone to have a care on the stairway and watch out for the loose tread near the bottom. Bartholomew screeched from his perch.

Meg would have followed the noisy troupe, but the earl caught her arm.

"Wait," he said calmly. "Let them manage this."

"But he's getting away!"

"Where will he go? He's penniless, family-less, homeless, and unloved. He won't get far, I assure you. Besides, we have some unfinished matters between us, I believe."

She lowered her eyes. "Yes... and I'm sorry."

"Sorry? Whatever for?"

"For the dreadful way I've treated you, my lord. I've been so very rude, and then I read through that book in the most hoydenish way, and I accused you of being a criminal, and I behaved like a... like a very loose woman with you!"

"And I would not for the world have you apologize for any of that. In fact, is there any chance I could get you to commit more of that last reprehensible transgression?"

She was confused by his words. "Last reprehensible transgression?"

"The one where you behave like a very loose woman with me."

Clarifying his words, he pulled her into his arms. Heavens! It was the place she most wanted to be so she folded herself into him instantly. And then he was kissing her.

His lips were much more insistent than before. Or perhaps it was hers that demanded more than just a simple taste of his essence. She pressed her body into his and gave in to the urgency growing inside her. This might be her last chance for the rapture of his kisses, his embrace, so she was determined to take all that she could.

She was weak from the feel of him—and perhaps lack of oxygen—when he finally pushed himself slightly away.

"My God, Miss Farrow, you are a very loose woman, indeed."

"I'll apologize again for it, if you like."

He tipped his head and eyed her suspiciously. "I think not. I'm worried that any more apologies might get us both into trouble."

"Perhaps your cousin is a good runner and they'll have to chase him halfway through the village," she suggested, eager to make the best use of whatever time alone they had left.

"I do not mean to limit my kisses to the time it takes Nigel to evade capture," he said. "Miss Farrow, I intend at the earliest possible moment to kiss you without any worry for pesky interruptions."

"I rather like the sound of that, Mr. Shirley."

He frowned at her. "And I'll thank you not to call me that. Shirley is my mother's name, as a matter of fact."

"It's going to take me some time to get used to calling you Glenwick, I'm afraid."

"Then don't call me that, either."

"What, then?"

"Well, my mother calls me Max and my grandfather called me Web. Once I was presumed dead I took to signing my letters to him with X..."

"You wrote that letter!" she exclaimed. "They lied to me about it."

"They did. I'm fairly certainly the lied about all of it. I'm sure when we look into things further, we'll find that no document exists at all that will tarnish your reputation, my dear. How could it? Nigel failed in his efforts with you."

"Indeed he did, Mr. Shir... oh, what did you tell me to call you?"

"I think I prefer Darling. Definitely Darling."

Whether he expected more pesky interruptions or not, he pulled her tight and kissed her again. Ah, but if he kept this up all the practice was going to make her very, very good at this sort of thing. Perhaps if she displayed enough expertise he would welcome further opportunities for more of it. She'd have to think of as many excuses as possible to visit at Glenwick Downs once he was installed there.

This training session, however, was called to an abrupt halt when Papa's violent throat clearing could be heard from the doorway. Her face burned as she pulled herself away from Max and stared shame-faced at the floor.

"Has Nigel been captured?" the earl asked, his voice as calm and assured as if he'd been caught reading his Bible.

"He has," Papa replied, not quite so calm and assured.

Definitely winded. "And some men have arrived from London looking for him."

Max nodded, as if he'd been expecting this turn of events, too. "I see. Very well. Let us get the unpleasantness over with. I'm sure there will be countless reports to write and people to talk to. Everyone will have plenty of questions for me."

"I know I certainly do," Papa grumbled.

Max piled the last of his things into his little bundle. The evening had dragged on and it was well into night. Candlelight flickered against the walls, sending grotesque shadows over the figurehead in the corner. Bartholomew slept peacefully on it.

Max almost hated to go. By God, he'd miss this tidy little room here at the parsonage, but Mr. Farrow was right. It would be most improper for him to remain under this roof now.

"And I hope I don't need to remind you the eternal consequences upon your soul should you not live up to your commitments, sir," the vicar said bluntly as he watched over Max's departure.

"No, no reminder is needed."

"You may be the heir to Glenwick and you may have the respect of men here in this world, but if you play fast with my daughter's affections, you'll answer to your maker for it."

"I know," Max said without any hint of the frustration he felt. "You've made your position quite clear."

"She deserves better than a man who shows up full of lies and deception."

"I know that."

"She deserves the luxury of time to make her decision.

She should not be forced to accept in haste simply because she was lured into a compromising situation."

"I understand, sir. I acted badly; I admit it."

"She deserves a man who can love her forever."

"Now there you will find no fault in me. I do love her. Completely."

"After a mere week of acquaintance?"

"Perhaps after a day. Maybe an hour, sir."

"Sentimental drivel."

"I can only tell you what I know to be true. I am in love with her and have every intention of begging her to have me for a husband."

"And if she refuses, or puts you off in any way?"

"I will make no complaint and I will not breathe one word of my ungentlemanly behavior to anyone."

That was an accurate recitation of the reverend's instructions. Max was beginning to feel a bit like Bartholomew here, being told what to say and how to say it. At this point he half expected the vicar to hand him a biscuit. He did not, though. Simply more rules and reminders.

"You will not use flattery or sugary words to sway her to your will."

"Of course not, sir."

"You will beg her forgiveness for your rash actions."

"Of course I will."

"You will promise her undying faithfulness and loyalty."

"Of course I will."

"You will grovel at her feet if she asks it of you."

"Of course I... wait, what?"

"Will you or won't you, sir?"

"Grovel? Oh, but now sir—"

"I believe God the Almighty would have you grovel,

sir."

"Oh, very well. I will grovel if it means she might have me."

At last the vicar's stern face finally broke into a smile.

"Very well, my lord. I think, perhaps, you just might be telling the truth. You *do* love her."

"I do, sir. More than I could have ever thought possible," Max replied, hoisting his things and standing ready to leave. "

"Good. Now go say your farewells, and God help you both."

The sounds of footsteps and baggage and low voices woke Meg. She roused herself quickly, not having intended to drift off but the late hour and the hectic events of the day made it impossible for her to remain alert. She glanced up, finding Max watching her from the doorway of the drawing room where she had tried to entertain herself with needlework.

"The carriage is here to take me to Glenwick," he said. "I'm sorry to keep the household up at such a late hour."

"I'm sure you'll be much more comfortable at Glenwick," she said, rising from her armchair but too timid to move toward him.

He was leaving. Papa had made his disappointment known when he found them in heated embrace and they'd not had one moment for private conversation since. And now he would be gone. He would be caught up in managing his new estate, he'd be courted by all the local gentry and she'd be lucky to see him on Sundays in church. Her efforts to find ways to be in Max's company would certainly be thwarted by Papa, and this dashing new earl would no doubt find plenty of other things to occupy his time.

"It's been years since I stayed at the Downs," he said. "But I suppose it's where I belong now."

"Yes," she agreed. "It's a fine home. You'll be quite happy there."

There was apparently nothing more to say. Meg could hear men in the entrance way, carrying Max's few things out to the carriage. Papa's voice was out there, too, as he directed them. Yes, Papa would be only too happy to see the man who had lied to them and taken liberties with her gone from their house. It was unlikely he'd ever be invited to return.

She stood dumbly, wishing to God she had the courage to say any of the hundreds of things that she felt. Max was silent, too. Finally he moved, and she involuntarily started. Instead of leaving for his carriage, he marched directly toward her, dropping the lone bag that he carried along the way.

"Dash it all, Meg," he said. "I won't be happy there. Not as long as you're here."

Further amazing her, he swept her into his arms and held her more tightly than he'd held that bag of priceless gems earlier today. She was limp for a moment before her startled body suddenly came to life and she threw her arms around him.

"You belong at the Downs with me," he said. "I promised your father I'd give you time to consider, to allow you to gradually know where your heart stood and make up your mind. I told him I wouldn't press you or use flattery or fancy words... but, by God, Meg, I love you. I want you to marry me, if you will."

He put her just far enough away from him that he could look down into her eyes. She had no idea what he must see there; her shock and surprise overwhelmed her. What had the man said? Had she heard what she thought she heard?

"I know we haven't started off very well," he went on. "I lied, I let you be endangered by my cousin when I should have protected you... I'm afraid I have very little obvious character to recommend me. All I can offer is a centuries old name, a grand title, a beautiful estate, and a pocket full of pirate treasure, but I can promise I'll spend the rest of my life trying to redeem myself in your eyes. Please, consider this groveling, Meg. I love you and I want you to be my wife."

By God, that certainly did sound like what she thought it sounded like. Now if only she could make some sound of her own, she would most definitely accept him.

"I... oh, good heavens," she said, catching her breath. "Of course I'll marry you! Even without all that title and treasure nonsense. I'd marry you if you really were just a parrot trainer."

She wrapped herself around him again. They were interrupted, however, when something loud and large crashed into Max's head, sending them both staggering sideways. He barely managed to hold Meg up from falling and she had to duck as large green wings beat furiously over her.

Apparently Bartholomew had awoken and found Max gone. It seemed he didn't like that arrangement and was now determined to latch onto the man and never let go. Meg could well understand the bird's emotion.

"He doesn't want you to go," she said when the uproar subsided.

"I thought he'd be happy to be rid of me."

"Clearly not. Maybe you really are a parrot trainer, after all."

"I'm going to be a parrot maimer in about a minute if he doesn't remove his claws from my scalp."

"He loves you," she said, trying not to laugh at Max's misfortune. "Perhaps you should take him—and that hideous figurehead—back to Glenwick Downs with you."

"No. Not for a hundred pirate treasures!"

"What? But... it's Bartholomew's home. He'd be so happy to go back there."

"If I take him and Old Dot back there, though, won't you be more inclined to want to stay here?"

Now she laughed, realizing he'd been funning her.

"Absolutely not. Do you have any idea what a madhouse this is? Papa brings in strangers off the street and hires them without references, spurious earls turn up twice weekly, and I can't go out of doors without encountering highwaymen! No sir, I'd much rather take my chances living with you and one singularly eccentric bird."

"Well, then, my dear, it is settled," he said, ignoring the bird on his head and pulling her back into his arms. "Bartholomew will return to the Downs and I will be a parrot trainer forever. And," he added just before he kissed her. "Once we are wed I can finally show you my references."

Note from the Author:

I think I had more fun writing this book than any of my others. Not only did I fall in love with my human characters, but Bartholomew kept me smiling the whole way through.
What's not to love about a big cranky bird?

Plus, I got to play with some really awful limericks. Incidentally, the term "limerick" was not used to reference the rhyme pattern that we think of today until later in the 19th century. This is why in this story, you will hear all of the verses referred to as "rhymes" when most of them follow the pattern that we think of as a limerick today.

And where did these dreadful rhymes come from? Some were dug out of history, but the majority were crafted by me to specially suit the purposes of this story. If you just can't get enough bawdy rhyme, please visit my website where I have kindly posted these groan-worthy limericks. Look for them in my Fun Stuff section at www.SusanGH.com.

Keep reading for a preview from another Regency Romance from Susan Gee Heino...

Miss Wheaton's Whiskers

by Susan Gee Heino...

London, England, May of 1813

Miss Elizabeth Wheaton was at her mirror, squinting and blinking at her reflection. She was not entirely displeased with what she saw, but certainly her chestnut curls could do with some arranging. Other areas of her life might be racing along somewhat out of her control, but she was determined her coiffure should not run rough shod over her. Not today, at least.

"Hand me that blue ribbon, if you please, Noreen," she said to her dearest friend.

It was quite a comfort to have Noreen here just now, actually. What good fortune for the girl to drop by this way, right when Elizabeth needed her most. But that was usually Noreen's way. She always seemed to be just what Elizabeth needed. Today, for instance, Noreen was delightfully quiet and had been sitting for well over half an hour, watching Elizabeth primp and listening to her rattle on about the day's expected drama.

Oddly enough, though, Elizabeth found her outstretched hand still empty as she waited for the arrival of the requested ribbon. A quick glance away from the mirror and she discovered why. It appeared Noreen was a million miles away and had not heard the request. In fact, Elizabeth was left to wonder just how much of the preceding discourse her friend had managed not to hear.

"Heaven's, Noreen! Wherever have you been wool-gathering?"

Noreen startled to attention. Her slight freckles went bright as she colored at the sudden discovery of her mental vacancy.

"I'm so sorry, Ellie. Please, go on. What were you saying? I'm sure it was terribly interesting."

"Obviously not," Elizabeth said, grabbing up the blue ribbon and flicking it playfully at her friend. "I don't imagine anything I might say is at all interesting when your mind has run off on some fancy with a certain young lieutenant we know."

Noreen's color went deeper, the freckles becoming nearly imperceptible. "I don't know what you could mean, of course."

"Oh, certainly not. You hardly think of Lt. Janiston at all, do you?"

Her friend gave a weary sigh. "I try not to."

"And what point is there to that? You know you've every right to think of him from time to time, considering how he's completely captured your heart."

"It's so very obvious, is it?"

"I'm your best friend, Noreen. Of course it's obvious. And I daresay the lieutenant has a bit of an idea on your estimation of him, doesn't he?"

Now her friend's blushing was nearly worrisome. Heavens, but how many shades of mortification could the girl turn? It wasn't as if she had anything to be ashamed of, after all. Lt. Janiston was quite a good catch. His brother was the very Duke of Asheford. True, the duke was an absolute horror, but once Noreen and her officer were happily wed they could no doubt find ways to avoid the man.

"Jeffrey has given me reason to believe he welcomes my affection," Noreen said, not meeting Elizabeth's eye. Instead she stared at her lap and nervously folded and unfolded the creases in her overskirt.

"Then I am overjoyed for you, Noreen," Elizabeth said, turning back to her mirror and weaving the blue ribbon into her unruly curls. "I've long known it's just a matter of time before you are married to the man."

"You believe so?"

"Of course it is so. While you have been blushing and making cow's eyes, I've been watching. It is my expert opinion that he's totally and completely besotted with you. Indeed, we can all expect to be wishing you happy any day now, I suspect."

"Oh, I wish it were so!"

"It will be so."

"But when? I've been waiting and waiting, but it seems... that is..."

"How impatient you are!" Elizabeth had to laugh at her friend. "Listen to you, as if you might expire from love in the course of a mere week or two. Oh, but I say I am glad I'll be well wed very soon without all this bothersome pining."

"You don't understand, Elizabeth, but... wait, what did you say?"

"Only what I've been trailing on about for the better part of an hour already! Silly Noreen, you haven't heard a word I was telling you, have you?"

"Perhaps you'd best repeat some of it. Did you just say you're to be *wed*?"

"I did! Rather soon, I imagine. I expect his proposal at any moment, as a matter of fact."

Now Noreen truly did look stunned. The blushing was long gone and she was, in fact, a bit pale. My, but the girl was a veritable chameleon these days.

"You expect a proposal? From whom?"

"Lord Fredrick Dothingley, as I've been telling you. He is expected to arrive and deliver his proposal this morning."

"Again? Hasn't he already proposed to you?"

"No, that was Lord Durbington. And I couldn't abide him at all, so of course I said no."

"But you like Lord Dothingley?"

"Not in the least. I like his house in Regents Square, though, and I've heard his estate in Kent is quite lovely."

"You would marry for the man's living quarters?"

"And his title, of course. He's an earl, after all. Durbington was only a baron. And my mother is quite fond of Lady Dothingley, Fredrick's mother. I could finally be done with Mamma's pestering if I were to wed her friend's son."

"But you do not love him!"

"No, certainly not."

"Then how can you marry him?"

Poor, mooning Noreen. She'd always been of a romantic nature, swooning and sighing over the least little thing. Elizabeth had never quite understood it all but assumed that at some point she'd run across some lucky fellow to make her heart melt and her pulse race at the merest thought of him. Apparently, though, such a thing was just not in her nature. Three years since her come-out and she'd never so much as melted an inch or pulsed more than a quick run up the stairs. Clearly she was not the falling-in-love type.

It was, in fact, Noreen's attitude toward Lt. Janiston that had convinced Elizabeth to accept the attentions of Lord Dothingley. She'd weighed it all quite carefully. If she was not destined for romance—and if Noreen's behavior was the definition of that, she was happy not to be—then at least she should be destined for a fine home and impressive social standing. As Lady Dothingley, she'd have both in high measure, and the groom was at least someone she could tolerate. In small doses.

Certainly marrying Fredrick Dothingley would be infinitely better than remaining single while Noreen went off to a blissful forever with the lieutenant and Elizabeth was stuck with Mamma's ceaseless harping. Indeed, no husband could be worse than enduring another year of that nonsense. Not even the weak-chinned, pinch-voiced Dothingley.

Elizabeth was spared having to defend her decision as the maid knocked at the door to announce the carriage was available to carry Noreen back to her home in Chelsea. The skies threatened rain so Noreen declared she'd best take advantage of this and make her departure quite soon. The maid left them to go inform the driver and collect Noreen's things.

Drat, but Elizabeth would be losing her dear friend and be forced to face Lord Dothingley alone. Oh, well. If she was going to marry the man she supposed she ought to get used to spending time with him. Perhaps accepting a proposal took less time than rejecting one and the man would be gone away quickly.

"Are you certain you want to marry Lord Dothingley?" Noreen asked slowly.

Elizabeth's reply was much quicker. Perhaps a bit too quick, in fact.

"He's a most excellent match, of course. I shall be quite happy with him, I'm sure."

"Oh, but I do hope so, Elizabeth. If I thought for one moment you might never know the joy that I've found after meeting my dear Jeffrey..."

"So it is Jeffrey now, is it? I had no idea things between

you had progressed so far already."

Noreen was blushing again. "I should not speak of him that way, I know. It's just that..."

"It's just that you're in love and you cannot help yourself. Of course I understand, even though I'm perfectly happy to admit this sort of emotion is foreign to me. That's why I'm quite content to marry for reasons purely practical, logical and intentional."

"And I would love nothing more than to simply marry, no matter how impractical it is. Oh, but what if Jeffrey does not care so much for me, after all? What if he realizes he should be like you, and marry someone with wealth and good standing? His brother is a duke, after all! He should marry far, far above me, I know."

"Lt. Janiston has no intention of marrying anyone but you, Noreen. I'm quite sure of it. He'll come around, you just wait."

"Waiting... oh, but how I hate that. The longer he waits, the more chance there is that..."

"That he'll lose interest? Not possible, Noreen."

"Unless his brother demands it. You know *that's* quite possible. It's likely, in fact. Everyone knows the Duke of Asheford is selfish and cruel. He could very well force Jeffrey to chose someone over me. Someone better."

"There is no one better than you. Your connections may not be grand, but your mother was a gentlewoman. Lt. Janiston knows this. Besides, he is of age, and he has his commission. Surely he is not entirely dependent on his brother."

"I fear he is. Plus, he puts great stock in his brother's opinion. If the duke were to set himself against me.... oh, there'd be no hope for us then, I'm afraid."

"Of course there is hope. No one should know that better than you, with your swooning and gaping and puppy-dog eyes. If you and Jeffrey are truly in love, no doubt you will end up together and the rest of us will be sickened by your endless mooning and sweet-talk. Blech."

"Oh, I do hope you're right, Elizabeth."

"Of course I'm right. Now help me sort this mess of my hair and then hurry to get your ride home. It would not do at all to get caught in the rain and die of the ague before you have a chance to waste away over love."

Noreen seemed to take the whole business entirely too seriously. "No, indeed it would not. Here, let me do the pins for you."

Well, at least Elizabeth's hair would look fetching when Lord Dothingley arrived. Heavens, but she was only too glad to be spared the wretched emotions that seemed to have overtaken Noreen as her heart had become increasingly captive to Lt. Janiston. Elizabeth might be doomed to an uninspiring marriage, but at least she'd have full use of her faculties for it. Noreen seemed to have nearly taken leave of hers. Apparently love did that to people.

A clever woman, she decided, was well free of it.

"A clever wife would solve everything for you," the Lady Anne declared over breakfast.

Her son, the Duke of Asheford, declined to comment. Instead, he concentrated on his soft-boiled egg. Dash it all, but he did not like soft-boiled eggs. However, it was better than engaging in conversation with his mother over this distasteful—and well-rehearsed—topic.

"If you would simply marry, then these fortune hunters would have no reason to plague you," she went on, ignoring his intentionally surly demeanor. "Honestly, Jack, you cannot expect society to turn a blind eye to this sort of thing. If you at least had a wife—"

"Then I would have two women thwarting my attempt at a peaceful breakfast, no doubt," he finally interrupted. "We've discussed this at length, mother. I have more than enough to do repairing the damage done by my late uncle's negligence and depravity. A wife—clever or otherwise—is the very last thing I need. Five very fine estates have gone to ruin and it's fallen on me to magically restore them. If you'd be so kind as to drop the subject of my supposed need for a wife, I assure you I would be forever quite grateful."

"And I suppose you think that girl from Worchester will just magically go away if you do nothing but ignore her."

Not that again. Bother, but this nonsense had gone on far too long already.

"I've assured you she has no claim. I have no responsibility to her or to her child."

"You bought her a house."

"No, I bought her grandfather a house. He had been a loyal retainer and deserved fair treatment after his long years of service. How was I to know his ungrateful granddaughter would turn up with child and start claiming it was mine, demanding money to cover the scandal?"

"And you gave in to her demands, as I recall."

"For all the good it did. I was hoping to protect you from finding out about it."

"Everyone found out about it."

"She was obviously desperate and it wasn't the child's fault its father abandoned them. I couldn't very well let it just starve, though I assure you I never laid eyes—or anything else—on that woman before she showed up making her wild claims."

"Oh, I believe you, of course. She's not your type at all. Still, people do talk and you know all too well what they say about us."

"They'd better not say it to my face."

"How can they? You keep yourself safely away from society. It's almost as if you invite the rumors and the whispering."

"I couldn't care less what these people say about me, Mother."

"Well, I do. You are the duke now. True, your father's family never dreamed the title would pass to you, but it did. Society will accept us now. You deserve to be accepted, and respected, too. Yet instead you thumb your nose and give people every reason to think badly of you."

"I've not needed acceptance or respect all these years, Mother. Besides, I hardly think playing toad to some puffed up noblemen will atone for all my imaginary sins."

"It's not the imaginary ones I'm worried about, Jack."

"Rubbish. They're all imaginary. I've lived like a monk since I've got this ruddy title and a fat lot of good it's done me."

"It's done a world of good. Why, just look how healthy and well-rested you are."

"A thing I can't say I'm particularly grateful for," he muttered.

"You're bored? Well then, start accepting some of those invitations you get. Attend a few balls, meet some new people. Find a good wife."

He bristled. He never quite knew how she did it, but the woman had an absolute knack for turning every conversation back around to that one topic. One topic he was determined to avoid. She, however, rambled on.

"Lady Nebbly, for instance, has a charming daughter just coming out this season. They are an old and respected family and it's an absolute shame how Lord Nebbly gambled away the family fortune. If you were to make an offer for the girl, they'd gladly give their consent and we'd be connected to some of the very best of the upper ten thousand."

"Good grief, Mother."

"I've seen her, Jack, and she's a pretty little thing. Young enough that she's likely not heard all the talk about my less than lustrous parentage and your so-called checkered past."

"I tend to prefer grown women, Mother. I'd rather not play nursemaid to my own wife."

"Ah, so you do have a notion of the sort of wife you want. Good. That will make it easier to narrow down the field."

"There is no field, Mother, and we are not narrowing it."

"Oh, but we don't have to. Mrs. Scott will do that for us. She is very highly regarded and her friends are some of the most influential members of the ton. Surely we can trust her guest list to include only the best."

"Who the hell is Mrs. Scott and what the devil does her guest list have to do with anything?"

"You're on it, of course."

"On what?"

"Her guest list. Her annual ball is coming up on Thursday and you are invited. We all are, in fact, and I've decided you will attend."

"You have? I will?"

"Yes. Now, I'd like you to look at this."

She surprised him by pulling a slip of paper from the sleeve of her morning gown. Flattening it, she scanned over a column of what appeared to be names. He knew he should not fall prey to this distraction, but he could not help himself. He had to ask.

"What is that?"

"It's a list."

"A list of what?"

"All the most promising young ladies who will be at Mrs. Scott's ball."

"You've got them bloody catalogued?"

"Watch your tongue there. And yes, I've got them bloody catalogued. We can't afford to be wasting our time on the wrong sorts of ladies, can we?"

He chose not to answer. Most likely his mother would not appreciate hearing his opinions on just how much time he wouldn't actually mind wasting on the wrong sorts of ladies. It was the right sort of lady, in fact, that he'd rather avoid. Like the plague.

"Ah, this is interesting," she said, pouring over her list. "It appears Lord Wheaton has two marriageable daughters this season. He's quite well off and high in the instep, I'm told. Hmm... he might be hesitant to let you near the younger daughter, but that older one has apparently been out for some time. Perhaps they are getting desperate and might be willing to entertain some attentions from you. We'll have to assure everyone that you're intentions are quite noble, of course, but..."

"No, Mother."

"Your intentions are not quite noble?"

"No."

"You mean you would approach these respectable young ladies with ignoble intentions?"

"No, of course not."

"Then your intentions *are* noble. Excellent. The parents will be glad to hear it."

"No! Stop this. You are intentionally misunderstanding me."

"What do I misunderstand, dear? Did you mean you'd rather meet Lord Wheaton's younger daughter instead of the older one? I thought you just told me you preferred women with slightly advanced years."

"I prefer women who are not intent on luring me into unwanted matrimony and right now you are the chief offender, Mother. I have no intention of meeting *or* marrying Lord Wheatfield's aged daughter."

"The younger one, then?"

"Good God, no."

"The elder, then. Wonderful. You'll escort me on Thursday and I will arrange a meeting."

Asheford gave up on his breakfast and snatched up his riding gloves. "I have an errand to attend. If you happen to see Jeffrey, tell him I'm looking for him."

"Good. You really ought to talk to him about that girl he's been rambling on and on about."

"Another opera dancer?"

"No, that was some weeks ago. Now he's all about some Noreen person."

Asheford grunted. "Don't know that one. Last I recall there was some daughter of a tutor he was pining after."

"I think this might be the same one. It seems Jeffrey is rather serious about her."

"He's serious about all of them until he moves onto the next. I told him I wanted to hear nothing more about it. The last thing we need is more scandal in this family. Thankfully, I have word that he's to be shipping out soon. Perhaps nipping after Napoleon's heels for a while might make a man of him at last."

"What? Oh, but I'll not have him going off to get himself shot at. No, you'll need to buy out his commission and keep him here. While you're at it, make sure he is free to leave his regiment and accompany us on Thursday."

"Thursday?"

"To Mrs. Scott's ball! Honestly, Jack, you really don't

listen well. We're going to the ball and perhaps I can find both my sons proper wives. Then I will finally look forward to grandchildren."

Good God, would the woman ever give up? He rubbed his temples but knew it would do little to ease the throbbing. His only hope was escape.

His mother called after him, but to no avail. He left the table and stormed out of the house. By God, he should have stayed in the country. The Season was just beginning with all the balls and activities and he should have known Mother would begin plotting this way.

If he had any sense at all, he'd find some excuse to flee London and head out to the peace and quiet of Asheford Lea. He'd be safe there; safe from rumors and scandal and, certainly, from meetings with desperate spinsters in ballrooms.

About the Author

Susan Gee Heino thinks the sexiest thing a man can do is engage in witty banter. If he happens to be wearing breeches and a cravat while he does this, all the better. If he comes with a noble title, a tortured past, and perhaps even dimples, then he is just about perfect.

Her lighthearted Regency Romances are full of quirky heroines who tend to feel exactly the same way—at least they do by the end of the book. Usually it takes a little convincing by the cravat-clad hero. But no matter what adventures ensue, the hero always ends up with his lady. And vice versa.

Ms. Heino lives in rural Ohio with her non-cravat-inclined husband, two very remarkable children, and an accidental collection of critters. She loves to hear from readers so please visit her website or connect on social media!

www. SusanGH.com

Love's funny sometimes!

www.ingramcontent.com/pod-product-compliance
Lightning Source LLC
LaVergne TN
LVHW020707110826
845149LV00012B/2142